HEARTS OF HONEYBROOKE COVE: A HEARTWARMING SMALL-TOWN ROMANCE

Welcome to Honeybrooke Cove!

THE BEST DARN PLACE IN WISCONSIN!

Victoria Banning's perfect California life falls apart when she loses her job and boyfriend, all in the same day. Finished with controlling men and broken hearts, she decides it's time to rewrite her story. New Chapter. New life. All on her terms. When she learns of her great-aunt Mags's financial distress, she decides to make a road trip. But she's not in time, and trouble follows her every step of the way when she moves into her late aunt's rundown cottage in Honeybrooke Cove. Thank heavens, there's at least one capable handyman in the small Wisconsin lake town to help her put the house on the market. Too bad, he's overly bossy for her tastes.

Surgeon, Barrett Collins, should have let someone else take his last case. When everything went wrong, he left the big city and rebuilt his life as a handyman in Honeybrooke Cove. He's up to his tool belt in repairs on Mags's house and everyone else who needs him. When Barrett learns Mags left her cottage to him and her headstrong niece, he's ready to ship Ms. Banning back to California. But there is something to be said for sharing a cottage with a beautiful woman. Especially when she desperately needs his help.

Life in Wisconsin's North Country can be harsh, and when someone wants Victoria out of Honeybrooke Cove, life is unforgiving. As Barrett helps Victoria navigate the elements, they learn to open their hearts and live again.

HEARTS OF HONEYBROOKE COVE

C C WILEY

C.C. WILEY

COPYRIGHT

"Anyone who has never made a mistake has never tried anything new."

Albert Einstein, 1879-1955

CHAPTER 1

Victoria Banning is a fraud. A complete failure.
The voices taunted her day and night. It had been a month since her world came crashing down, and still those voices refused to shut up. She couldn't take one more sleepless night. She had to do something to stop the chatter.

Being laid off from her dream job and then discovering her lying-cheating-snake-in-the-grass-boyfriend-Connor was kissing someone else was a hard thing to swallow. Discovering all this in a single day, by noon, made her want to curl up and eat her weight in potato chips and chocolate.

Victoria took a sip of the steaming coffee and wished it was spiked with something stronger. However, that would just make her a drunk, cranky caffeine hound. All before noon. She blew the unruly bangs out of her eyes. *A lonely, exhausted, caffeine hound. Way too much like my father.*

Her reflection in the glass patio door stared back at the rumpled pajamas and ratty pink slippers that Connor had threatened to give to the dog down the hall. Greasy, mouse-brown hair hung limp over her slumped shoulders. "Suck it up, Cupcake," she sneered.

The closet door down the hall slammed shut. Her muscles tensed, preparing for the next punch to her heart.

Victoria tapped her nail over the coffee cup's ceramic ridge. Connor knew she hated surprises. And yet, he'd shown up at the condo and let himself in as if nothing had ever happened. According to him, he'd given her sufficient time to cool off and get ahold of her emotions. All was forgiven. *Not.*

The scraping of the dresser drawer, the one that always stuck halfway, echoed into the living room. The soft *whump* of a suitcase hitting the mattress came from their—correction—her bedroom. A lead anchor lay at the pit of her stomach.

This was real. Their relationship was over.

A wave of loss clutched her chest. Her breath caught. On paper, they had been the perfect couple. Connor, the handsome young attorney, and she, the bright financial advisor. He used to make her laugh. They had laughed and planned their future together.

She glanced over at the kitchen. The empty Chinese take-out boxes were stacked on the counter. The bag of garbage needed to be taken out—Connor's one and only responsibility around the condo.

Somehow, the implosion of their perfect relationship had become her fault. She could still hear Connor's *woman du jour's* squeal, the crash of the wine bottle hitting the tile floor. And Connor, yelling at Victoria for coming home early.

Eyeing the wine stains on the wall, she made a note to give Connor the cleaning bill. Court liaison, her white fanny. To think he actually tried to tell her that they were only going over his briefs. Maybe those CSI dudes could follow the spiked-heel wine dots out the door and pin some crime on that cheating lawyer and his court researcher. The crime? Death by broken heart.

Connor strode down the hallway, his outrage palpable. He dropped the suitcase near the door. "Call me when you've got your head back on straight."

Her nostrils flared before she painted the forced smile on her lips. If she had to, she would fake it until the wounds lost their sting. Indifference settled over her shoulders like a warm blanket. "Not happening," she muttered.

His radiant smile, the one he used in front of the jury, never reached the ice in his eyes. The telltale tick in his square jaw revealed the anger he kept in check. "V, it doesn't have to go down this way."

"Let the doorman know where to send the rest of your things," she said. Another layer of stone formed around her chest, shielding her from his penetrating glare.

"I'll be back." His fingers curled. They were stark-white in contrast to the cell phone's black leather casing. "I—we've invested too much to just turn it off."

Victoria stood, adjusting the belt to her comfy old housecoat.

"Come on." He took another step deeper into the room, reaching for her arm. "You know you have to forgive a little mistake."

"No, Connor. I don't. And I have the pictures to make sure that I never forget." She sidestepped out of his reach. The bruised imprints of his hand around her arms from that terrible night were still too tender. On the outside, she maintained the cool and calm mask she'd learned to wear since she was a kid. It hid the turbid soup of emotions swirling on the inside. She held up her phone so that he could read the 911 on the screen. "Get out now. Or your career as an attorney is down the toilet."

"Don't do it, V." He paused, his eyes darting from her to the phone. He backed toward the door, grabbing blindly for his bag. The scent of his cologne trailed out the door behind him. "You'll regret it when I come back."

She ran to slam the door shut, throwing the deadbolt in place. "Step One: Lose the loser." Her hands shook beside her head pressed against the door. "Damn. He still has a set of keys."

———

"I'm sorry Mr. Collins, but you know the procedure. The bank has to put Mags's cottage into foreclosure," Jack Dorner, the bank's manager, said it as if he really was sorry.

Heck, everyone in Honeybrooke Cove had a tender spot for Margaret Ellington, known and loved by most of the cove as Mags. Barrett wouldn't be surprised to learn she had helped Mr. Dorner at some point in his life.

"How much time do we have?" Barrett Collins asked.

Mr. Dorner lifted his shoulders and pressed his palms into the walnut desk. The sun glinting off the lake cast shadows over the banker's face. "Depends on the buyer and the financial agreement. But the clock's been ticking for a while. Mags kept promising, sure something or someone was gonna turn up and pull her through. I've already put my neck out for her. Stretched it nearly clean off too."

Barrett dropped his head into his hands. "Yeah. I know. Mags had been praying for a miracle. She had her heart set on some distant family member coming out for a visit. I'd hoped it would help her to hang on."

"She pushed well past eighty, Barrett. This town will surely miss her." Mr. Dorner shuffled the papers on his desk and swished them into a filing cabinet. "We'll see what we can do."

Barrett lifted his head, his eyes narrowed. He bet Mags had mailed dozens of letters. Not one response. If he ever got ahold of those people in Los Angeles, he'd gladly straighten them out. But right now, he needed to clean up the mess Mags had gotten herself into before she'd passed away.

That was one promise he intended to keep.

CHAPTER 2

Victoria huddled on the couch. Her cell phone lay against her hip. Although the building security had promised to change the locks, they couldn't promise when they'd fit it into their schedule. After several attempts, she had them convinced of the urgency. What was another hour or two?

She twisted the corner of the pillow, rolling the edge between her fingers. There'd been something different about Connor. He made her jumpy. Somehow he had it all figured out that the breakup was her fault. And he was actually furious instead of contrite.

Victoria's gaze landed on the laptop beside her. Taking a deep breath suitable for diving into the Pacific Ocean, she cracked open the silver lid and renewed her search for employment.

She glanced at the emails from the contacts she'd already made that week. The job market in finance and investments had dried up in Los Angeles. Not only did everyone fight for their job, they fought for your job as well. No one was safe. Worse, now that she was free for hire, she was considered damaged goods.

With no prospects for immediate employment, she'd have to dip into her investment funds to tide her over until she could figure out what to do. She had some accounts earmarked for buying her own place.

Her hand paused over the mouse pad. She'd been walking through a room full of hidden landmines for longer than she cared to admit. Maybe, deep down, an internal warning bell had gone off months ago, and she'd refused to pay attention to it. A faint ember of confidence sparked. She wasn't a complete idiot. Just blinded by love. A mistake she would never make again.

Her cell phone rang. The specialized ringtone *Bwah-hah-hah* warned her of her father's call. No need to hear what he had to say. She eyed it, waiting for him to leave a message.

Guilt nudged her hand forward to hover over the phone. Time for her to play the game of chance. She shut her eyes and blindly touched the screen. Her stomach clenched as the phone when silent. Did that mean she hung up on him or had she picked up the call? She opened one eye. "Shoot."

"Victoria." Donald Banning had his no-nonsense bank president voice on full throttle. The clipped tones carried through the airwaves. "Pick up the phone."

Resolute in her previous stance with her father, she licked her lips. "What?" The single word sounded harsh even to her ears.

"I talked to Connor. He explained what happened."

She did not want to do this. Again. She shifted the cell phone. "Okay."

"You know I love you. Been there for you. Even during that time when you were unreasonable after your mom died."

"Yeah." She caught the flash of gnashing teeth reflected back at her in the glass door. *"Smile,"* was a single word mantra that stuck with her from childhood. She jabbed the air, twirled her finger for him to hurry up and say what he had to say.

"Connor's sorry," he said. "Just a big misunderstanding."

Awkward silence slithered between them. She flexed her fingers, slowly pumping energy into the joints. The burning behind her eyelids increased. She made an involuntary noise in the back of her throat.

"Look into your heart," he continued.

She glared at the phone. That little strangled sound must have been enough of a response to encourage her father. He was just getting started.

"Forgive him." Hope warmed his words, slowing them down. "He's too good of a catch. You don't want to let him go. You'll never be lucky enough to snag another like him."

Victoria stood up. Her lips flattened as she took a deep breath. She paced the room, wandering the condo that she used to think of as their home. "Why are you apologizing for him? Did he ask you to?"

"What does it matter?" her father snapped.

Her finger grazed the binding of one of Connor's law books. It lay on top of a stack of envelopes. Mail over a month old. She'd been too busy working, long hours and late nights, to look at it. Too busy building a perfect life that had always been out of reach, like capturing the elusive unicorn.

An ache between her eyebrows alerted her to the deep frown etching into her face. She picked up a law book to drop in the box holding the rest of Connor's belongings.

"Victoria. It's time to get over it."

"No."

"The man made a mistake. You'll never find anyone else that is half as good as him."

"Jeez. Thanks for the confidence-building speech, Dad." She played with her mom's engagement ring hanging from the silver chain around her neck. The warmth in the metal was a poor replacement for Diane Banning's famous hugs.

"Okay," he huffed into the phone. "I'll let him know you need to take a little more time to rethink things."

"I have nothing to rethink on that score. He knows that."

Victoria heard him take a deep breath. Like a sailboat captain repositioning his sails, searching for another way to land his boat. She braced for the landing.

"Look," he said. "Your bank account won't last long with one income if you're living in Los Angeles. If you can't figure anything out...well...you can answer phones at my bank. You could...you could move in with me. Until you get back on your feet."

Check herself into her own personal hell? She shivered. Not likely.

The phone nestled between shoulder and chin, Victoria flipped through the mail, buying time. "Ah, huh...well—" She paused over the white envelope. The address was handwritten in sloping cursive. A real letter? The name above the return address didn't ring any bells. But the address did. Honeybrooke Cove, Wisconsin. Eureka, she found something to derail his fatherly advice. "So, Dad, what do you know about Honeybrooke Cove?"

"Where?" His voice scraped the speaker. "Sounds like some Podunk place in Loserville to me."

Victoria knew a stall when she heard one. "Really? Hmm." The envelope tapped against her leg. She had a hazy memory of her parents arguing over a relative living in Wisconsin. Dad had called her Crazy Mags and refused to let her mom go and visit. The memory was vivid, even after all these years, because they didn't speak to each other for over a week. Soon after, Mom got the cancer report and nothing else really mattered.

"When should I schedule the movers?" Dad went on.

"What?" Guilt pinched her thoughts. She'd move in with her father when pigs flew, or in her case, when her heart healed. Never. Half-listening, she held the envelope up to the light. "Um, yeah, I still need some time to work things out."

"Excellent. I'll speak with Connor. Smooth the way. Let him know you're reconsidering your overreaction."

"Look, I, uh, gotta go, but I'll let you know. Okay?" Her mind no longer on the phone call, but on the letter inside, she added, "Bye."

Dropping to the couch, she tore open the envelope. Inside, contained a sheet of yellow lined legal paper, folded in thirds. She withdrew the letter and a faded photo fluttered to the floor. Time had faded the gray tones to sepia, but it was a woman and a teenage girl. Her mom's ring swung on the chain around her neck. It caught the sunlight, radiating fire across their smiling faces.

Victoria bent to retrieve the photo and flipped it over. Two names written with scrolling penmanship were on the back. Mags and Diane. She snapped it over, examining the two people, standing arm-in-arm, grinning at the photographer.

Her hands trembled as she smoothed the yellow paper out on her knee. The handwriting had bruised the fibers, leaving an indentation in its wake as the anonymous writer made clear their distinct thoughts. Rereading it didn't change what it said. She and her father were not only selfish; their behavior was appalling and unconscionable.

Her great-aunt Mags needed help and no one from her family had responded to the numerous attempts to contact them. Victoria counted back the dates the author gave as proof. Mags had been writing for a year.

Victoria checked the date stamped on the envelope. It had been sitting in the pile for over a month. How did she miss the other letters? Oh, yeah, The-One-That-Got-Away client. All those extra hours she'd put in to close a new client. And Connor had handled all the mail, controlling what came in and went out.

Victoria set the coffee cup down and read further. She pinched the bridge of her nose. How desperate could her great-aunt Mags's situation be? If it was that bad, she could have called her. Or emailed her. Had her dad received the same letters? The sound of his guilt-laced voice replayed in her head.

This required a face-to-face father and daughter meeting.

————

Victoria flipped through the financial magazine, the paper snapping as she turned the pages. She'd been sitting in the reception area for an hour. She should have made an appointment with her father before taking the time to battle her way through the traffic on the 405 Freeway. It had never crossed her mind before.

She glanced up, narrowing her eyes to examine her father's too perfect gatekeeper. Irritation seethed just under the polite surface. The woman did her job with militant attention and should receive a commendation. Was this the woman her dad wanted her to replace? Or worse. Work for her?

"Not happening," Victoria muttered. Carefully, she replaced the magazine before spinning on her heel, calculating the distance between Ms. Perfect and the double door. The gatekeeper watched her, holding her position, knowing she was about to breach the barrier. She had a chance if she kicked off her pumps and ran.

The doors swung open, releasing a volley of men and women in suits. They blindly rushed past her. Their cell phones already in use.

"Victoria." Donald Banning's dark brown eyes beamed back at her. "Speaking twice in one day. We're breaking records."

"Yeah, I know."

They stood awkwardly in the foyer. Neither one moved in for the perfunctory hug and air kiss. Ms. Perfect kept covert watch over her commander.

He glanced at his watch. A pinched line formed at the corner of his mouth. "Getting out is a great sign. But you should have called first."

"Sorry." Victoria shifted the leather purse, comforted by the normalcy of its weight on her shoulder. Appearing at his office seemed to put him off schedule. The longer she took, the worse it would become. She took a deep breath and jumped in. "Have you heard anything about Mom's Aunt Margaret? Recently."

"I thought she finally got the message. Is that why you asked about Honeybrooke?" He shook his head, shoving his hands into his pockets. "Still coming around after all these years too."

"You knew she needed help?" Victoria's stomach clenched. Whatever he was going to say would leave a bad taste in her mouth. But she refused to let his hard gaze pierce her resolve. "Mom would have wanted to help her."

"Not here." He grabbed her elbow, propelling her toward his office. Victoria slid into the leather chair. The mantra he'd enforced in her youth emerged. *Smile!* She flinched when the door closed behind her.

"Look, she caused nothing but arguments between me and your mom," he said, coming around to perch on his desk. "Once I got her out of your mom's life—our lives—the trouble was solved."

Devoured by the oversized-chair, Victoria raised her chin to look at him. Her grip tightened around the upholstered leather. The tension in her jaw made her muscles ache. "What does that poor old woman need?"

"Eh…." He rose to claim his throne behind the desk, fanning the air with his hands. The wooden barrier in place between them, he rested his elbows on the smooth surface. He picked up the sterling silver Montblanc pen, rolling it through his fingers. "Help paying the bills. Last I heard she had some issue with mortgage payments. Just like a whole lot of careless people. In too deep."

"And we did nothing?" Victoria's eyes were riveted on the pen. It gleamed in the office light. Her mom had given him a pen like that for Christmas. The last one they had together as a family.

His pen-play stalled. "Loaning money to family doesn't make good financial sense."

"Isn't that what you offered to do for me this morning?"

"It's different." The pen began to tap an impatient cadence into the desk blotter. "It was a job. Work. Not a handout."

"Like it or not, Dad, the way I see it, family is family."

"Exactly." He grinned back at her. "You're my family and she is not."

Victoria leaned forward, rising from the chair. "If Mom were alive—"

"Well, she's not." The pen rolled across the desk. The shadow of guilt sharpened the edges in his bone structure. "Besides, I talked it over with Connor. We agreed it was best to stay out of it."

"You talked it over with—" Victoria choked on Connor's name. She blinked. What else had they discussed? What other decisions had Connor made without her knowledge? Panic formed. She rubbed her chest. *Heart attack at thirty?*

Had she barely escaped something that had already gone seriously wrong? She gathered her things, scrambling to put distance between them. "What gives either one of you the right?"

"Victoria. Come back here."

Hugging her purse, she pushed through the door and marched past Ms. Perfect. "Here." She tossed the visitor tag on the receptionist's desk. "I won't need this anymore."

Victoria shivered despite the ninety-degree temperatures radiating in the parking structure. The dashboard dials glowed in the dim light, flaring when she turned the key in the BMW's ignition. She was safe in her car. Donald Banning may yell, but he never chased after anyone. Especially her. But after today, maybe he was capable of doing a lot more than she anticipated.

How had she allowed two men she could barely tolerate to control more of her life than she even realized? There had to be something she could do. Her brain refused to work out a solution. *Aneurism?* She shook her head. Giving in to Connor and her dad was *not* an option.

She glanced in the rearview mirror before backing out of the stall. Despite the circles entrenched under her eyes she still looked like her mom and Aunt Mags. Withdrawing the photo from her purse, she stared at it. Her heart ached. "I miss you, Mom."

Memories washed over her. Laughter. Hugs. Happy family holidays. It seemed like forever since she'd felt like she truly belonged. Whole and happy.

Maybe a quick trip out to see Aunt Mags would do both of them some good. Although she no longer held her financial advisor position, she still had a talent for making money. She'd give Aunt Mags a hand in working out her finances. And maybe, seeing her aunt would fill the empty place where her heart used to be.

A quick search on her cell phone proved that a same day flight out to Wisconsin would be too expensive for her bank account. Driving her BMW out to see Aunt Mags made the most sense. If she drove hard, she could be there in a couple of days. She had plenty of time to set things right.

Victoria pulled out of the parking structure, embracing the rush hour traffic. The searing sun created heat waves over the pavement. A smile tugged at the corner of her mouth. She was making a road trip. To Wisconsin. Heck, she might even extend her stay.

"Step Two: Get on with your life."

CHAPTER 3

C ar dancing to the song on the radio, Victoria drove her red convertible down the highway. She tapped her fingers on the steering wheel in time to the country beat. Somewhere lovers were swingin' and swayin' close to their sweetie.

The cell phone buzzed on her seat and Victoria yelped. Her heart sent an SOS code against her rib cage. Connor's phone number flashed on the screen. He'd been silent for the last couple of days. Today, he must have decided that break was over.

She eyed the flashing number like it was a snake with a rattle on its tail. The last text messages had taught her not to pick up her phone. It was a good thing he'd stopped when he did. One more message and she would have reported his harassment. He probably figured she knew enough to keep them as evidence.

Her cell phone flashed. Ten calls in the last two hours. The phone beeped, announcing a new voice mail. Connor finally dug into that tainted well of pride and wanted to talk to her. Victoria swallowed and turned up the radio.

North of Madison, Wisconsin, the clouds began to break up. Wind turbines scattered the horizon, their white blades spinning like giant pinwheels. Sunlight sparkled on the lush green fields. Tails of steam rose from the damp earth. Grazing cattle dotted the green hillside, oblivious of the drivers whizzing past on the winding roads.

Victoria followed the directions the gas attendant gave her the last time she'd filled up the car. Eager to meet her aunt Mags, she was like a horse racing to its stall. She took the exit, tires squealing. Her breath caught. Butterflies tumbled, tickling her insides.

The sign arched over the road announced she was entering the town of Honeybrooke Cove, Best Darn Place in Wisconsin.

Weary, she flexed her fingers and lingered a little longer than necessary at the stop sign at the corner of Vine and Main. A little thrill spun down her spine. A new beginning. A new chapter to her life.

She couldn't wait to explore the little town. But first, she had to find Aunt Mags's house.

She took a deep breath and pressed down on the accelerator. Main Street spread out before her like a Norman Rockwell painting. Mike's Gas & Garage sported an oval red and white enamel sign offering full service with a tank of gas. The only restaurant in sight was The Duck Blind Corner Café. A blindfolded duck tapped its way across a store marque. Ironically, there were two empty storefronts between the corner and the café. Maybe the duck was lost.

The neighboring post office was linked to the local watering hole, Tank's Bar. A neon mug of beer flickered next to the "We're Open" sign. Beside it, someone had taped a large poster in the tavern window, announcing the next Church Fall Festival.

Quaint picket fences lined the houses along Main Street. Mags's address was supposed to be somewhere on the lake side of the road. Victoria stopped at the curb and pulled out the map for the hundredth time since she'd left California. She peered at it from the dim interior light. She'd nearly worn the ink off the paper. The directions took her as far as Main Street then became vague because of the private roads threading around the lake.

"Next time, I buy a car with GPS." She patted the old red BMW's dashboard. "Sorry, girl, no offense."

They had been together since the day of her graduation from college. It had her the moment its top came down. It was her way of celebrating, since her father never showed up for commencement. Ten years ago, her decision to buy the convertible had been based on what she could easily afford and not how much of her property she could load into it. Now, a new car with GPS and the ability to stream her music over the audio system was a luxury she could no longer afford.

She dug in her purse and looked at her phone. Still no service. And that meant no GPS. The signal had dropped off when she went over that last hill about thirty miles back. The good news, if she could find some in the mess her life had become, was that she finally got a break from Connor. He was probably having a coronary right about now. She supposed she would have to listen to his messages eventually. Then she'd tell him where he could stick his cell phone.

Victoria leaned her head on the headrest. What she wouldn't give for a drive-thru coffee shack and a double shot of espresso.

Aunt Mags had yet to answer her calls and she had begun to wonder if she had the right number. Her visit was definitely going to be a surprise. She prayed the old woman's heart could take it.

She glanced out the window and wiped the perspiration beading between her breasts. About halfway through the flat stretch of Iowa the temperature had skyrocketed. She had decided to leave the convertible top up and attempt to keep some of the hot air out. With the air-conditioner up as high as it could go, Victoria prayed the little car would turn into a small fridge. Unfortunately, the elements outside were winning.

Late in the day, a red orb, radiating in fuchsias and brilliant yellow stood out on a backdrop of smog-free blue. The beauty of it shifted out of focus. Soon she'd be driving into the unknown without a working phone. She never stepped out of the condo without a fully charged phone. The exposed rawness made her want to lock her doors.

"Come on, Cupcake, pull it together. This is Honeybrooke Cove, not the big city."

The rapping knuckles on the passenger side window made her jerk, hitting her kneecap on the steering wheel. "Ack!" An automatic need for survival triggered the lock switch on the door handle. With the neckline of her shirt gripped close to her throat, she peered toward the person lurking outside her car.

All she could see were lean, jean-clad hips adorned with a plain leather tool belt. *Nice.* The logical side of her brain screamed that some serial killers like to use tools. Hammers. Those quick-tie-thingies. She slid her hand to the car horn. If she didn't arouse attention then she'd at least leave him partially deaf.

He wore a loose black t-shirt, exposing muscular forearms. Knuckles rapped the window again. *Strong hands.*

The cell phone she held in a death grip was useless. No 911 phone calls made with that thing. Its best use would be to chuck it at him if he made a move. No, wait! What if he threw her in the trunk? If he drove toward civilization, she would find a signal.

"Can I help you?"

Victoria jumped. Her weapon slid from her hand and landed between the seats. She looked up while frantically searching for her phone.

The owner of the t-shirt bent down, revealing the curl of hair brushing his neck. Shadows danced off his jawline. It looked like it had been several hours since he last shaved. He squinted through gray-blue eyes. "Are you lost?"

His voice, deep and velvety, broke through her blind search for the cell phone. Even though she didn't have a clue how to drive to

Aunt Mags's house from here, she shook her head, denying any need for directions. How had she, a once successful woman of the city, failed to fine-tune the directions to her great-aunt's home? Seriously. What did she think? That someone would leave her a trail of breadcrumbs? What had happened to her brain cells in the last month?

"Are you ill?" He made a rolling motion with his hand. "Can you manage to open your window?"

Victoria shook her head.

A crease deepened between his dark eyebrows. His jaw clenched. He tried the door, prying the handled away.

"Wait!" Protecting her precious car like a momma bear, she tossed away all fears for her own safety and hit the window switch.

Mr. T-shirt bent low, following the window's path. Grayish-blue eyes glittered back at her. "You're not ill?"

"No." She shook her head.

His head dipped so that Victoria couldn't see his face. Just the shadow of ridiculously long lashes brushing his cheeks. He drew in a deep breath and let it out.

"I'm sorry. I...I just needed to stop. Get my bearings," she said.

He tipped his head. A tanned, chiseled jaw framed his full mouth. His glance bounced off her belongings stuffed in the car. "You must be way off track. You're miles from the freeway." One work-roughened hand rested on the window ledge, the other swept off his Cubs baseball cap. He knocked the shaft of dark brown bangs from his forehead with the back of his hand. "Where are you headed?"

The exasperated tone in his voice made her nerves bristle. "I'm not lost. Just...lacking information for the final leg of my trip. This is where I'm going." She withdrew the sheet of directions, pointing to the address. "Margaret Ellington's place."

Mr. T-shirt, her wanna-be rescuer, straightened and snatched the paper from her grasp. "You're the one?"

"Hey, give that back." Victoria unbuckled the seatbelt and leaped out of the car. "Who do you think you are? That's private property."

She winced, racing around the back of the car. Days before, the chocolate-colored, high-heeled sandals had made her short legs look amazing. Now they made her feet complain with every step.

"Give it." She held out her hand. It hung in the air, waiting for the delivery.

"Name's Barrett." He returned the paper.

She crumpled it in her fist. "Victoria Banning."

Barrett folded his arms over his wide t-shirt covered chest. "You're the one Mags has been writing to. A relative." His eyes narrowed. "Or something."

"Margaret Ellington was my mother's aunt."

"Mm, hmm. People in Honeybrooke know her as Mags. Everyone who cares, that is." His scowl deepened. "How long do you plan to be here?"

She rested a fist on one cocked hip. Her fingers curled around the paper in her hand. In a matter of seconds, the humidity made it feel like a wad of Kleenex. His lack of welcome felt just as damp over her arrival. She swatted at the mosquitoes that buzzed around her head like bees drawn to a flower. "I intend to stay as long as I need to, Mr. ..." A heated flush swept up her neck. "Mr. Barrett."

"Barrett's my first name, Ms. Banning." He indicated the tools slung on his hip. "Barrett Collins. Handyman."

"I see." The irritation in his clipped tones scraped across her nerves. Victoria wiped her damp hands on her capris. Daylight was slipping away, and she was still no closer to her aunt's home than when she'd stopped to look at the map. "As much as I enjoy meeting a local, I'd really like to reach Aunt Mags's cottage before dark." She softened her words with a smile. "Can you give me the directions?"

Barrett sighed. He adjusted his tool belt and pointed to his pickup truck. "Follow me in."

Before she could agree, he marched off to his truck, assuming she'd follow like a meek lamb. He was buckled in and ready to go.

"Jeez, what's got your undies in a twist, Mr. Handyman?" Victoria muttered. Her heels clicked on the pavement as she limped over to settle behind the wheel. She didn't know what kind of driver he was, but she had no intention of being left behind. She already regretted asking for his help.

———

B arrett tossed his tool belt into the truck cab and climbed in. The buttery leather sighed as it took his weight. He did his best not to slam the door. He took a few deep breaths, settling his long legs into position. The hot steering wheel felt good under his hands, soothing his joints and his jangled nerves. Mr. Dorner, being the banker and attorney for Mags, must have finally gotten through to the relatives and informed them of the reading of the will. What kind of cold-hearted person wanted to see the cottage before paying their respects at the gravesite?

He studied the pretty woman slipping into the convertible. Her pants tightened around slim thighs as she bent to accommodate her high heels. She daintily lifted her feet, tucking them inside the little car. He should've known the moment he saw the car with California plates parked next to the curb that it was part of Mags's family and not some lost tourist. The convertible stood out like a bright red apple in a pile of potatoes. In snow, that thing would be about as good as a bear on stilts.

He bit the inside of his cheek. He may have just met the woman, but he knew her kind. Easy on the eyes, but shallow as a dry creek bed. Some way or another, women like that had just enough information to get themselves in trouble. He had a long list of ex-girlfriends like her. Each one taught him to stay out of their way. When he decided to leave Chicago, he'd made sure to leave them all behind. He never thought one of their kind would end up in Honeybrooke. The cove would be a prettier sight, but all the more dangerous too. If he didn't pay attention, he'd end up falling into that sinkhole.

He caught her gaze. She was watching him through her rearview mirror. Her chocolate eyes widened. Her brow lifted, waiting, questioning. With a twist and turn of her wrist, she had her caramel-colored hair up in a hair clip. She looked like a caramel and chocolate sundae. Maybe a cherry on top. Whipped cream.

"Cold-hearted," Barrett muttered under his breath. "And nuts."

He slipped the gearshift into place. He had that feeling, like ants running up his insides. Something about the woman told him to forget his promise and run.

Except this time, he couldn't. He'd promised Mags he'd take care of her place. He'd thought he had lots of time. Boy was he wrong. The bank and that woman were in for a surprise. No matter what was in Mags's will, he was not going down without a fight.

————

Headlights pulled away from the curb and wrapped around her. Victoria followed, memorizing the landmarks that would help her find the way back to town. They turned off Main Street. Just three roads down. Had she trusted in herself she could have avoided meeting one of Honeybrooke Cove's locals until she was ready. In particular, that bossy, albeit handsome, handyman driving ahead of her.

Victoria followed at a safe distance. She hunched over the steering wheel to see the moon rising over the hillside. Shadows clung to the maple trees lining the road. The numbers on the odometer reported they had driven a couple of miles. But these miles held hard curves and made the road ahead difficult to see.

The truck's brake lights flashed as a deer dashed in front of him. Barrett's pace slowed as if he'd let off some steam. He braked and jumped out. The arched gate swung open with a single push. Victoria frowned. She made a note to speak with Aunt Mags about ramping up the security. It now held second position on her to-do list. The first one was finally meeting her great-aunt.

He hopped back in the truck and put it in gear. His lights crept down a lane lined with piles of stone. A jet-black surface glittered to the right.

"This is it," Victoria whispered. "Family."

The lane bent to the left. Tall maple trees surrounded the back of the gray structure. The cottage stood by itself. A smaller version looked like a gardening shed.

The headlights caught the cottage. Victoria's eyebrows shot up. Not gray, but peeling, dirty white paint. And there were mounds of stones, stacked one on top of the other.

"Okay. Maybe Mags is a tad eccentric." She clenched and unclenched her fingers in an attempt to calm them enough to unbuckle her seatbelt.

Barrett was at her car door before she could gather her things. He held out his hand to help her. "Watch your step."

Operating on automatic, Victoria slipped her hand in his. His fingers were callused, strong. Steady. Warmth rushed over her, filling her with the need to lean into him. She took a step away, breaking the hold. New chapter. New life. Time to heal. Without complications.

He scrutinized the cottage. "Do you know if you have power hooked up?"

"Mags doesn't have power?" Victoria frowned. Aunt Mags was in worse shape than she thought.

"I thought you knew."

"Knew what?" Victoria kept her head down and concentrated

on stepping on the flat stone in the pathway. The last thing she needed was to break a heel or fall into the tall handyman striding beside her.

Barrett stopped and turned to stare at her. "Ms. Banning, Mags passed away a couple of weeks ago."

Victoria stumbled, grabbing his forearm before she hit the ground.

CHAPTER 4

Barrett turned the key in the lock and swung the front door open. Hot air, steamed and dusty, blasted Victoria's cheeks. Sneezing, she fumbled along the wall until she found the light switch. She flipped it. Nothing.

Her stomach churned like a ride on the tilt-a-wheel. She would have to contact the power and gas companies tomorrow. Sleeping in a strange place, without the ability to see, would make her seek out a hotel. Provided Honeybrooke had one. She didn't recall reading about it on the internet. Another spin, her stomach twisted. How could Mags have passed? If only she had known. Tears burned the corners of her eyes.

"Look." Barrett grabbed her wrist and led her into the living room. "Mags kept a flashlight under the sink." He turned, the shadows played over his face. "Might even have some candles somewhere. Stay here while I go look." He paused before placing the flashlight in her hand. "It'll be okay."

Obviously familiar with the cottage, he moved in the dark to locate the kitchen. The creak of the floorboards, then a bump and curse, pulled her attentions to a doorway. The door swung back and forth on its hinges. It made a whispered swoosh-swoosh as it brushed the floor.

"Are you all right," Victoria called out.

Met with silence, she shot the beam of light over the room. The living room was cozy. Someone had the foresight to protect the couch and overstuffed chairs with a linen covering.

Barrett returned with a flashlight and several half-melted candles in hand. His work boots struck the wide-plank flooring with sure purposeful strides.

"Sorry it took me so long." The extra light created a glow around their heads. He shoved the candles into her hands. Sweat glistened over bands of muscle collaring his neck. "It's weird. They weren't where she normally keeps them."

"Maybe I should find a hotel room," Victoria said.

"Suit yourself. Though I imagine Mags would have liked you to stay a bit." He set one of the candles on the fireplace ledge and pulled out a box of matches from his pocket. The wick came to life.

Standing over six feet, Barrett's wide shoulders stretched the t-shirt, drawing Victoria's attention. The jean material strained over his thighs.

He turned with a mission-accomplished smile stretching his lips and lighting up his eyes. Then just as quickly, like a wall switch, the wariness was back. "That should do it." He wiped his hands on his jeans. "Want me to stay until you've checked things out?"

"Oh, I'm good. Thanks. You've helped me enough already."

He shook his head. "Haven't done that much. You have things to bring in, right? Familiarize yourself with Mags's..." He paused, struggling, searching. "Correction. Your place."

"My place?" Victoria squinted at him through the dim light.

"Figured it is. You being her only family."

Victoria closed her eyes, focusing on the second bombshell of news he dropped on her. "I can't stay here," she muttered under her breath. "I might be trespassing." She snatched her purse from the couch. "I'll find someplace else to stay."

Barrett hooked her arm, stalling her escape. "The nearest hotel is probably an hour down the road."

Victoria shook him off and grabbed for the door. She couldn't possibly drive another mile. Exhaustion threatened to choke her with tears. "I didn't know the woman. How could I possibly be the new owner of this cottage?"

His gaze scraped over her face. "You really mean it, don't you?"

She did her best not to roll her eyes. "Like I told you already, I didn't know her. I came to meet her. To help her."

He blew out a deep breath. "Listen. Stay here. Let me make some calls. Maybe Jack Dorner is available for an emergency meeting tonight."

Victoria stared at his retreating shoulders. She licked her lips, tasting the salty perspiration. "Hey," she called. "Who is Mr. Dorner?"

Barrett paused and rested his wrist on the top of the truck door. "He's a one-stop-shop in Honeybrooke Cove. Banker. Executor. And foreclosure agent."

"Foreclosure?" Victoria gripped the doorframe as if holding onto the rope of the sinking Titanic.

"Don't worry." He lifted his hand. "I'll take you to his place so you can get back to California as soon as Mags's will is read."

"Thanks," Victoria muttered through a stiff smile.

B arrett and Victoria stood outside Mr. Dorner's office. The building was a mix of business and country cottage, brick and clapboard, decorated with a pair of bent willow rockers on the front porch. They turned as the long white Cadillac pulled beside the curb.

Jack Dorner unfolded his legs and pushed his girth out of the vehicle. After the perfunctory greeting and sharing of identification, he let them into his office.

"Come on in, Ms. Banning." His balding scalp caught the porch light as he pushed open the door. "Can't say I was expecting to hear from Mags's family so soon. Not after all this time." He wiped his brow with a handkerchief and turned a side-eye toward her. "Course, death and wills have a tendency to catch people's attention."

Victoria moved slowly, feeling like a participant is some soupy dream. Caught in a situation she had a feeling she wouldn't like.

Barrett offered her a reassuring smile. "Don't worry. He's actually one of the good guys."

Victoria slipped past Mr. Dorner. Old leather and wood permeated the shadows, reminding the visitors that this was not his first financial meeting. She settled into the overstuffed leather chair. Her heart thumped hard against her rib cage.

"Barrett," her aunt's attorney growled. "You better get on in here."

"What?" Barrett dropped the magazine on the coffee table.

Mr. Dorner held up the legal-sized file. "Mags wanted you in on this too."

The whooshing in Victoria's ears increased.

The town handyman sat down next to her. He gave her a confused glance and shrugged. Their knees almost touching, they stared at Margaret Ellington's attorney. They listened to him read the will and discovered their lives were now joined together by a meddlesome old lady from the grave.

The roaring in Victoria's ears crashed like waves hitting a rocky shore.

———

B arrett and Victoria gazed up at the cottage that had officially become their responsibility. He lifted her hand, turning it up and dropped the key in her palm.

"Thanks." Victoria closed her fingers around the cool metal.

"I'll carry in the bags." Barrett spun on his heels, headed to Victoria's car.

She opened her mouth to refuse his help, but his rigid back was already slipping into the night. Mr. Dorner had promised to move heaven and earth to get the power on as soon as possible. For now, she would have to light every candle in the cottage just to find the bathroom.

Her hope renewed, comforted by the warm glow in the living room. Did Mags really leave her the cottage?

She scrunched her nose. Their new home. That's how her aunt's will read. She and Barrett Collins were now co-owners of a house in desperate need of repair and on the verge of foreclosure. The bank's clock was ticking.

The flashlight she held in front of her like a sword, cut through the dark, leading her on the tour of the house. She pushed the swinging door and stepped into the room. Multiple light fixtures hung from the ceiling, offering the promise of a well-lit kitchen. Over the sink, windows encased the outer wall. Cabinets with antique frosted-glass panes flanked two other walls. The appliances looked like they were energy-guzzlers from the 1950s. She prayed they'd last her a while. At least until she had income flowing in. From somewhere.

Where did that come from? This was supposed to be a quick visit. Mend the family fences. The flashlight's beam washed over the kitchen as Victoria mumbled to finish the thought. "Just a road trip to see an old woman from my mom's youth."

The first door off the kitchen led to the guest bedroom. The walls were a mint green that might have been in vogue back in the

70's. The purchase of several gallons of interior paint went on Victoria's to-do list.

A plaque hung over the empty space where the bed once stood. 'Dreams can come true, if you've the courage to pursue them.' Someone had removed the beds and left only the dresser. The promise of a bed had been something that made her push on all day. It had also been something that made it easier to walk away from the bedroom suite she and Connor had shared. That, and there was no way she was going to sleep where he had probably sweated it up with someone else.

Victoria tipped her head, trying to loosen the kinked muscles that seemed to get tighter by the moment. She would get through this. The lack of power and no bed was just a small hiccup. The death of her great-aunt Mags? Yeah. Now that was a huge surprise.

The tour down the hall revealed a second bedroom. Someone had painted the master-bedroom walls a fuchsia and then tried to cover it up with a coat of Pepto-Bismol pink. It failed miserably. Victoria scanned the room with her flashlight. The bedframe, four-posted, honey-gold oak, rested against the pink wall. The mattress was gone.

The view from the double-paned window was too hard to see. Draped in clouds, an empty blackness covered the moon and stars. An oily finger slid into view, bobbing against the window. It made a skin-shivering scrape over the glass. Victoria gasped. The flash-light hit the floor, clattering over the wood planks, and rolled to the corner of the room.

A giggle sputtered in her throat, fighting for space with the tears. She retrieved the flashlight and added tree trimming to the list. No need to look in the closet. She'd deal with it in the daylight.

Victoria pulled the door shut and returned to the living room. Barrett had already stacked her belongings by the front door. The small mound represented what she deemed necessary for a road trip. The rest she had stored in the care of the starving college students employed by The Meat Masters Moving Company. Connor's things were still in the condo. It was time for him to deal with his own stuff.

The small pittance of personal effects looked like she intended her stay to be brief. Not move in. Maybe that was why Barrett grinned back at her. He thought she'd cut and run as soon as the opportunity hit.

"Just tell me where to put the boxes. Then I'll be on my way."

Victoria tore open the box that held her favorite blanket. "No need. I'll manage."

She swung open what looked like the linen closet. Two pillows, packed neatly away in protective bags, shined like a beacon to a weary soul.

Standing on unsteady legs, she began to clear the linen covering from the couch. Victoria spun around, set on removing the others from the two chairs. Dust swirled in the air, making her sneeze. The candle flames wavered, casting shadows on the flower-wallpapered room. Ever since the reading of the will, the awkwardness between them seemed to grow.

"It's late in the summer." Barrett lifted the linens from her hands and folded them in tight squares.

"So I've heard," Victoria said. "Who knew? We California city folk know the seasons, too."

"It takes a little more than switching out your flip-flops." He swatted at the cushions. "Won't be long before the critters come in. Looking for a place to hole up for the winter."

"Nice try." She eyed the sofa and chairs. Was he trying to scare her off? "I'm staying. Besides, I'll see that the power will be on tomorrow."

Barrett turned to her, one hip cocked, his eyes stormy. "Didn't say you weren't." He pointed to the sheet and pillows. "Want a hand, Ms. Banning?"

"How'd you know I don't intend to sleep in one of the bedrooms?"

Barrett shrugged. "Doesn't take a rocket scientist. The couch will make a better bed than that hardwood floor. Besides, you looked like you had a mission to complete. If it bothers you, Ms. Banning, I'll get out of the way." He did as promised and stepped back.

"Victoria."

"Pardon?"

"Now that we're partners in this cottage, don't you think you should call me Victoria?" She looked up from tucking the corner of the sheet over the cushion. The warmth of his smile actually reached his eyes. Heat slid under her sleeveless blouse and straight up to her ears. Her breasts pebbled under his gaze.

"Well now, Victoria, it is a pleasure."

Victoria steeled her shoulders, waiting for his, 'But…'

It never came. He stared at her. The smile had already slipped, replaced by a frown. Here it comes.

"Ms. Banning. Victoria," he corrected. "You sure you don't want to stay someplace else? Where there's power?"

"I'll be fine." Even to her own ears, she didn't sound very convincing.

Barrett tilted her chin so that she looked straight into his blue-gray eyes lined with the longest eyelashes she'd ever witnessed on a man. Her gaze dropped to his mouth. She hadn't noticed how full his lips were. Probably because she'd been too busy being bossed around by that mouth. Although she wasn't one for kissing a complete stranger, she wouldn't mind if he took it upon himself to kiss her. Just this once. She leaned into him. His arm tightened. Her stomach growled like she'd been impregnated by a Sasquatch.

He gave her a quick brotherly hug and left her standing by the hearth. Victoria blinked, grateful that this time any tale-tell signs of embarrassment were hidden by the shadows.

"Welcome to Honeybrooke Cove," he said. "I'll be back to check on you later."

Victoria scrubbed her temples as his truck lights arched and slipped into the night. What was she thinking? She just met this man. *Desperate?* No, just tired. And definitely weary of men.

CHAPTER 5

Victoria triple checked the locked door, then stripped off her clothes and tossed them on the chair. After rummaging through her overnight bag, she pulled out a pair of shorts and a pink tank top. She snorted. It was almost the same color as the bedroom walls. Who puts that on a wall?

Aided by the glow of the candles, she found the bathroom and washed the grime off her face with tepid water. A hot shower in the morning would require a miracle. She skated her feet over the smooth hardwood floors. They were cool to the touch. Wanting the caress of fresh air over her skin, she slid her hand to the window sash and tugged on it. Stuck. Sweat dripped from her brow. Her legs braced, she muscled one window open.

The breeze lifted her hair off her shoulders. She tilted her head to look up at the stars and breathed in the night air. Only the chirp of crickets broke apart the silence. "I'm sorry, Aunt Mags," she whispered into the late summer air. "If only I had known sooner."

The makeshift bed on the couch called her name. So did the other half of a cheese sandwich she purchased almost a day ago.

She dug through the bag until she found it. Dry as dust, the bread crumbled in her hands. She picked off the cheese and nibbled what she could before giving up on the inedible mess.

Her legs stretched out, she leaned back into the corner of the couch and stared at the wavering shadows on the wall. How had her simple plan to rediscover and help her great-aunt become so complicated? There had to be an easy solution to inheriting a run-down cottage. Eyes heavy, her head nodded. A deep sigh emptied out.

Victoria's eyes snapped open at the sound of floorboards creaking.

Something thumped against the back porch and dragged across the flooring. She shivered and pulled the blanket up to her shoulders. The candles on the hearth had melted down to puddles of wax, and cast wavering shadows across the room. How long had she been asleep?

Victoria grabbed the poker as the doorknob turned, and the door swung open. "What do you think you're doing?"

Barrett had the nerve to glare back at her. He shifted the paper bag in his arm and closed the door. "Figured you were hungry. Thought I'd better get to the Duck Blind before Lyle closed for the day." He held out the bag as a peace offering. "Best burger in town."

The savory perfume coming from the bag called to her like a drug. Barrett must have been a snake charmer in another life. Victoria stepped closer as the Sasquatch in her stomach rumbled again.

Grinning, he reached into another bag and pulled out three more candles. "Brought these too." He motioned for her to set the poker down. "Stole them from Lyle. He won't mind though. Not much use for candles until February."

Victoria caught the twinkle in his eyes. She couldn't resist. "Why February?"

"That's when Fred serves his special Valentine's Day meal. Liver and onions."

"That's disgusting." She scrunched her nose and fought back the vision.

"Maybe." Barrett put the bag on the coffee table and pulled out the takeout container. The smell of beef and french fries was pure ambrosia to a starving woman. "But Lyle swears by it. Says every time he had liver and onions with his lady they ended up with a baby nine months later."

"Doesn't he know it's not the liver and onions that make the baby?"

"He's sworn off liver." Barrett shrugged. "Hasn't eaten a bite of it in over twenty years. But every Valentine's Day he puts it on his specials board and has a disclaimer for everyone to read and sign."

Victoria took a bite of her sandwich and sighed. It might be the best darn burger she'd had in a long time. Barrett was watching her. Just in case he had some crazed notion she was going to share, she held onto the burger, refusing to release it from her grasp. She licked her lips, dreading the answer to her next question. "Do you want a bite?"

Barrett shook his head. "I'll eat at home."

Home. She tried to catch a glimpse of his left hand. No ring. Nor was there a faded tan line where his ring was supposed to be. Still, he might have someone waiting for him. Connor sure didn't seem to have an issue with that little detail. The bite of sandwich in her mouth grew, turning into a ball of dust. She choked it down.

"Have you eaten the Valentine's special? Any babies I should know about? Or a special someone to share your liver with?"

Barrett chuckled. It was a warm, velvet caress on her edgy nerves. "Never had a reason to be there on Valentine's Day." He rose, scrubbing his faded jeans with his hands. "I better get going. Tilly's waiting for her supper."

Tilly. Victoria mulled over his answer and followed him to the door. So, he did have someone waiting at home. Maybe not as bad as Connor, but he had no business hanging out with her. Still, he did bring her some food to get through the night. She should be grateful.

He snapped his fingers. "Wait here." He jogged off to his truck. Victoria couldn't help noticing the way his jeans molded over his backside when he bent over the seat. His thighs stretched the material, showing off muscular legs.

He jogged back. A thermos in his hand. "You'll need this."

Victoria gazed at the worn and dented thermos. She looked up and could have sworn there was a blush crawling up from his collar.

"Coffee. If you keep it sealed, it'll be good for in the morning."

"Coffee," she whispered. She cradled the thermos like a baby, hugging it close to her chest. Tears burned, threatening to embarrass her. She rose on tiptoes and touched her lips to his. She lingered a little longer than she intended. "Oh." Puzzled by the buzz running through her body, she wondered if she'd get another opportunity to see if it happened again.

Barrett cleared his throat before tucking a wave of hair behind her ear. "I'll see you tomorrow."

Mesmerized by his touch, all Victoria could do was nod. She was too busy refusing her body's plea to leap into his arms and demand that he have his way with her. She licked her lips, prepping them in case he read her mind and came in for another kiss. What was she doing?

It had been a while since she'd made out on a couch with a handsome man. She and Connor always made sure to go to the bedroom. Lights always off. He didn't like the idea of messing up the living room. Funny, that was not okay, but cheating on her didn't seem to bother him.

Barrett gripped the top of the doorframe with one hand and leaned toward her. The thermos stood like a guardian between them, blocking any close contact. His mouth, those full lips were close to hers. "I brought you a cooler of ice too."

She felt the brush of his breath on her cheek. Her mom used to call it butterfly kisses. A whisper of a breeze nuzzled the hair on her neck, cautioning her to slow down.

Victoria nodded, leaning in with a Jezebel sway to her body. "I thought I heard you dragging it over by the kitchen. Thanks."

A confused look darkened his eyes. "I put it on the front porch." He paused, his fingers edging toward her shoulder. "Look, if the power company gets it right, the house will have juice in a day or so. Maybe even ice in your freezer by afternoon."

"Okay." She didn't know why he felt the need to move it from the back of the house to the front, but she was grateful for his help. Grateful enough to kiss him one more time before he left. *To go home to someone else,* her inner voice hissed.

She took a swift step back. Oh no! They may be forced into a partnership for now, but that was all. She was not going to be the new bimbo in town. Had she lost her senses? For cripes' sake, what was Aunt Mags thinking when she drew up that will?

"Smile!" her father's voice shouted in her head. Obediently, Victoria's lips stretched into a pleasant mask. "Good night, Barrett." She grabbed the door and started to shut it in his face. She sure hoped he'd remove his hand from the doorframe in time.

"Victoria."

Her name rumbled under his breath, causing her to freeze. Enthralled, she couldn't move. He leaned in. Their lips touched. Lightly. He shifted. One hand pulled her waist closer. He drew back. Then having second thoughts, he returned to linger on her lips. He tasted of coffee and...man. Definitely trouble.

Victoria shivered when he pulled away.

"Good night," he whispered. "Partner."

She blinked. He was in his truck and backing up before she could remember to breathe. He was headed home. To Tilly.

She shook free from the trance.

The wind had picked up. Leaves swirled under the trees, creating what Californians called dust devils. Did Midwesterners have a name for them? She held the blanket tight around her shoulders, more confused than ever, and slowly closed the door. The deadbolt clicked into place.

She glanced at the clock. Ten o'clock. Too early to sleep for this west coast girl. She sat down on the couch. The breeze had pushed out the heat, making the house feel cooler.

Despite the time, her eyelids grew heavy. She'd need toothpicks to keep them propped open. Sighing, she settled deeper into the cushions.

The scraping sound came again. It was at the back of the house, again, by the kitchen porch.

Victoria's heart skipped. "Barrett?"

She ran to the window. Outside, it was dark and unwelcoming. No headlights cut a swatch out of the night. Nothing but darkness.

The fireplace poker was back in Victoria's hands before she realized it. Barrett's warnings of wild animals and all the horror movies combined to make a scene of razor-sharp nails and teeth.

As soon as she got to the kitchen the movement outside stopped. She turned off her flashlight and squatted next to the ancient refrigerator. The clouds drifted past the moon. Moonlight shined through the window, illuminating the plaque Aunt Mags had hung on the wall.

Victoria read the words slowly. "Lord, help me change the things I can, accept the things I cannot change, and the wisdom to know the difference."

Right. Point taken. Without Aunt Mags, she had no reason at all to stay in Honeybrooke Cove. Starting tomorrow morning, she would meet with Mr. Dorner and find out what it would take to put the house on the market. Convince Barrett it was the smart thing to do. Then she'd get in her sweet little car and head back to California.

She tilted her head against the wall. A tear slid down her cheek. Guilt and loneliness swept through her. Victoria took a deep shuddering breath. She didn't want to end up like Aunt Mags, in trouble and alone. But isn't that what waited for her back home?

CHAPTER 6

"Hello-o-o!" the voice cawed like a crow sitting on a dumpster.

Victoria jumped, sending the poker skidding across the white kitchen tile floor and straight for the 1950s gas stove. She glanced at the list of things she needed to do that morning. She'd had all night to think and write. The page was nearly full. Meeting a new neighbor was not on the list. Moving back to California was.

Although she had been miserable in California, she at least had electricity and a cell phone that worked. And a lying-cheating-no-good-snake-ex-boyfriend. But who wants a perfect life?

"Hello-o-o!" the woman called out again. This time she didn't stop there. She started scratching and tapping at the windowpane. The woman had her hair teased into a short cap that must have required a can of hairspray. Every single day.

Victoria scrubbed her weary eyes. Except for the head-bobbing moments, she hadn't slept all night and didn't feel like talking to anyone who wasn't on her list.

The order to 'Smile!' echoed in her sleep-deprived brain. She took a deep breath and sucked in the last drop of coffee Barrett had left with her. Silence. Victoria looked up.

The woman stood at the window ready to pounce on her prey. "I'm your neighbor. Mrs. Tewilliger." A tray of cookies came into view. "I brought something over for you. Thought you might be hungry."

Slowly, Victoria lifted her hand in defeat. She was stiff from sitting on the hard kitchen chair for most of the night. Her throat was parched. Humid air filled the house, making it damp and sticky. She'd love a huge tankard of iced tea, but the cooler was outside. And so was that thing that kept dragging and scrapping across the porch. It kept it up until about two in the morning. Thank goodness, the flashlight batteries hadn't drained out.

The smile firmly in place, she unlocked the door. "Good morning, Mrs. Tewilliger."

The woman bustled past her. The tray of oatmeal raisin cookies presented before her as if they'd won first place in a bake-off. She pushed everything on the table out of the way. Victoria caught the flashlight before it rolled off the table.

"Dear me!" Mrs. Tewilliger fluffed her helmet-hair, patting it in place. "I saw a light moving around and thought I should come over before I go to work at the market." She took in the the kitchen's state, Victoria's smeared makeup, and the pad of paper on the table. "Not an early riser, I see."

Victoria wondered if the woman intended on counting the silver in the drawer. Provided there was some. She hadn't noticed. "Thanks for the cookies."

"Well, I figured I should be neighborly. Our properties practically butt next to each other." Mrs. Tewilliger fanned her face. "Lord have mercy! You like it hot in here."

"Most of the windows won't open."

"Why not?" Mrs. Tewilliger's eyes widened. "I know I saw Barrett Collins's truck parked here last night."

Victoria wrapped the blanket tighter. This was just one more thing to add to the plus side of leaving Honeybrooke Cove. No neighbors taking roll call of visitors.

"You call that Barrett," Mrs. Tewilliger continued. "He'll fix it for you. Surprised he's not here already."

"I imagine he'll want to wait until the sun comes up." Victoria could feel her smile slip. "Besides, I don't have power."

"No power?" Mrs. Tewilliger marched over to the light switch. She flipped it up. The light bulbs exploded into life. "Looks to me like you have it just fine."

"Oh, my! Mr. Dorner must have worked his magic with the power company." In the glare of the lights, Victoria looked at her kitchen, really seeing it for the first time. Cupboards filled one side of the other wall. The window over the sink and counter banked another. It was a kitchen designed for cooking big meals. Too bad, she was a terrible cook.

"Do you have coffee?" Her new neighbor popped her head into one of the cupboards. "Mags preferred tea, but I'm willing to bet she has some coffee stashed away for company." Head tilted, she contemplated Victoria's taste. "You look like a coffee drinker. You'll want to come over to the market and stock up on things. Mmm-hmm."

Victoria ran her finger over the edge of the cookie tray. "I don't think I'll need much. I don't intend to be here much longer."

Mrs. Tewilliger stopped her rummaging. She peered out from her bangs. "What do you mean? You're leaving already?" Her neck began to turn a mottled shade of pink. The color swiftly rose to her cheeks. "After what you put your aunt through, not being there when she needed you most, and then you go off and leave?" She snapped her fingers. "Just like that?"

A vehicle rumbled up the driveway. Somewhere in the yard, a car door slammed shut. It barely registered; Victoria had an irate elderly woman in her kitchen, and she had no idea what to do with her.

She stood. A better defense than allowing that woman to point her finger in her face. "I'm sorry. Thank you for the cookies. It was a...pleasure to meet you."

Mrs. Tewilliger refused to budge. She dug in her heels, intent on delivering her feelings. As Victoria's father liked to say, 'and strong message to follow.'

"Let me tell you, this just won't do." She took a step closer.

The granite countertop pressed into the small of Victoria's back. "Mrs. Tewilliger, I didn't know…"

"Suppose you intend to knock it down," Mrs. Tewilliger said. "Take life right out of this cove. That's what folks like you do. Don't know what they want. Don't know what they got until it's gone."

The door swung open. Barrett stuck his head in. "Hey, there."

Victoria sighed, grateful to see his handsome face. He'd know what to do with the unhinged woman in her house.

"You'll ruin it for him too," Mrs. Tewilliger said, pointing in Barrett's direction.

Picking up on the energy in the room, Barrett moved cautiously into the kitchen. "Mrs. T, you're up bright and early. What's going on here?"

"Just welcoming Mags's relative." Mrs. T moved the pad of paper toward Barrett. The list of two columns, Pros and Cons, stood out on the white paper. "Ms. Banning says she's leaving Honeybrooke Cove."

He picked up the pad and flipped the pages over.

"Hey!" Victoria stood on tiptoes and tried to yank it from his hands. "Give it back."

"You really intend to leave? I bet you haven't even looked outside." He dropped the pad on the table. "Have you?"

Victoria folded her arms across her chest. "It's just there are things…"

Mrs. T looked like she was about to pop. She went to work leaving the cookies on a paper towel. "If only Mags were still alive…"

"We don't intend to pressure or pry, do we? I'm sure Victoria has her reasons for wanting to leave so soon after getting here."

Barrett gently steered Mrs. T to the door. "Don't you worry. I'll take it from here."

They watched her march across the backyard. Her lips were still moving when she turned at the side gate and sent a seething glare toward the kitchen window.

"Well, good morning, Partner." Leaning against the kitchen sink, hands planted on his hips, Barrett drew in a deep breath. "Thought maybe you'd like to join me for breakfast."

Victoria chuckled, swallowing grateful tears. "I don't...I haven't had a chance to clean up."

"Look." He scrubbed his chin and pushed off the counter. "Give us a chance." He paused. "I mean Honeybrooke."

"I don't think..." She shook her head. "This is not what I—"

"Shew, it's still hot enough to melt iron in here." Barrett motioned outside. "I'm going to my truck and get my tools. I'll open some windows while you shower."

He had turned for his truck before she could refuse his invitation. Victoria looked for reasons to deny him but the idea of a meal before she hit the road made too much sense. Maybe over breakfast he'd explain what had Mrs. Tewilliger all worked up. Then she'd fill him in on her plans to dump the financial monster on someone else.

Unlike the rest of the house, the bathroom was a pleasant surprise. Recently updated, it had all the modern conveniences. The cabinets were solid oak. Granite and tile surrounded the deep tub. The shower was separate, deep and roomy enough for two people.

Victoria shivered and let the cold water cascade over her shoulders, down her back. Even the water heater didn't work. The house was in worse shape than she realized.

She didn't feel like offering up herself like one big target of crazy, but maybe there'd be a way to talk to Barrett about the sounds throughout the night. In the daylight, standing in the gorgeous bathroom, her determination to leave began to dissolve.

Her stomach growled, making it obvious that she needed a good meal before she made another bad decision.

Clanking and hammering echoed through the air ducts. Barrett continued to work on the windows. A few muffled words rose through floorboards.

She wrapped the towel around her hair, flipping it into a turban. It's funny how Barrett knew to arrive like a shining knight. Although in his case, he rode a pickup truck, saving her from the neighborhood dragon lady.

Her hands slowed. How did he let himself in the front door? It was locked. She was sure of it. She had neurotically checked it throughout the night.

CHAPTER 7

The hum of water through the pipes turned Barrett's head. Victoria must have taken his advice and headed to the shower. He washed the dust off his hands in the kitchen sink and suddenly realized the water heater wasn't functioning. Feeling a tad bit guilty he'd been the one to send her to a cold shower, he leaned a hip against the counter and waited for the city girl's shriek.

The pad of paper Victoria had been working on yelled at him like a hooker on the streets. 'Pick me up. You know you want to.'

He yanked the paper towel off the roll, wiping away the cottage's years of grime. He and Mags had gone round and round about the need for repairs. Their last conversation about the state of the house ended with her telling him he was a fool. It was time; he'd better decide if he intended to stay in Honeybrooke Cove or head back to his other life. Even in death, Mags had pushed home her choice. He hated being forced to do anything.

He shoved his fists into his back pockets to keep from sticking his nose into something that wasn't his business. It'd be all for the better if Victoria packed up before she started to think about putting down roots.

Barrett dropped onto the kitchen chair. The sound of running water, hitting the new shower door he'd recently installed, caught his attention. The remodeling job had taken him longer than he had expected. He imagined it was partly due to Mags wanting to talk to him while he worked.

The humming in the pipes ceased. The quiet echoed in the kitchen. He supposed she'd want him to look at that too. A cabinet door slammed. The heated towel-closet. He'd been meaning to check the hinges before anyone used it. Those seals were so tight they'd catch your finger like a snapping turtle.

He couldn't help smiling. Once, after a brief stay in the urgent care center, Mags decided she needed warm towels at home. Most patients liked to cozy up to something warm when they were feeling poorly. Man, she could not stop talking about having a warm and toasty towel. He wished he could have finished it in time for her. Instead, a stranger was the first to experience the luxury.

His fingers thrummed on the smooth tabletop. He never expected Mags would actually leave the cottage to him and a stranger. Family or not, the city girl from California was a stranger. She didn't know her aunt and didn't understand the gift she'd been given. If she did decide to put the house on the market, he'd find a way to buy her out.

He caught the corner of the pad of paper with his finger. He spun it around in a lazy circle. The words whirled together. She'd listed two columns. On the top were the headers, Pros and the Cons. Not much was in the Pros column. Just one word. Home.

Barrett grunted. That must have been wishful thinking on her part because the Cons column filled its side of the page. He flipped the paper. She'd listed more on the back.

"Well, if you don't like it here, then let me help you find the road out of here." He tossed the pad down on the table, smacking the surface.

He glanced down the hall toward the bathroom. Victoria had

been in there forever. He rubbed his jaw. "Who does she think she is to come into town, and in one night pass judgment?"

How Mags thought attaching his name to the cottage along with her long-lost niece was a smart decision was beyond him. The complication quotient just multiplied tenfold.

He clenched and unclenched his fingers, always mindful of the importance of keeping the joints loose, his hands strong and steady. His stomach rumbled. The longer he sat and waited for her highness to emerge from the bathroom, the madder he got.

He stood and began pacing. He had a list of things to do of his own. A man had to eat. Soon. Walking down the hallway, he stopped at the bathroom door. "Victoria?"

A squeal erupted. "Don't come in!" The lock hit home.

Barrett glared at the door. What made that woman, sexy though she might be, think he would do a thing like that? "Are you coming out anytime soon?"

"I'm sorry. I just need to dry off. It's taking me a while."

An exasperated sigh escaped. He'd had the same hellish experience waiting on his little sister when he was a teenager. He was too old to hang out by the bathroom, pounding on the door to hurry it up. Didn't help then. Wouldn't help now. He took a deep breath. She didn't have that much square yardage of flesh to towel off. "Look. If you don't want to go with me, just say so." She mumbled something. By the hissing, he had a feeling it wasn't pleasant.

He shut his eyes, wishing he had x-ray vision. Thoughts of a naked Victoria, no towel anywhere, flashed in his food-starved brain.

Her wet hair, darkened by the shower, was smooth and shiny. It coiled down her back. A little stream of water snaked down her shoulders, to her rounded hips. He pressed his forehead against the wood doorframe and did his best to shake the vision from his thoughts.

"Lyle is going to be impatient. I already told him to expect us.

For breakfast. Not lunch." *Smack!* His head bounced where she hit the door on the other side.

"I said, I want to go but can't until you find me something to dry off with."

"Towels are there in the cabinet." He wondered if her eyes glittered when she was angry.

"Oh no, they're not," she snapped. "And I am not going back in there until that finger-guillotine is fixed."

"I put them in there a couple weeks back." He rubbed his jaw. He knew they were there. "Look. Race out. Get your stuff. Whatever you need. I promise not to peek." He hoped he could fulfill that last one.

"Barrett," she said, her voice rising, barely in control. "Bring me the sheet." She added as an afterthought. "Please."

Too hungry to argue, Barrett stalked back to the couch where she'd left the rumpled sheet. He flipped it over his arm and knocked on the door. "Here." He presented it to her, bowing like the queen's lowly servant.

Victoria cracked the door open a little wider. She turned, wrestling the sheet through the opening and around her breasts. It slipped when she stepped away, showing him her backside.

"Need some help?"

The glare she shot over her shoulder could have been lightning bolts. Barrett grinned. She looked better in real life than in his imagination. Before he could think of a compliment that didn't make him sound like a stalker or a country hayseed, she slammed the door in his face.

Barrett frowned. Her cheeks may have been a pretty pink, but he hadn't missed the fear sparking out at him. He eased away from the door. He had definitely been out of circulation for far too long.

———

Victoria stepped onto the porch. She wore a pair of jeans and a cotton t-shirt. A gauzy button-down shirt opened up, gave her a sense of protection. Her smile wobbled. "I'm ready."

She appreciated that he'd sat outside to give her some room to finish dressing. The debate to lock the doors and leave him out there was tempting. Having clothes on and standing in the light of day gave her more courage.

"Hey," Barrett rose from the porch swing. He gave her lots of space and eyed her as though she was a crazed woman.

Victoria held her hand out. "I need the keys."

He towered over her. "What?"

"Do you have a key to my home, or not?"

"You mean our house." He jammed his fists into his jeans. "And no, I don't have another key. Figured we'd make copies later today."

"How did you get in this morning?"

His look told her he really did think she was crazy with a side order of nuts. "Lady, I came by this morning and the front door was unlocked. When I heard Mrs. T giving you the third degree, I came on in."

Victoria's legs began to tremble. "I locked the doors. I know I did. I checked every hour on the hour last night." She gripped her purse strap, trying to make sense of the unlocked doors, the scraping outside the window.

"Hey." Barrett cupped her elbow and put his hand around her waist. "Are you all right?"

"Sure," she said. '*Smile!*' her father commanded. Victoria swallowed. She couldn't do it. Not this time.

"Come on." He took the key from her hand and locked the door. He rattled the doorknob to prove it was solid against intruders. His arm still offering support, he led her to the pickup.

They climbed into the cab. Both stared out the windshield, silently watching the cottage. Sunlight danced over the lake. Shade trees swayed in the breeze. And Aunt Mags's old house called to her despite the aching need for so much loving attention.

Victoria closed her eyes. "This is my home," she whispered the mantra under her breath. Then she forced the addendum as a dose of reality. "For now."

Barrett gripped the steering wheel and nodded. "Let's go to the Duck Blind. You can tell me why you're so jumpy while we fill up on Lyle's pancakes and stiff coffee."

Taking a deep breath, she turned to search his face. "Just so we're clear, Partner. I'm not leaving Honeybrooke until I'm good and ready."

"That's what I like to hear." Barrett put his hand on the seat next to hers. Their fingers didn't touch, but tendrils of heat danced up her arm. "In the meantime, you better prepare for more neighborly attention. Everyone is curious about you."

Victoria didn't need an order to smile. It came on its own. "I'm ready for my close-up."

CHAPTER 8

They pulled up to the Duck Blind Corner Café. The dark wooden sign hung on the post outside. With every gust of wind, the well-dressed duck, sporting a pair of sunglasses and a shotgun, appeared to be walking to the door.

"A little rude, don't you think?" Victoria muttered.

Barrett looked up at the sign. His eyebrows arched as if he'd never noticed it before. "What's wrong with it?"

"There is a sign of a blind duck. Isn't that enough?"

"A duck blind is what hunters stand behind to bag a duck during hunting season." His glance slid over her. "Lyle just liked the play on words." Barrett opened his door and hitched his leg out. He stopped. "Lyle doesn't even hunt."

Victoria felt the heat rising up her neck. "Well, it's cheesy."

He shook his head at her and snorted. "It's Wisconsin. Everything is cheesy here." His lips twitched. "It's what we do best. Beer, cheese, and football. What else is there?"

Victoria caught his joke and chuckled. She was in the land of cheese. "Good thing," she said, climbing out of the cab. Looking across the truck bed, their eyes locked, sharing the lighter mood.

Aware of the heat growing between them, Victoria sucked in a breath of crisp morning air. "I'm starved."

Barrett broke the spell and dipped his head. "Well, come on."

Releasing her hold on the truck bed, she skirted the bumper. Her feet screamed at her for abusing them another day with those fashionable sandals. They seemed like a good choice when she slipped them on. At the time, she'd been angry, focused on ripping into Barrett. They were the first thing she could find, and she had no intention of unpacking her suitcase. She was leaving. When she was good and ready.

Barrett was nearly to the door, oblivious that she was walking a little slowly. Head down, his pace to the café was like an accountant jonesing for the first cup of coffee. His work boots crunched over the gravel, eating up the parking lot. He paused at the door and held it open. His face registered surprise when she wasn't right beside him. "You are coming, California?"

"Only in my dreams," Victoria muttered under her breath. She hitched her purse strap, squaring her shoulder, and set off in toe-pinched, rapid steps. Gravel rolled under her heels, wobbling her determination to look perfectly happy and calm.

Barrett watched as she picked her way across the parking lot. His impossibly long lashes fluttered against those cheekbones.

Heat gathered up her neck. He'd braced the door open and the only way in was to walk under his arm. There was hardly any room. She'd have to brush against him. No big deal. If you're crammed into enough elevators, you're bound to brush up against someone. Been there. Done that. No big deal. Right? Just one more elevator in life.

"Glad you could make it, California," Barrett said.

His breath brushed her cheek as she made her way through the gauntlet. His scent was clean, made of freshly laundered clothes and mint. Like a bright fall morning. The crisp air. The sun offering warmth and hope. It would be a perfect way to start every day for the rest of your life. The hem of her shirt caught his belt buckle, slowing her progress.

"Victoria…I, uh…" Barrett said.

"Shut the darn door." The deep baritone voice shook Victoria from her stupor. She yanked her shirt free, ducked past Barrett, past his scent, and into another world that caressed the senses.

She inhaled. Coffee, dark and rich, steamed from mugs and carafes, greeting her with the promise of caffeine. The tables were busy with conversations. The buzz drew down to a low hum as they moved toward the reception podium.

"Morning, Lyle," Barrett said.

"You know the rules," Lyle said. He raced past, balancing a tray loaded with plates piled with sausage and biscuits, and a side order of bacon. The perfume of breakfast wafted in the air as he whipped by. "Sit anywhere you want." He pointed with his balding head in the direction of the corner booth. "That one's yours if you want it."

Victoria felt the café patrons' eyes follow her to the back of the restaurant. She would have preferred the table closest to the door. Keep it simple. Talk to no one. Easy in and easy out.

Instead, she felt like the morning floor show. The hunger gnawing at her belly vanished in an instant. She wished she could do the same. She hated that "new-girl" persona. Where everyone sized you up. You were the new pariah in an instant.

Barrett's fingers brushed the small of her back, leading her to the booth in the corner. On their way to the oasis, they passed plates of eggs and stacks of pancakes. Side orders of sausage, biscuits and gravy, squeezed onto any available spot.

Conversations paused as they passed. They took up again just as quickly, a little more animated.

"Mornin' Barrett."

"Good morning, Harold. Mrs. T, it's good to see you again."

"Barrett. Ms. Banning." Mrs. Tewilliger offered them a pinched smile. "Out and about, I see."

Victoria gave her most gracious smile. The one she used when greeting a new client. "Thank you for the cookies."

Mrs. Tewilliger rested her fork on the edge of her plate and daintily wiped her mouth on the napkin. "When do you think you'll be taking off for California, Ms. Banning?" She took a sip from her coffee mug, apparently waiting for an answer. "Don't want to delay too long. Snow will be here before you know it."

Victoria shivered. As far as she was concerned, the winter storm was already inside the café.

"Oh, now, Helen," Harold set his mug on the table. His rosy ears peeked out of a cap of gray curls. He pushed out his chair and held out his hand. "It's a pleasure, Ms. Banning."

He switched on a gleaming smile and enveloped her hand in bear-sized paws. "Pay no attention to her. She doesn't mean any harm. Do you, Helen? We think you are a downright lucky lady. Gett'n that cottage and all while this whole town was snooz'n. Yup, one lucky lady." He held on. "We own the Cove Market. You come on over. Anything you need, we have it. If you don't see it, we'll get it."

"Thanks, but actually, Barrett is—"

"Harold," Lyle called out across the room. "Let them sit down. I have breakfast to serve before lunch service begins."

Victoria didn't think it was possible, but Harold's ears turned a deeper red. They were almost purple. He let loose of her hand and tossed a twenty-dollar bill on the table.

Helen rose, jerking her jacket over her shoulders. "Time to go to work. Barrett, your special order came in. You'll want to stop by." Her head snapped down. "Ms. Banning." She didn't wait for a response but spun on her heel and marched out, leaving Harold in her wake.

"Give her time," Harold said. "She's struggling with change, is all."

Barrett leaned close, touching Victoria's arm. "Coffee's waiting."

Relieved to do something besides have the townspeople's attention, she followed him to the booth. If not for the siren's call from the steaming mug, she would have lit out before anyone could say another word to her. A sigh escaped as she sat down. The worn leather seats were as welcoming as a church pew.

Wrapping her hands around the ceramic mug, she sniffed the rich life-giving liquid and imagined she was back in California at her local coffee shop. She took a sip and closed her eyes. A hot jolt of energy coursed through her veins. It cruised right up to her brain. Her eyes snapped open. Barrett watched her, wariness on his face. Why? He was obviously well-liked, but definitely in the doghouse for being nice to the new girl.

She took another sip. "What was that all about?"

Barrett played with the teaspoon on the table. He spun its bowl, the stainless handle clicking softly against the water glass. "It's bad enough that Mags is gone. Left a sizeable hole for some of us."

"Why didn't you tell them Mags left the house to you too?"

Barrett shrugged. "They don't need me telling them. The news will get out soon enough."

Lyle strode up to their booth. Beads of perspiration coated his balding pate. His pen hovered over the order pad in his hand. He nudged the menu toward Victoria. "Find something to order?"

"She's been promised your pancakes, Lyle. Plus, all the sides you can shove on the plate. Make mine the same."

Lyle grinned, his brown eyes snapping with excitement. "A woman after my own heart." He flipped the book closed and raced off to put in the order and check on the other tables.

"Bring a pot of coffee too. Will ya?" Barrett called.

Lyle acknowledged the request with a wave of his hand.

"I didn't know I was that hungry," Victoria said. She watched Lyle scoot around the room with an efficient lightning speed. "The man should have roller skates." Her gaze slid over the dining room. The Duck Blind Corner Café was anything but on the corner, but the rest of the décor was pure duck. There were ducks on the wallpaper hanging above the wainscoting. She rotated the mug in her hand. Even the dishes had mallard ducks on them. A man cave that served food.

"He works hard." Concern edged his voice. "Maybe too hard. He's a one-man show. I've been trying to get him to add some help, but he says staying busy makes him happy."

They sat in silence as the room began to empty out.

"I thought they'd never leave," Barrett joked. He scooted forward in the booth seat. "I saw your Pros and Cons list. Not a whole lot of good listed. And a whole page full of reasons why you should go. Pretty weak ones if you ask me." He quit playing with the spoon and sent his focus all on her. "Why do you really want to leave? You haven't even given Honeybrooke Cove half a chance. So why come here in the first place?"

"I thought I could help my mother's aunt. Get to know her. I didn't plan to stay here. It's supposed to be a quick visit."

"So, you knew about her troubles and just decided to pop in at the last minute? Too little, too late. Right?" Barrett's fingers curled around the salt and pepper shakers. The glass caught the sunlight and cast a rainbow over the tablecloth.

"It's not like that." Victoria didn't know what to do. She was out in an ocean and had no idea how to get to the shore. "I didn't find out about Mags's financial trouble until about a week ago. Her health wasn't mentioned in the letter. Just her needing help."

"Seems to me that a year of letter writing should have gotten your attention."

Victoria flinched. She narrowed her eyes, wishing she could strike him just as easily. "I came as soon as I could."

"And that was still too late." Barrett abandoned the shakers and searched her face. "At least you arrived just in time for the reading of the will. Too bad I'm stuck to the house with you."

"What the…" Victoria sputtered, fighting to tamp down the desire to throw the wretched saltshaker at his smirking mouth. "If

I wanted to see my family purely for financial gain do you honestly think I would claim a rundown cottage about to go into foreclosure?" She began gathering her things and scooted out of the booth.

"Well, it's just that—"

"No, Mr. Collins. I would not. Because that would make me a financial idiot. And that, I assure you. I. Am. Not."

"Wait."

She stared down where he snagged her wrist. Infuriating tears blurred her vision.

"I'm sorry," he said. "Please. Sit back down." He gave a gentle tug, then released her. "Please."

Despite her misgivings, she sat down but drew the line on relaxing into the back of the booth seat. She clutched her purse, ready to escape.

"Look. I'm sorry. Give me another chance." Barrett shoved his fingers through his hair and waited.

Victoria folded her hands and nodded. "Okay. Go for it."

"The will was a surprise to me too. I never thought I'd be a part of Mags's crazy plans. But I also never thought she'd bequeath it to a relative who never responded to her letters." He took a deep breath and went on when she didn't have anything to say. "Financially, if we had any brains, we should let the bank sell it off. And I know the house has seen better days. But it has good bones. It's like Mags would say, 'If you've got a good foundation, good bones, then you can rebuild anytime you choose.'" He covered her hand with his. "Stay a little while longer. Snow won't be here as soon as Mrs. T thinks."

Victoria was so tired. Weariness seemed to counteract the coffee's brief adrenaline boost. "It's not just the finances."

"I know having the power off was a rough start. But, it's back on."

Victoria laughed, searching his face to see if he really thought that was the worst of it. "I think learning of Mags's death and then finding out I'm part owner of a house in trouble, might top an already *craptastic* couple of months."

He cocked his head. "That bad, huh?"

Working for flippant, she ticked off the list a finger at a time. "No boyfriend, no job, dead aunt, a falling down inheritance." She paused and pointed to her middle finger. "Again. No job, remember? Oh, and I am being eaten alive by mosquitoes the size of condors in the middle of freakin' Wisconsin. And someone is messing with the locks on the doors." She waved her hand in his face. "Hello. Meet *craptastic*."

Wide-eyed, he had the intelligence to look empathetic. "Sorry. Didn't mean to pry." He took a sip of fortifying coffee. "As far as the keys go, you can always change the locks."

"It's not just that." She tilted her head and sighed. "I know that I locked the doors. Someone had to have been there without me knowing it."

"While you slept?"

She rolled her neck. God, what she wouldn't give for a massage. She weighed her next complaint. He might brush off her concern. What she heard last night was real. If he did, she would walk back to the cottage and load up.

"Not just while I slept. Which was very little, by the way." She laced her fingers, covering her face. "Someone was outside. Dragging something across the porch."

"Wild animals."

"All night long?" Her hand slapped the table. "It didn't stop until after 2 a.m."

A country song wailed in the background, spinning a tale of young love and cheating hearts. Connor's face drifted to the forefront. He wouldn't have believed her either. She shoved the annoying vision away. "Someone was out there."

Lyle arrived with the plates piled high with food. "Welcome to Honeybrooke Cove. Best Darn Town in Wisconsin. Go on. Dig in before it gets cold." He refreshed their coffee, setting the carafe on the table. "Why the serious faces?" He hooked a leg over a nearby chair and sat down to chat. "Don't mind Mrs. T. We all loved Mags. It shook us up. Change is good. Makes you grow. If Mags was here, she'd say the same."

Victoria trailed the table surface with her fingernail. "I can manage Mrs. T. She seems harmless enough. It's just some of the other things that are bothering me."

His brows raised, Lyle leaned in closer. "Trouble at the cottage?"

"Victoria heard something last night." Barrett said. "I'll check on it when I take her back." He looked up, catching her attention. "Mags never complained of vermin problems. Probably nothing. Maybe a wild animal has made a nest under the porch."

Lyle's thin frame rested back against the chair. "If Barrett's looking into it, you're in capable hands." He winked at Victoria. "Would trust him with my life."

She did her best not to roll her eyes.

———

Barrett glanced over at Victoria. Why did he ask her to stay? Hell, he nearly begged her after doing a fine job of insulting her character. She hadn't said much since they'd climbed into the truck. Actually, the increasing silence started after their conversation with Lyle. She didn't like that he discounted her trespasser theory. He wanted it to be a wild animal with his whole heart. The alternative meant she did have someone who wanted to send her packing...well, besides him. And he wasn't so sure anymore. If Mrs. Tewilliger was up to mischief, he'd have to make a visit to Harold.

He made the turn through the gate. There was something about those misplaced candles and towels that kept poking at him. He was certain he'd put towels in the bathroom. Those emergency candles were always under the kitchen sink.

He pulled into the drive and parked the truck. Victoria didn't move. She stared out the window. The sun caught glints of auburn in her chestnut-colored hair. Daylight revealed the dusting of freckles sprinkled across her nose, the shadows under her eyes.

"Have you changed your mind? Are you going to stay?"

"This is my home," she whispered. "Technically, yours and mine. But I refuse to leave easily. Not this time."

Barrett reached out, surprising them both, and cupped her jaw. His lips found hers, brushing over the soft flesh. "Great. You do that."

Victoria exploded out of the cab and was already heading toward the garden. Those ridiculous sandals didn't hold her back this time. Her jeans molded smoothly around her hips, cupped her bottom. She moved like a squirrel, scampering across the grass, doing her best to get away from him. Too bad. He wasn't going anywhere either.

Barrett groaned. He had no business kissing her. He hopped out of the truck close on her heels. His steps slowed to the realization that he might not have wanted her there to begin with, but he was darn glad she was staying. Even if it meant he might still lose the house.

One of Mags's lectures came back to him as soon as he crossed into her rock garden. 'Memories are what you make them. Good ones. Bad ones. Up to you to decide.' Her parting shot was always the same. It was time for him to get back to doing what he was born to do.

Victoria stopped in the center of the garden. Her hands on her hips, she turned. Her cheeks were pink, eyes snapping out those lightning bolts.

Regret already flooded in, washing away her warmth from his lips. *Memories.* Maybe Mags was right. Maybe he did carry too many bad memories. He chose to keep them. That way, no one else would be harmed by his hands ever again.

CHAPTER 9

The sun glinted off the lake behind the cottage. Victoria cocked her head and listened. Birds trilled in the trees, oblivious of the humans standing in their sanctuary. The soft, rhythmic slap, slap, slap of the shoreline hitting the dock soothed her bound up nerves. The scent of humidity was in the air. It penetrated the soil, moist, ready to close one season and prepare for another. Quieting. Peaceful and filled with hope.

Hands on her hips, Victoria turned, surveying the garden. She took in a deep breath, breathing in the earthy scents. This could be her home. Her sanctuary. The view from a work-from-home office desk began to form. If she stayed, she'd find a way to make it work. For now. Until she sold the place. Provided Barrett agreed. She'd make him understand. It was the best choice that made financial sense.

She scrunched her face. The yard needed a ton of work. The to-do list in her mind began to fill. As far as she could tell, she wouldn't need to deadhead any flowers. There wasn't a plant in sight. Just the large shade trees and piles of rocks. She'd have to hurry and bring in some flowers. It was early enough for roses. Bulbs for spring. With any luck, she'd be long gone by then.

The rocks would be her first priority outside. She had never seen so many stones. They littered the backyard, piled in different heights, no obvious pattern.

Barrett walked up to her, his rolling stride shuffling through the yard. His athletic build spoke of endurance and agility. At some point, he'd strapped on his tool belt. It hugged his hips gunslinger-style, angled, and ready for his next fight. Funny, she'd never thought that as sexy before.

Victoria felt the rush of heat over her neck again. Avoiding eye contact, she dug in her purse to find a pen and a pad of paper. "I'd like to hire you. Today."

Why did he fluster her? She snapped the pen, popping the cap on and off.

"You want something beside the windows worked on?" A wary frown popped on his face, digging edges around his mouth.

Victoria cleared her throat. Yes. There were all sorts of things she wanted. "We have a lot to do. I've a list started in my head. Come to the kitchen. We can start there."

With a lingering look at the lake, and a promise to get down to the dock and check it out, she turned for the back door. If there was any chance for a decent night's sleep, she needed to have whatever kind of varmint that made its home in her cottage removed. And the locks checked.

Barrett kept pace as she made her way around a mound of stone. Her heel caught on a rock and rolled. Victoria grabbed whatever she could to keep from falling flat on her face. His bicep bulged as he broke her fall.

"Steady." Barrett braced her against his thigh, his long fingers wrapped around her waist. He pointed to her sandals. "You know, those make your legs look sexy, but they'll cause you to break your neck. You need to put solid boots on that list of yours."

Victoria's mind staggered under the compliment. How long had it been since Connor had said she was sexy? Right after she helped him out by paying for a semester of law school? Just because Barrett said it, didn't mean she was. But it felt good to be told.

"Boots?" She cringed when the single word came out breathy. The heat flowing through his shirt was too tempting to hang onto. She took an unsteady step, putting distance between herself and Barrett's bicep.

"We have real weather here. You'll need to get some winter boots. And, rain boots. Those rubber ones that won't slip. Add work boots to that pad of paper you keep scribbling on."

Before Victoria started tallying up his recommendations, he examined her t-shirt, rubbing the material between his fingers. "Do you have winter clothes?"

"Sure." Relief washed over her. This she had. Last winter, in Los Angeles, she had gone on a buying spree. She vaguely recalled why. Something to do with a snide remark that Connor had made. Something about looking dowdy. That was also right after he'd gone on a ski trip with his "bros" from the office.

Her breakfast pinched her stomach. She'd never met these friends. Never questioned him further when she'd paid his credit card bill.

Victoria yanked her arm away. How could she have been so blind and stupid? She couldn't get to the back door fast enough.

"Victoria?" Barrett stopped her and spun her around. "What's wrong?" He tipped her chin. Catching a tear, he cleared it away with his thumb. "Whatever it is, I'm sorry."

"Not you. Me." She pulled out the keys from her purse and started to turn the bolt. Her hand froze. Someone had left the door unlocked, and it swung open. No, she made certain to lock it before they left that morning.

Barrett put his hand out. "Stay here," he ordered. He moved the door with his toe. The only weapon on him was a hammer and screwdriver.

Victoria bit her lip. Her stomach did aerials, flipping and twisting. It was her house too. But she didn't want to be that dumb girl in the movies who always walks into a serial killer's lair. "Wait." She grabbed his jeans pocket. "Let's just get back in your truck and call 911."

"Cells have crappy signals here. Remember?" Barrett sighed, squinting at the neighboring houses. "My place is too far. Look." He caught her wrist, tugging her close. "There's a car in the Tewilliger's driveway."

Victoria scrunched her nose. "I thought she was supposed to be at work?"

"Maybe she is." Barrett was already beating a path to their doorstep, knocking on the door. "Could be Harold came home for something."

Victoria hoped so. It was evident that her new neighbor wasn't her biggest fan.

When Mrs. T answered the door on the first knock, it appeared everything was perfectly in place. Except her light blue eyes were red-rimmed, her mouth was pinched. She smoothed a hand down her slacks. "What do you want?"

"Sorry to bother you, Mrs. T. We need to use your phone." He took a hopeful step forward. "Need to call Chief Graham."

"Mercy! Whatever for?"

"Looks like someone broke into Victoria's cottage while we were at breakfast."

"Mags's place?" Her face paled under the stiff sprayed hair. She gripped the door, clinging to it as if she needed help to stand. "That's ridiculous. Never had a problem like that before."

"Please," Victoria said. "We don't mean to be a bother. Once we make the call, we promise to be out of your way."

Mrs. T took a breath, looking like she'd been on the verge of sinking and had come up for air. "Well, then…." She swung open the screen door. "Come on in." She smoothed her slacks again, brushing the fabric with fluttering hands. "Phone's over there, Barrett."

They left Victoria to stand in the front room. Picture frames littered a baby grand piano. Victoria lifted one, examined it closely. A man and woman grinned back at her. They held a towhead boy, maybe two or three, squeezed between them. The happy family stood on a dock, the lake glistening behind them. Fishing tackle, baskets, and poles rested at their feet.

Victoria looked up. The view outside the bay window led to the lake and a dock.

"That's me and Harold."

Victoria jumped, caught in the nosy task of researching her neighbor. "I'm sorry." She returned the frame to its spot on the piano. "It's a beautiful photo."

"Yes, well, that was a beautiful time."

"Is that your son?"

The pinched twist came back to Mrs. Tewilliger's mouth and followed down her hunched narrow shoulders. "Tommy," she said, stroking her finger across the boy's image. "He died." Her head bobbed toward the window. "Right out there."

Barrett walked into the room. "Chief's on his way. Thanks, Mrs. T." He embraced her shoulders, giving her a gentle hug.

Unable to respond, Mrs. Tewilliger kept her gaze on the view outside and nodded.

———

B arrett sat in the truck with Victoria while they waited for the sheriff to come out to the cottage. He would have liked to go in, see if anyone was actually there.

He hated to bring Chief Graham out for no reason. Thankfully, they didn't get much crime in Honeybrooke. The man was getting up in age and needed to rest more. He'd prescribe more fishing time if he thought Graham would heed it.

Prescribing a fix and getting the patient's cooperation wasn't always the easiest part of the solution. The woman next to him needed to eat more, cut out the caffeine, and quit watching horror movies. He bet her overfed imagination had every serial killer known to movie history hiding in her basement.

He withdrew her hand from her mouth. "You're not going to have any left if you don't stop it right now."

Victoria looked down at her ragged nails, surprise dawning on her face. "Thanks. Nasty habit."

Barrett liked the feel of her hand in his. He didn't release it, just gave a gentle squeeze.

"Won't be long. Graham will be here soon." He squinted at the cottage. Shadows danced over the sun-glazed windows. The place looked buttoned up and peaceful, ready for a fall day. "Are you certain you locked the back door?"

"Of course, I am." She bit her lip. "Pretty sure." Casting a sideways glance his way, she opened the truck cab door.

"Hold it!" Barrett jumped out of the truck and drew her back, toward the bumper. "Where do you think you're going?"

"I'm thinking that even if someone had been here, they're long gone. We both have too much to do and neither one of us wants to sit and wait for something that's not there." She took another deep breath. "And that maybe, you're right and there is only some wild animal hiding under my porch."

Tires crunched on the gravel behind them. Chief Graham parked his patrol car and slowly climbed out. Barrett prayed they didn't have to chase anything down. He'd left his running shoes back at his place.

"Graham, this is Victoria Banning."

Graham's salt and pepper mustache matched his full head of curling hair. Except for the two blotches of color on his cheeks, his face was nearly as gray as his hair. "Ms. Banning." He held out his hand, consuming her hand in his grip. "Heard you made it into town. Shame you didn't make it here before Mags passed."

Victoria chose to ignore his little jab. They were starting to become as annoying as mosquitoes. She slapped at one buzzing her neck and wished she could do the same for other irritations.

Instead, she plastered on her best smile. "Chief, thanks for coming by."

He turned to Barrett. "What's going on here? You say there's an intruder?" He sucked in his lips and puffed them out. He examined Victoria like she was the one to leave behind fingerprints at a murder scene. "Pretty unusual. Don't get crime here like they do in Los Angeles."

"Tell you what, Graham, let's walk around the place. Make certain everything is safe, nothing's been tampered with, and then you can be on your way."

"I'm going with you," Victoria announced.

Barrett raised his brow and glared in her direction. His jaw muscles ticked as he worked to chew back the words. "See that you stay behind us, okay, Partner?"

CHAPTER 10

Satisfied with his search of the cottage, Chief Graham tucked his notebook into his back pocket and hitched up his gun belt. He clicked his pen and slipped it into his shirt pocket.

"Like I said, Ms. Banning, we rarely get intruders of the two-legged variety. Nine times out of ten, it's your four-legged varmints." He turned, his call out to Mags's place completed.

"Yes, Chief," Victoria nodded. She'd had just about all his advice she could take for the day. His idea of search and discovery was to note that the place needed a good cleaning and Mags would pitch a fit if she knew her floors were dirty. She wanted to tell him to grab the bucket and mop and help out, but that would have kept him there longer than she wanted.

She matched Barrett's pace, escorting the sheriff to his car. The little amount of walking through the house had left Chief Graham winded. The harsh breath pushing through his lungs sounded like dry leaves rustling against bare twigs. Barrett walked on his other side. Victoria wondered if it was out of fear the man might not make it back to his patrol car.

"You go out. Buy yourself some catch and release cages. Harold will know what you need. Can tell you where to set 'em, if like you ask him real nice. And next time you think someone is in the house…and you're by your lonesome," he pointed his index finger and cocked his thumb. "You call me. No need to take chances."

Victoria and Barrett stood side by side, their hands nearly touching. Not quite. She could feel the heat from his body taking up the space between them, connecting them. Like a couple.

Chief Graham cast a bushy gray eyebrow up to Barrett. "Course, if you're around you'll know what to do." He chuckled and a cough erupted.

Barrett bent over, resting his wrist on top of the car. "Graham, when did you say your appointment was?"

Graham waved his hand, shooing him away.

"Look, I can go with you—" The roar of the engine coming to life absorbed his offer. Barrett smacked the car and stepped back.

Hunched behind the wheel, Chief Graham backed the car up and pulled away. He tossed a salute out the window before the red taillights curved through the gate and down the road.

A breath she hadn't realized she'd been holding escaped and passed over her lips. She shoved her fists in her back pockets. Barrett stood behind her, studying her with those watchful blue-gray eyes.

"Looks like you were right. Nothing to worry about but maybe a ground squirrel." She rubbed her forehead with the back of her hand. "I must be nuts."

Worry creased the lines around his mouth. "Glad I'm right." His mouth tugged up. "I wouldn't have been any good chasing anyone. Not so soon after eating a short stack of Lyle's pancakes."

———

After Chief Graham left, Barrett dredged up the nerve and scouted out the dark underworld of the porch. He declared the porch clear of wild varmints trying to take up residence. He couldn't say that about spiders and shuddered just thinking about the cobwebs.

He looked over Victoria's list, calculating the time it would take out of his schedule. He'd have to move around a few jobs. Push them back maybe a day or two. Some of his clients would not be happy with the delays. Victoria was watching him. Her eyes, dark like hot chocolate, beamed at him. Hopeful. He cleared his throat.

"This is quite a list." He scrubbed the back of his neck. She had enough work to keep him busy through the winter. "Which one takes highest priority?"

"All of them." Victoria chewed on her lip. The sun beamed through the kitchen window, catching the dust of freckles on her nose. The fading sunburn pinked her cheeks.

"Tell you what. Choose two, maybe three jobs. Then we'll go from there."

She crunched her nose in thought. "If you pick up some of the paint for me, I can help."

Barrett checked his watch. His day was getting away from him. "I have an order to pick up. I'll grab some swatches for you to choose from."

Relief lighted her eyes. "That'd be wonderful." She followed him to the kitchen door. "Barrett?"

Her fingers brushed his arm. The touch warmed his skin. Heat swept up his neck. It scorched a dry patch in his throat. He worked his parched tongue past it. "Yes?"

God, he croaked like he'd just hit puberty. He cleared his throat.

Victoria snatched her hand back. She tilted her head, studying him. Her full lips tipped up in an unsteady smile. "You've been more than kind." She gripped the door handle as if it would hold her back from leaping off to somewhere unknown. "I just wanted to say thank you. And..." The tip of her tongue, pink and luscious, swept over her lips. "Um, I'll see you later."

Barrett tucked the wisps of honey-brown from her brow. The whole time he leaned in, he knew he shouldn't, but he did it anyway. He was drawn to her. The sun-kissed freckles. Her idiotic ankle-twisting sandals. He brushed his lips over hers. Felt her sigh tickle his mouth. Tasted the sweet strong coffee she liked so much. Barrett broke away. It was too soon. Right?

"Oh." Wide-eyed, she stood on the threshold, hanging onto the door for dear life.

Afraid of losing his balance altogether, Barrett swept his ball cap off and shoved his hands in his hair. Where did the ex-boyfriend fit in? Were they just taking a break? He wasn't about to steal someone's girlfriend. He stepped back, putting Victoria safely back in their new partner-zone. "I'll...I'll check on you later today."

———

P ad of paper and pen in hand, Victoria stood in the center of the living room. She traced the spot where Barrett had tasted her lips. He'd planted a breathless kiss on her and then left as if he expected an irate father to charge out the door. His tires had scattered the gravel as he took off down the drive.

She shook her head. For heaven's sake, this wasn't the first time she'd been kissed. She'd lived with Connor for nearly two years and their kisses never threatened to spin the world off its axis. Her fingertip scraped over her lip again.

However, this was the first time a simple kiss rocked her speechless. Would it have gone any further with Barrett? Maybe they'd find out the next time they saw each other.

Victoria glanced at the clock on her cell phone. Without a signal, the voicemails remained the same. The bulk of Connor's messages weighed heavily on her. She'd have to find a signal as soon as possible. It was as if she was in another land, cut off from the rest of the world. Hooking up the internet and ordering a landline phone went on the list.

Enough time wasted on daydreaming. If she intended to sell the cottage, she had to get started today.

She uncapped her pen. Where to begin? Each room needed a coat of paint. The kitchen needed a good cleaning, and she needed to take stock of the pantry. If she decided to stay, she'd have to contact The Meat Masters Moving Company and let them know whether to store or ship her things. Plenty of time to cover the Pepto Bismol pink paint in the bedroom.

The couch would do for a makeshift bed for a few days, but she had to find a mattress store. The threat of several more nights twisted on the couch sent her to work.

The list complete, Victoria snatched the keys off the counter, and headed to the car. She'd start at Jack Dorner's office. There was enough in her savings account to stop the foreclosure proceedings. Barrett probably wouldn't like it, but he could pay back his half of the bill when he had the money.

Then she'd go to the Cove Market and see what she could find. If nothing else, someone would be able to send her in the right direction.

She stepped off the back porch. Caught in the heat and humidity, the sun beating down on the stones, the garden took on an unearthly personality. The haphazard piles of rock glistened in the daylight. Shade trees cast wavering shadows over their surface.

Victoria pulled out her pad of paper. Plants. Flowers. Pots. Gloves.

The little garden shed stood in the back, nearly covered by more rocks. Creeping ivy covered the peeling, faded-white siding. Small windows twinkled from the shade. She was pleased to find the panes of glass were intact.

She shoved and the door opened on squeaking, rusty hinges. The afternoon light pushed its way through. Cobwebs clinging to the rafters fluttered in the gentle breeze. Victoria danced around, spinning, swiping at the cobwebs tickling her cheek. "Please don't let there be any black widow spiders," she prayed. A nature guide to Wisconsin was added to her list.

Her gaze caught on the odd shapes hanging on the wall. Rusted shovels, rakes, and hoes, were lined-up like soldiers, retired from duty. Wheelbarrows crowded the corner. A garden hutch, its paint peeling and faded, held hand trowels and spades. Clay pots, dried dirt clinging to their insides, their mouths open like hungry baby birds huddled together. A crystal chandelier lay abandoned and forgotten on its side.

The miniature house was cool there in the shade. A tingle ran over Victoria's skin. She rubbed her bare arms and pictured parties. Gatherings in the garden, shared with friends and family. It didn't matter that she was all alone. That little fact didn't keep the vision at bay.

The flower garden, overflowing with roses and lavender, filled her imagination. Peonies. Iris. She could smell the roses and see the vases filling every empty corner of the cottage.

Victoria tugged on a hutch drawer. Old seed packets, filed in alphabetical order, spilled out onto the counter. They were past their date but ignited another list. She could create a vegetable garden. Rubbing a skim of dust off the windowpane, she searched the yard. The best spots were in the sun. Exactly where Mags had piled the stones. Did the old woman intend to make a wall and forget what she was doing? Had she suffered from some type of dementia?

"What did the chief find?"

Squealing, Victoria spun to see Mrs. Tewilliger hovering in the doorway. Her heartbeat thumped in her ears. She shoved her hair back with both hands. "Lord, Mrs. T, you scared me half to death."

"I'm sorry. I knew Graham and Barrett left. Saw the door open. Wanted to make sure everything was as it should be." She cast an appraising look over the dusty room. Her gaze stopped on Victoria. "Thinking about taking up gardening? Mags loved her garden. But never much appreciated flowers."

"Why's that? I think that's the best part of a garden. Don't you?" Victoria tucked the old seed packets back into the drawer and closed it.

"Oh, they have their place. Mags liked her rocks. Said they were solid and never faded like flowers. Me, I like a nice swing or a comfortable chair to add to the scenery."

Victoria wiped her hands on her jeans. Thanks to Mrs. Tewilliger, the garden dream had faded. She picked up her purse, hoping her neighbor would take the hint. "Thanks for checking on me."

"Looks like you have the tools. Just need a bit of tending." She nodded toward her house. "Putting them to use will be the best remedy for them. Course, if you want, Harold has some oil that will help take off the rust."

Mrs. Tewilliger walked beside her. She paused at Victoria's convertible. Her eyebrow rose. "Imagine that is a fine ride in the warm weather." She patted her hair. The hairspray didn't allow it to move under her hand. "Though I'd have to get my stylist, Betty, to make house calls."

Victoria couldn't help but laugh. "If you change your mind, I'm happy to give you a spin."

"Well now, that's very nice of you." Mischief lit up Mrs. Tewilliger's eyes. "Would have to be pretty soon. Before the snow falls." Her mouth drooped, her shoulders dipped toward the cottage. "Will you be gone? Or do you intend to call this place home?" She held up a hand. The diamond in her wedding band caught the sunlight and sparkled with the movement. "Now, I don't mean to pressure you. Harold finds out I asked again, he'll give me a piece of his mind, and a cold shoulder tonight."

"I don't have any plans to leave," Victoria said. "At least, not yet." The warm breeze pushed her hair off her neck. She tucked her hands in her back pockets and let her gaze caress the yard. Maybe, just maybe, she'd stay at least through the summer.

Mrs. Tewilliger smiled, tears pooling, threatening to fall. "That'd be nice. It gets lonely out here when I look out on the lake. Remember when we lost our Tommy." She fumbled in her pants pocket for a Kleenex. "Margaret Ellington...Mags, helped me remember the good times we had." She pointed to the pile of stones that divided their gardens. "Tommy liked his rocks. The sparkly ones. Mags and I gathered stones that we thought he would have liked. Helped us remember how precious our days were with him. His stones, along with the memory of his laughter, will never fade."

The pile of stones winked in the sun. They caught the movement of leaves, the dance of shade and light. Victoria could almost hear the childlike giggles of a small boy. She blinked away the tears, covertly swiping them off with the back of her hand.

Mrs. Tewilliger patted her arm. "You best get into town, pick up a few things. I'll call ahead and let Harold know you're coming."

"Thank you, Mrs. Tewilliger."

"There now, you call me Helen. Or do like Barrett and the others and call me Mrs. T." She paused, smoothing the material on her hips. "In case you're interested. The women of Honeybrooke get together once a year and have mammograms done."

"All the women?" Victoria's brows rose. A mammogram was nowhere on her to-do list. She had visions of women lined up on a conveyor belt, pulling the handle on a slot machine. Cherries, you get a pass. Aces, you get the big C on your chest. She guessed her mom must have come up Aces. "Like a support group or club?"

Mrs. T nodded. "Something like that."

Victoria swallowed, fearing the giant thing that had taken her mother away when she was a kid. She couldn't help herself. Being one of the Honeybrooke Women didn't really mean that much. Did it?

CHAPTER 11

Pleased with her conversation with Jack Dorner, Victoria skipped down the bank steps, the weight of losing Aunt Mags's cottage lifted from her shoulders. Barrett may not like owing her, but he'd have to get over it.

Following Mrs. T's directions to the market, she turned the corner off Main. It was as Mrs. T had said. She couldn't miss the Cove Market.

The log building was bigger than any cabin she'd ever seen. Most of those had been in a magazine. Even some of the lodges up in Big Bear would have been put to the test. This place looked like it should hold just about everything she needed. Maybe even a mattress.

Two elderly men sat around a small table in the shade. She blinked. Sure enough, they were playing checkers. A tall sign stood beside them announcing that there would be brats, beer, and bluegrass music every Saturday night until fall. She didn't know if bluegrass music was anything like folk music, but it might be fun. The next show was in three days. Too bad, she had too much to do to check it out.

Victoria stood at the bottom of the steps. The sun beat down in the sweltering heat, bouncing off the parking lot and searing her arms.

One of the men paused in his move. His game piece wavered in the air. "Afternoon, miss," he said. He caught his partner's eyes and did a shoulder nudge in Victoria's direction. His bushy, peppered brows rose, questioning.

Wary of their scrutiny, Victoria gripped the railing. Each step brought her closer to the porch and the two judges.

"Hi!" She held out her hand. It hung in that agonizing space of time that swings between welcome and rejection.

"Hey there," Mr. Checkers, with the blue-striped golf shirt, scooted back his chair and rose.

His calloused, work-worn hand wrapped firmly around hers. A hug couldn't have felt any better.

"You must be one of Ol' Mags's people from California." Blue eyes twinkled brightly over his rosy cheeks. Reading the question in her eyes, he whispered, "Saw your plates. Figured it was you. Welcome to Honeybrooke. You looking for Harold?"

Resettling in his chair, he motioned to the cooler of beer by their feet. "You want one?"

"Thanks." Although the thought of a cold beer sliding down her throat sounded wonderful, she shook her head. "I have a lot to do before I can take a break." She paused. "Maybe next time?"

"You betcha. That'd be right nice," he nodded. "Name's George. You stop by and sit a spell, next time you're in town. Anyone who can beat Barrett out of a sure thing is bound to offer me a little checkers competition." Eyes still gleaming he lifted the bottle to his lips, tilted it and sighed. "Least ways more than this fella here. Right, Fred?"

His checkers partner grunted. "You gonna talk all day, George? Or what?"

"Oh...I—" Victoria hitched her purse on her shoulder. A sure thing? Were they talking about the cottage? So far, everyone she met assumed Barrett should have been given Mags's place. Their attitude didn't exactly make a woman feel welcome.

George and his grumpy partner had already turned their concentration back to the game board and arguing about the weather. It was mind-boggling what some people found interesting.

Perspiration trickled down Victoria's neck and between her breasts. How hard could it be to tell what the weather was going to be for the day? There would be heat. Humidity. She slapped at the insect dive-bombing her head. And, more heat to follow with a dose of mosquitoes. A dusting of salt coated her upper lip. It tasted like the rim on a margarita. Somewhere a huge bucket of ice had her name on it. She pushed the door and walked into heaven.

Air-conditioning. God's answer to escaping the humidity.

Victoria's list grew instead of shrank. As soon as she marked one thing off, she wrote down two more. The fire pit was a bit of an extravagance, but she'd always wanted one. At least the Cove Market would welcome her. They saw a good thing coming through the door. A customer with a little money, and like her father used to say, 'she had round heels.' She was an easy bet.

"Will you be at Mags's place to receive your order?" Mr. T braced his palms on the counter. He looked at the wall calendar next to the photo of him standing next to a dead deer. "We can bring over some of the items this afternoon. We'll have to let you know when other things come in."

"You don't have it all?" Victoria tore her gaze from the image of the proud huntsman. Thank God, the poor animal's head didn't hang on the wall behind him. She glanced at her watch, judging how long it would take her to get to civilization and back home before nightfall.

"Well now, shoot, we have most, but we sure don't have a mattress lying around here. You're gonna have to go into town, maybe as far as Sturgeon Bay. Course," he rubbed his chin, "if you know what you want, I guess you could buy it on the internet.

Probably take a couple of weeks, maybe even a month, to get here."

"Provided I had internet," she snapped. "Which I don't." Victoria felt her shoulders marching up to her ears. She pushed them down, drawing them backward into a stretch. Mr. T's eyes widened and all too late, she realized that little stretching exercise pushed her boobs out. She glanced around, noting who stood nearby, watching her like she was the new monkey at the zoo. Judging. The onlookers turned their back, caught in mid-gape.

Mr. T held her list out to her. "We'll do what we can." His cheeks were as ruddy as his neck. Victoria bit her lip. If he were a cartoon character, he'd have steam coming out of his white collared shirt and fogging up his glasses.

"Thanks," she mumbled. She shoved the paper in her purse and looked for the nearest exit.

"Victoria," he called, waving her back.

Despite her leaden feet, she dragged herself back to his counter. Maybe he found a mattress behind his storehouse. "Yes?"

"Listen, it'll probably take a little while to hook up internet at your house. Hell, we don't have it, and the wife and I've been there for over thirty years. Don't think they even come out that way. Course, since we have it here, never saw a need for it besides business."

Dismayed, Victoria saw her work-from-home window closing. Without access to the internet, her plans would be dead in the water and so would her bank account. Mr. T's voice became white noise. What had she done? Some form of madness must have taken over for her to empty her bank account into Aunt Mags's cottage. Maybe Mr. Dorner hadn't processed the paperwork. Panic began to buzz in her head, muffling her ears with cotton.

"—if you need to, you can come here. I'm sure Helen wouldn't mind. We'll work around her. Least till you have things sorted out."

The white noise dissipated. "Come here?" Hope fluttered in

her heart. Panic receded, returning to that place where it waits for another moment of despair. "Oh, Mr. T!" Victoria leaned over and gave him a peck on his cheek.

"Hey," he sputtered.

Leaping back, she knocked the rack of greeting cards with her elbow. "I'll take you up on your offer." She grabbed his great bear-like paw and squeezed before running out the door.

The walk to the car felt long, nearly as long as the walk of shame she did once in college. This time, instead of spending a night of raw naked sex, all she did was get a little too appreciative in front of the town gossips. She had a feeling those two checker-playing goats sitting on the store porch were the worst ones. Their bleating could be heard clear across the parking lot.

Victoria forced her steps to a stroll. Pausing at the car door, she looked around for a place to regroup. There was a little garden shop next door to the market. The sign on the archway leading to the entrance read, We Aim to Bloom.

An oasis of flowers. Thoughts of healing her barren garden at home overruled the left side of her brain. Flowers were more important than the numbers in her wilting bank account. Flowers would make her happy.

Despite the two sets of eyes following her trail, she marched through the archway covered in vines. Hints of rosemary scented the warm summer air. Barrels of rose bushes and trees lined the sides of the fence. Wind chimes caught on the breeze, rang out a solemn call.

She wandered the small yard. The stock was limited. Evidence that fall was coming. Bare root roses were stacked in rows. Each one had the promise of their future posted on cards. Their description, color, height and width. David Austin's English Roses, the ruffled pink Queen Anne. The red long stem American Beauty Tea Rose.

"Hello." A pretty, jean clad woman came out to greet her. Her red hair poked out from under a sunhat. She tugged off her dirt-covered gardening glove and held out her hand. "I'm Teresa."

Victoria warmed to her wide smile. "Victoria. Just moved here. Temporarily."

Teresa nodded. "Figured as much. Don't get many tourists in this time of year."

"That's the second time someone mentioned them. Do we get that many?"

"Lord, yes. We're the gateway to Door County. Once they discover our little cove, they keep coming back. Besides, you can't beat the location. By the time they get to us, they usually have to make a potty break and need something to eat. The Duck Blind will be hoppin' in the spring and early summer."

Victoria wiped the sweat from her brow. "Still hot enough for summer."

"It'll cool off before you know it." Teresa sized her up. "What are you looking for?"

Wary, thanks to Barrett and the Tewilliger's first reactions, Victoria hesitated. She squared her shoulders. Darned if she would apologize for rescuing a cottage and making it more attractive. "I inherited Margaret Ellington's cottage." That part was true. No need to add that Mags had made Barrett her partner.

Teresa nodded and blew a puff of air to dislodge the hair from her forehead. "There's a project." She held out her hand. "Come on. I'll show you what we got left for the season. I'll warn you. There won't be much you can do, except plant some bare root-stock roses and some bulbs." Teresa paused. "Maybe a tree or two." She shoved open a greenhouse door. It had to be twenty degrees warmer than outside. "Then you sit back, pray for winter to come and go so you can plant more in the spring."

————

After declining Teresa's offer to deliver her purchase, Victoria waddled to the car with the plants. She couldn't wait to dig holes, shove her hands in the dirt and dream how the plants would fit together. The garden was her palette. Her muscles would be her paintbrush. Giddy with excitement, she had to hurry to be home when the market made their delivery.

Her darling red car stood out in the sea of white pickup trucks and sedans. Like a red rose in a field of dry dandelions. She leaned the roses against the car. They didn't look anything like a live plant, their bare roots and stems splayed out, but Teresa promised they would indeed make roses.

Unlocking the door, she considered the daunting task of loading everything into the car. There was a passenger seat and that was it.

She lowered the convertible top and stood back. The two apple trees she'd convinced herself that she had to buy that very hour, would have to be strapped down, or they'd blow out the first turn she took. She hated to have to lug the things back to Teresa, especially since her dreams for the evening would evaporate with that tiny detail.

"Tight fit in that hot little number."

Victoria squealed, twirling, catching in the rosebushes' woody-fingers. Barrett caught her by the elbow, steadying her before she went down. His arms wrapped around her waist. She bet there'd be hand-shaped brands on her backside if she didn't get out of the way. Dang, he felt so good. Too good.

"What?" Gasping, Victoria searched for words that wouldn't feed the gossip mill. The milliners sat in hearing distance on the porch, looking like they were ready for the big play to begin.

Barrett's smile tugged at the corners. "The convertible. That car's a classic. But not worth a hill of beans in the snow. Nor for hauling stuff."

"Nothing like a compliment and a put down in just a few

sentences." Offended for her baby, Victoria wiggled, sidestepping out of his grasp.

"Better hang onto that one, Barrett," George hollered. His comment collected a couple of hoots and 'You betchas!' from his pals. Cackling with his cronies, he raised the beer bottle in a toast.

"I'll do my best not to throw her back," Barrett returned. He tipped his baseball cap from his forehead. His blue eyes twinkled, looking like a little boy who had devilish plans that included a frog and a squeamish girl.

Victoria slid her palms over her jeans. Squeamish had never been used to describe her, and she wasn't about to let it start. "George," she flipped her hair off her shoulders, turning to hit him with her best beam-worthy smiles. All teeth. "What makes you think I won't throw him back first?"

Barrett folded his arms, fists under biceps, plumping up his muscles. Except he didn't need to do any artificial maneuvers. His shoulders, yoked with bands of muscle from neck to arms, were real. They led her to his biceps, forearms dusted with sun-tinted hair. She could visualize his arms, pulsing with strength, lifting, tugging, warming. Holding.

"Guess, since I've been tossed back, I'll pull my offer to load and carry those trees to the cottage."

"What?" Thoughts of making a personal examination of his arms dissipated. "You never offered."

"Meant to." Barrett shrugged his yoked shoulders. "Got a little distracted."

"But..." The heat she'd been feeling rushed up to her ears. "I'm sorry. Just joking."

He leaned against the car. "You didn't think I'd just leave you to manage this all alone, did you? Course, now that I've been thrown back, maybe I'll move on down the road."

"But..."

"Now who can't take a joke?" He turned and lifted a tree to each shoulder.

Victoria followed behind. Her eyes drifted to his jeans. The waistband rode below his waist, hugging his hips. His tool belt hitched to one side. He had a gunslinger gate, strong thighs and long legs, striding comfortably to his pickup.

There were several boxes and bundles. A fire pit and two bent willow rocking chairs. A huge red and white metal cooler stretched across the truck bed.

Barrett shoved the boxes over and secured the trees near the cab. He stood on the tailgate, surveying his load. Sweeping his cap off, he swiped the sheen of perspiration from his forehead.

Victoria craned her neck to look up at him. "Thank you."

Barrett grinned, the smile reaching his eyes, turning them bluer than the Caribbean Sea. He hopped down, landing next to her. "I mean it." He brushed loose strands from her face, tucking them gently behind her ear. "If you're gonna be here this winter, you'll want to rethink your hot little number with something that can handle the snow."

"If?" Victoria's lips pressed together. "Don't you worry. I'll be here." She blinked, suddenly aware that her mind was set. She was extending her stay.

Her cell phone trilled an incoming call. Stunned that the thing actually worked, she grabbed it from her purse. Connor's number flashed out.

"Lucky you," Barrett grunted, and waited with his hands shoved in his pockets.

Victoria stared at the phone. The text message slid over the screen. It felt like a grenade, explosive and harmful. The text message screamed at her. She hit the delete button, silencing Connor's tirade. She dropped it into her purse. Her fingers tightened over the strap, hiding the trembling.

She shrugged, giving Barrett her everything-is-perfect smile. "Least I now know where to stand for a signal."

"Are you okay? If you need to—"

The cell phone trilled again. Victoria gripped the handbag in front of her. Connor had quickly given up on the texting and headed straight to voice. She spoke over the annoying sound. As soon as she got in her car, she was putting the thing on vibrate. "I'm heading to my place. Come when you're ready."

Barrett searched her face, looking behind the smiling mask that she'd been so careful to put in place. After numerous rings, his eyebrow lifted, arching in curiosity. "Aren't you going to answer it?"

Her throat squeezed, choking back the words. She shook her head.

"Victoria?" Barrett wrapped his hand around her shoulder. He bent, tipping her chin to see her face. "What is it? Do you need help?"

She took a shuddering breath that seemed to shake her from the spine out. "I'm fine. You...you just be sure to bring a healthy appetite."

Victoria spun on her heel and headed for her little red beauty. She slid in. Warmed from the sun, the buttery leather seats wrapped around her like a shawl. Tilting her head back against the headrest, she let the sun warm her skin and draw away the pain.

CHAPTER 12

Barrett sped down the country road to his house. Humidity rose from the blazing pavement. Dappled sunlight caught the windshield. The pickup bounced between the cool of the shade and the heat of the day. He planned to drop off his shipments and shower before heading to Mags's cottage. "Our cottage," he muttered, correcting himself.

He pulled into his drive. The gravel rolled and popped under the wide truck tires. He hopped out, calling Tilly on the way to the back door. The golden retriever leaped from the deep shadows of her dog run. The shade tree kept her cool and caught the breezes that ran in the afternoon. Her automatic water bowl was full and ready for another big slurp after an hour of ball chase.

"Sorry, old girl," He patted the top of her head, moving his scrunching massage down to her hips. "Not tonight."

He couldn't say that he had a date with a beautiful woman. The invitation was a combination of shattered nerves and a huge case of guilt. He'd worked with less.

After filling up Tilly's food bowl, he headed to the shower. He stripped down and stepped into the stream of hot water. He went into automatic and shaved for the second time that day. His eyes locked on his reflection in the mirror.

He'd done his best to put that crawling feeling out of his mind, but there it was again. He didn't know what was going on with Victoria, but he'd bet his stethoscope that she was in some kind of trouble.

Something was up with the beautiful woman from California. She'd tried not to show how badly the phone message had disturbed her. But he saw her fingers tremble around her purse. Rapid blinking sprouted under the stress of the continuing rings. And that smile never lit up her chocolate dipped eyes. She had set it up, made it look like she had it all under control, but he knew better.

He had to figure out a way to get her to open up. Whether she liked it or not, he'd find a way to help her before she returned to California.

———

G lorious, hot, steaming water sliced into Victoria's shoulders and back. It cut through the frustration and fear. Fingernails dug into her scalp. Tears mixed with the face soap and shampoo.

Reliving Connor's betrayal was bad enough. Her mind didn't stop there. It spun in circles, pointing out the obvious. Connor was the quintessential shark. He had been disrespecting her and mistreating her long before the betrayal, and she had ignored it and then learned to accept it. The manipulations and claims to a relationship had to stop.

The strong cell phone signal at the market had allowed all of Connor's messages to download onto her phone. On her drive home, she'd thought she could listen to the messages and then close the book on that chapter of her life. She'd flipped the phone to speaker and listened to all fifty missed phone calls. Some were hang-ups. Some recorded a curse word before he cut it off. The others, Connor vented his anger, dripping bitter condescension for her choice of running away to failure. By the time she heard the last message, she was trembling so hard that she had to pull over to the side of the road. Something had changed in Connor's world. His rage had ripped through her, reaching out of the phone to grab her by the throat, squeezing until she spilled out of the car and threw up in the ditch.

Tilting her face, she directed the shower spray into her chest. She doubled over. A sob tore through her, a broadsword through her torso.

Connor's text messages made it clear. He intended to make her pay for leaving him. It wasn't a broken heart that bothered him. He wanted the condo, and he needed her to pay for it.

Did he really think she'd give in to his threats? Whether she stayed in Wisconsin or returned to California, it was her decision. No one else had that power over her. Not anymore. Not her Dad and definitely not Connor.

Victoria directed the shower handle to cold and let the icy water sluice over her body. Her head clearer, she stepped out, and dried off with one of the fluffy towels she had purchased that day. The towel tucked around her body, she walked through the house.

Ignoring the shuddering pink walls, she hauled her suitcase into the largest bedroom. She'd ordered a soothing soft beige paint that reminded her of the white sandy beaches of the Florida Keys. It would brighten the room and show off the *café au lait* stained floors.

With her arms full of hangers and clothes, she twisted the knob, popping the closet open. Catching the light switch with the tip of her finger, she flipped it on. "Oh, gosh." Air wheezed out of her lungs like a balloon with a hole in it.

Handwritten notes wallpapered the closet walls. Victoria hugged the clothes to her chest and stared at the multi-colored pieces of paper. The handwriting began in precise, well-formed letters. Scrawling cursive, half-formed letters and sentences filled the others. A few had lost their stickiness and had fluttered to the floor.

The clothes slid from her hands. The towel sagged, then dropped away. Victoria twisted her damp hair and slung it behind her back. She stepped over the towel and picked up a faded piece of paper.

Remember.

———

V ictoria looked up from the pile of notes and unfolded her legs. Barrett would be there soon. She dug through the hangers and clothing abandoned on the floor and dressed on automatic.

She glanced at her reflection. Shorts and a t-shirt, flip-flops, and a ponytail. That should complete the look that says "this is not a date."

Dark circles under her eyes proved she'd had little sleep in the last week. She pursed her lips. Actually, a full night's sleep had evaded her for over a month. A little vanity was good for the soul. After applying makeup with a light hand, she stood back and surveyed her work. It would do. Not too much. Just enough.

Victoria returned to the bedroom closet. She squinted at the walls, trying to see a pattern. There were several, newer notes, that bore Barrett's name.

She chewed on her thumb. They were puzzle pieces without a picture to give her clues. A puzzle of the community and Mags.

She scooped up the loose notes and put them in her overnight bag. One thing was obvious. She couldn't leave her things piled on the floor. She hated wrinkles too much to rock the super casual "I don't care" college look.

Victoria took out her cell phone and shot pictures of each note, then walked to the window and checked the images, making certain she could read the handwriting. There were over a hundred shots added to her photo file. Blank spaces were noted too. The missing messages were bound to be in the ones she'd found on the floor.

Confident she could recreate the layout, she carefully peeled the notes off the wall. First the left side. Then the right. Stepping deeper into the closet, she pushed back empty hangers and ducked under the wooden rod. Taped to the back wall were another fifty faded yellow notes.

One spelled out a quote in graceful handwriting, *There is a price for freedom. Accountability always follows.*

Victoria traced the faded blue ink with her fingernail. There was truth in those words, but why write the note and then hide it in a closet?

Tires crunched over gravel, announcing company. "Darn it!" She whipped out her phone. The time on the home screen told her she'd been messing with the stuff in the closet for over an hour. A pickup door thumped shut. The solid *thunk* of a tailgate being dropped down soon followed.

"That's probably Barrett." She chewed on her lip. "Perfect."

There wasn't enough time to compile shots of each note. She'd have to return to it when there was privacy. Sharing what she found with Barrett wasn't an option. She took a few more pictures and stepped back to examine her work. Her hanging clothes covered Mags's secret.

Barrett. Why did Mags write his name on one of her slips of paper? Was it to help her remember?

Victoria dug her hands into her shorts pockets and glanced out the window. Barrett was outside, hauling boxes out of the truck bed. He'd changed clothes. His chest and shoulders stretched the fitted, red t-shirt. He still wore jeans, but they lacked the tool belt this time. Too bad. It actually enhanced his hips, giving her a valid reason to look at his backside.

She should go out and help. At least direct him where to put her purchases. A crumpled note, stuffed in her pocket, poked into her thigh. She pulled it out.

One of the first ones she'd picked up. Funny, she forgot when she put it there. Barrett's name was scrawled across the front in a shaky hand. She flipped it over. *Needs what's missing.*

———

B arrett straightened from picking up the last load. With a self-satisfied grin, he set the bent willow chair in the shade. It joined the other three he'd grabbed on his way out. Yes, he was right. The bent willow chairs from his workshop looked perfect under the maple tree.

The back door slammed shut. Energy blew past him, raising the hair on his arms. His gut spun like a tornado.

He turned to watch Victoria walk across the yard. Her long legs ate up the space between them. She'd changed out of jeans and had on a pair of shorts that barely covered her sweet behind. The faded t-shirt, draped around her body, directing his gaze to the cleavage peeking over the V-neck. A breeze lifted her hair, revealing hints of auburn fire.

The woman had something on her mind, and he had a feeling he wouldn't like whatever she had to say. Every fiber in his being said to run. Instead, he stood rooted to the ground. He didn't have a choice; his legs wouldn't move.

"Barrett," her voice rose over the sun-warmed earth.

He cringed. Maybe she was annoyed he didn't ask her for her permission to bring over the chairs. Hell, it was just an idea. Evidently a dumb one. He braced his legs, waiting for impact. It was as if he was witnessing an impending train wreck. He knew he should look away, but he couldn't tear his eyes from her. She was just too darn fun to watch. He shoved his hands in his front pockets. Maybe she wouldn't notice the compass in his pants, pointing at her like she was the freakin' North Star.

"Barrett, where did those come from?"

"Look," he shrugged, "if you don't like them, I can take them back."

"Take them back?" She looked up, tears welling. Her radiant smile brightened the darkest corner of the barren garden. "Don't you dare! I love them!" She slid her hands over the arching bentwood, her fingers trailing over the back. Stepping away, she examined their details. Victoria snared his gaze in hers. She grabbed his wrist. Her touch electrified his skin. The air squeezing Barrett's lungs sizzled loose.

"Thank you," she whispered.

He caught her like it was second nature to have a woman jump into his arms and wrap her legs around his waist. A floral scent, flowers and citrus, floated from her hair.

Pride lifted his shoulders. Barrett couldn't suppress the satisfied grin. "Glad they make you happy," he said into her crown. "Must have made them just for that spot."

Victoria drew back. She cleared her throat. Surprise registered, raising her brows, widening her brown eyes. "You made these?"

The summer breeze cooled his skin when she pulled away. A trail of fire slid from her fingertips. He was certain she'd branded her handprints on his ass. He didn't mind that thought at all.

CHAPTER 13

Victoria leaped down, putting much-needed space between her body and Barrett's. She bit the tender flesh that had come so close to latching onto his mouth.

Embarrassment flooded her thoughts as she rubbed her thumbs over the points of her elbows. Forcing her focus on the beautiful chairs, she worked to examine Barrett's craftsmanship. She bent down to stroke a curve in the bent willow. Peeking up through bits of hair that caught in the steamy breeze, she watched his expression shift.

He had looked like a little boy who'd surprised his mom with flowers from the yard, hope shining in his eyes. The radiance had already begun to fade, mingling with the barrier she tried desperately to erect. The shades dropped down, protecting his thoughts from further examination.

Flashes of dear old Dad's disdain, his obvious confusion over how to accept a gift graciously, tap-danced inside her head. Had she become the very person she vowed never to become? Callous. Self-indulgent. Scared to death of being trampled underfoot by someone you loved.

Barrett moved cautiously toward her. He had that wary,

narrow-eyed look. Uncertain if she was friend or foe. Unsure whether he was the hunter or the prey. Otherwise known in most circles as that-woman-might-be-crazy syndrome.

Her fingers slid over the chair arms, wrapped around the legs, rounded over the arched back. The workmanship was that of an artisan. She'd almost missed the nuances of the simple pickup driving handyman. He'd built this piece of art with meticulous care and passion. Her Grinch's heart swelled, threatening to burst open the box she'd worked so hard to keep closed. "They're," her voice croaked. "Beautiful," she whispered.

Victoria ached to be the object of that much attention to detail, the receiver of that much passion. Warmth rushed to her neck. Who knew she'd get that hot and excited over a set of outdoor furniture? Her eyebrows arched. Not her; that's for sure. That part of her had died when Connor broke her heart.

So why did she feel so much appreciation for a couple of chairs? Appreciation? No, it went deeper than that. And that was what scared her, shook her to her core. He had thought of her, had seen a need and took a chance. It had been a long time since someone cared beyond the toddler mentality of wanting to know "what's in it for me?" Her soul warmed, burning her eyes with a surge of senseless moisture.

She turned to stare at the lake shimmering behind them. She hadn't even been down to her very own private boat dock. That had scared her too. God, when had she become so afraid?

Barrett stood beside her. Silently, he looked out at the lake.

The summer breeze lifted her hair from her neck, caressing Victoria's skin. She closed her eyes. Lord, but the brush of their bodies had jangled her nerves all the way to her toes.

Rocking on the balls of her feet, she scrunched her toes in the ends of her flip-flops. What would it be like without all that clothing wedged between them? She shivered, wanting.

Mirroring Barrett, she shoved her hands into her back pockets. Her fingers curled, wanting desperately to return to his shoulders, his finely formed ass. Instead, they curled around the useless iPhone fighting for space in her pocket. Its presence reminded her of the nasty messages. It squeezed out the liquid warmth that rushed through her body.

Why couldn't she have met Barrett before Connor? Of course, Barrett would have been living in Wisconsin's backcountry. So that wouldn't have happened. She needed to get herself together. Her new life didn't have room for more complications.

Barrett smoothed her hair back from her face. "The...uh... groceries are still in the back of the truck." His long fingers trembled where he cupped the base of her jaw. "And, we, um, need to get the cooler out of the sun."

Victoria's eyes shot up to his. Iridescent blue-gray irises ringed his dilated pupils.

Oh, God. Bowling-ball-sized nerves flattened the crazed notion of a passion-filled night in one strike. The thought of cooking had completely evaporated from her brain cells. And, "they" said *men* lost brain function when aroused. She nodded numbly. Cooking meant something more than peeling open a microwavable meal. What was she thinking? Did he want food now?

A buzzing sound came from his hip, and he glanced at the satellite phone on his belt. Victoria made a note to find out his service. It seemed to be the only wireless technology that worked around the cove.

"I'm sorry," Barrett said, "but I have to run."

"Sure." She wanted to ask what kind of handyman emergency came before sex or food. Then again, she wasn't exactly a sure thing. Was she?

The corners of his firm mouth pressed into a thin line. He scooped up a bag and tossed it on top of the cooler. "I'll help you carry it in before I go."

"Thanks."

Victoria yanked out her cell phone and glanced at the time. Relief washed over her in waves. One would have thought she had gained a reprieve from walking the plank. She had a few hours to pull a recipe out of the internet. Her stomach fell. No service. No recipes from the ethers. Somehow, she'd have to create something from memory.

Covertly moving the canned foods around, she glanced at their labels. Maybe there was a recipe on the back. The only one that came up was lasagna. In this heat, she had no desire to fire up the oven.

Victoria set her jaw, resigned to having to make something up. She muscled in two large cardboard boxes, placing them on the kitchen counter. "Lord, I don't remember buying so much stuff." She blew a puff of air to cool her skin. "I hope I have enough room for everything."

Barrett stood, legs braced, fists at his hips. "Did you buy out the market?" His eyes sparkled back at her. He wiped his upper lip. "Where is the rest of the cove supposed to buy their groceries?"

He lifted the lid and peeked in the cooler. "Dinner looks like it will be amazing."

Victoria eyed the stacks of food as if they were the enemy. Now was the time to confess. Her best source for prepared food had been through the phone. Dial a meal and have it delivered. If she really wanted to impress, she'd pick it up herself.

The clock on the wall struck four. "I hope you don't mind eating late. It will take time to put everything away."

The skin stretched over his cheekbones. His eyes searched the yard. His mind led him out the driveway before he was even in the truck. "No rush. I may be awhile."

"Trouble?" She bit her lip. Barrett dodging a date before it even occurred hit a nerve that Connor had left jagged and raw. "Rain check?"

Barrett snagged her waist, pulling her closer. There may have been inches between them, but Victoria swore she felt the heat scorch her belly. His mouth covered hers, hungrily nibbling, drawing her in. He stole her breath, all thought processes, and the ever-present fear of being hurt again. Her fingers curled around his shoulders, bunching his shirt under her palms.

The shrill beep of his sat phone went off at his waist. Barrett and Victoria jumped apart. Technology sliced through their building heat with surgical precision.

He jerked the phone up and read the number. "I'm sorry about this, but I've got to go." He grabbed her again. The kiss absorbed her. Strong and powerful as the man. Barrett released her and jogged to his truck.

Victoria pressed her fingers to her mouth, rubbing the swollen flesh. She watched the taillights flash as he braked. Maybe he was coming back. Her heartbeat began a stuttered jitterbug when he jumped out of the cab.

Stepping off the porch, she forced her steps to take it slow. She was not about to toss what little dignity she had left on some backwoods repairman. There would be no racing to him. Her steps quickened. Meeting him in the middle was definitely an option.

"Victoria," Barrett trotted up to her.

Hope swelled despite her efforts to remember they'd just met. "Yes?"

"I should be back in a couple of hours. Two, maybe three, tops." He paused. "Is that too late?"

The beeping sounded again. He didn't wait for her answer but spun on his heel and ran to his truck. Gravel sprayed out from the tires as he shot out of the drive.

Victoria stood in her yard, speechless. Her toes scrunched into the soft soles of her flip-flops. Too late? For dinner or a booty call?

———

One hour later, Victoria stood in the middle of the kitchen. The moment the groceries were in their respective spots, it felt like someone lived there. It became hers. Too bad, she didn't know how to fix any real food in it. She was certain she'd find inspiration once she had everything organized.

Victoria nibbled her nail. Didn't she read somewhere that with a little organization the cooking muse would find her? She couldn't help herself. As soon as she unearthed the label maker from her suitcase, she started making sense out of the chaos in her life.

Two hours later, the pantry was organized. Individual canisters for all the basics, lined up, labeled, and ready to produce amazing food. However, the muse had yet to show up. *The lazy bitch.* She shrugged. The ingredients to a perfect meal would have to hang out on the shelf until she figured out what to do with them.

Victoria moved on, taking inventory of the drawers, examining the kitchen utensils. Some might as well have been used in a surgical ward, because in the kitchen, her knowledge was limited to a spoon and a spatula. "Another day," she promised, stroking the shining stainless steel.

One eye on the clock, she flipped opened the last cabinet. The truth to her incompetence in the kitchen would soon be all too real to Barrett. He'd be here soon, and she had nothing figured out. Granted, she could boil water. There was a bag of spaghetti and a jar of sauce.

Thankfully, she had packed a couple of bottles of Central Coast pinot noir. Maybe man could live by bread and wine alone.

She envisioned Barrett, his tool belt slanted on his narrow hips, ready to take on the homeowner's emergency. His tools sang like the jingle of a gunslinger's spurs.

Victoria shook her head. A man that used his body in physical labor needed a meal with substance.

Gasping, she knelt down to worship at the feet of the hidden treasure inside the cabinet. The shelves were loaded with Mags's cookbooks. She traced her finger over the bindings. Some stained and worn, showing frayed edges of use.

She pulled them down, flipping through the pages. Notes,

scribbled hastily along the edges of recipes, spoke of meals and dinners shared alone and with friends. They revealed a life of the woman everyone in Honeybrooke Cove seemed to miss.

Before she knew it, three hours had passed and still no recipe, no meal, and no hungry man walked through her doorway. Despite Mags's fascinating cookbooks, the cooking muse was unavailable. Victoria gave in. Tonight would have to be a simple offering of spaghetti.

A half-an-hour later, she added a salad and set a bottle of pinot noir on the kitchen table.

Victoria stepped back. It wasn't bad. Not exciting, but no one would starve. She glanced at her cell phone. Still time for a quick shower.

———

By nine o'clock, Victoria did the math in her head. Barrett had said he'd be two, maybe three hours. So far, he had pushed dinner to four hours. The cold spaghetti had congealed into a lump of tangled starch. Tomato sauce was past saving. The entire meal would go *en masse* into the trash. Just like her night.

The useless cell phone rested on the table. She spun it with her fingertip and watched the apps spin in a kaleidoscope of color. No connection to the outside world was driving her nuts. For all she knew, Barrett would have called if he could. A prayer for his safety went up automatically. Maybe he'd had second thoughts on that promised kiss.

Mags scribbled notes crept up to remind her of Barrett's missing pieces. Victoria popped the cork on the wine and grabbed a glass. Flicking off the kitchen light, she headed to the living room.

She had a few missing pieces too. One was her heart. She'd misplaced it a long time ago. Her fingers pressed the deep V in the neck of the navy blue tunic she'd slipped on in anticipation of Barrett's arrival.

The sip of deep red liquid warmed her tongue and slid down her throat. The half-full bottle stood at her elbow. She leaned her head against the couch's deep back. Her father's command echoed in her head, *"Smile! No one wants to see you cry."*

Victoria tipped the bottle, pouring the liquid promises into her glass and lifted a toast. "Thanks, Dad, you always know just what to say."

Restless, she rose from the couch. Wine in hand, she went to the kitchen sink and stared out the window. The lake water glistened in the moonlight. Shadows swirled over the glassy surface. Bank fishing was supposed to be safe. Maybe tomorrow she would go to the Cove Market and buy a fishing rod.

She picked up Mags's cookbook. Judging by the looks of its stained and worn pages, it looked the most loved. She flipped it open to a burgundy ribbon marker. Mags had written beside the casserole recipe, "Trials are temporary. He will wipe away any tears from our eyes." At the bottom of the page she wrote, "Comfort food."

Victoria held the glass up to the light and swirled the wine. When she paused, the wine legs stretched and grew until they returned to the base. A wistful smile tugged at her lips, and she emptied her glass down the sink.

———

B arrett smacked the flat of his hand on the steering wheel. A single light shone in the front window of the little cottage. It was past midnight and he was bone weary. The night had sucked every bit of energy out of him. Knowing Victoria had waited for him dug into him until it ached like a sore tooth.

It had taken over an hour to convince Chief Graham to seek medical help. Someone who still practiced medicine. Not him.

Hadn't he told Graham, in a weak moment, that he never wanted the responsibility of someone else's life again?

Instead, that fool decided the only doctor that knew anything was Doctor Barrett Collins. Graham had spouted to the urgent care doctor, 'That fella may have escaped Chicago, but never medicine and his physician's oath. Knows more than you and ten others put together.'

Barrett put the truck in gear and backed up. He wasn't about to lay all this on Victoria. Tomorrow would be a better day. And then, he planned to tear into Graham for behaving like a fool.

CHAPTER 14

Victoria rolled the wheelbarrow toward the first pile of stones she had to move. She set the barrow down and stood in the cool of the shade tree. The burning muscles in her neck and back ached from another night on the couch. She was beginning to think sleeping on the floor or in the car would be more comfortable.

She dropped into one of the bent willow chairs. Wrapping her fingers around the ceramic mug, she breathed in deep and let the steamy aroma of coffee penetrate every brain cell.

It was a new day. If Barrett could have a change of mind, then so could she.

That revelation came in the middle of the night as she read Mags's...correction, according to the inscription inside the beloved cookbook, Margaret Ellington's cookbook. That little bit of knowledge made the eccentric aunt real to Victoria. She understood the woman who felt the need to list and jot down thoughts. Apparently, she had a part of the woman's DNA swirling with her own.

Reading the cookbook had been like reading someone's

personal journal. She could only hope that some of the suggestions would help her learn to cook.

Margaret Ellington had been meticulous in taking notes. She was a woman after Victoria's heart. Lists and observations were everywhere. Not just about the food. Mags wrote about the people she served. And, she wrote about how she felt when she ate alone.

Tilting her head against the backrest, she watched as the green mass shifted in waves of light and shade. The leaves whispered in the breeze. Victoria understood the loneliness. It was one of the reasons she was useless in the kitchen.

She had tried to recreate the meals when her mother first passed away. They were a miserable failure. Her father spent more time walking the plate to the trashcan than he did sitting down and eating with her. She figured it was her cooking, so why try.

There was something about the cookbooks. She was eager to get back to them. They made her want to try again.

Victoria took another sip of coffee. The Tewilligers's lights were on in the house. The couple were probably preparing for another day at the market, ready to fulfill the needs of the locals and the tourists.

Maybe she would bake something and take it over as a thank you for using their phone. Mags had scribbled a side note that snicker doodles made quite the impression on the Tewilligers. Victoria pulled the small pad of paper out of her back pocket and added the cookie offering to her list. If they are inedible, Harold could use them for bait.

Sighing, Victoria rose and turned her attention to the mounds of rock littering the garden. It was exhausting to think that she'd have to move almost every pile. They were right where she wanted to plant the David Austin rosebushes. The Old English roses would catch the morning sun during the summer and have protection from the frigid winter winds.

A screen door slammed at the Tewilligers's home. The woman never seemed to stop moving. Expecting a glance and a half-wave,

Victoria smiled, surprised that Mrs. T hurried across their immaculate lawn. Her legs stretched the narrow skirt. Her sensible shoes kept her from toppling over the uneven ground.

"Victoria," Mrs. T hollered. "What do you think you're doing? You can't move them!"

Victoria pushed at the ache in her lower back. "Mrs. T, I promised I wouldn't move Tommy's memory stones. But these," She pointed to the pile that she'd loaded into the wheelbarrow. "These weren't anywhere near that pile. And they're right where I want to plant a rosebush."

She grinned, excitement with her plans made her want to share her vision. "Wait until you see it. I've laid out a garden that will turn these rocks into an actual garden. I have a few hardscapes I intend to use." She waved to the shed. "I want a water feature over there to draw our eye to the lake, give us something cool and soothing to listen to when we sit under the shade tree. I'll enlarge the path to the docks. Build a rock wall. Maybe even with some of the larger stones."

Mrs. T's glaring silence made Victoria rush on with her garden ideas. "And I have a couple of trees to plant. More David Austin roses. I think they are the prettiest and have the best-perfumed scent. Don't you think?" Victoria swallowed. "I'll mix in some perennials too."

Mrs. T's eyes narrowed. The woman looked like she chewed on barbed wire. "Mags put those rocks there for a reason." She spat the words out, the barbed syllables striking where they hit. "You don't have a clue what you are doing." She jabbed the air with her finger. "Each one has a story. You better find out what it is before you tear down a memory."

Victoria's cheeks heated. Her heartbeat thrummed in her ears. When would this cove come to grips with the fact that this was no longer Mags's place? "But they're in the way of what I want to do."

"*Hmpf!* That's why we didn't want a stranger coming in and

destroying what Mags had built." Suddenly aware she had crossed the line of civility, Mrs. T's eyes widened. A flush of pink crept up her neck. "You'll thank me, Victoria. Trust me. You will."

Her piece said and confident that Victoria would rethink her plans, she spun on her heel and left.

The wind caught Victoria's hair, lifting it from her brow. Thoughts of baking cookies dropped to the bottom of her list.

Thanks to Mrs. T, Victoria would never be able to turn off the questions until she had answers. If she wanted a decent night's sleep, she would need to find out why the towers of memory stones were there in the first place. There were five in all. Not that many. One was Tommy's. That left four to go.

She rubbed her thumb against a broken fingernail. Dirt stuck to the creases in her skin. There had to be a way to keep the mounds and create the garden that she wanted.

———

B arrett pulled into Victoria's driveway. No one had seen her for several days. He told himself it was partly her fault he didn't call. It would have been easier if the woman had a cell phone that actually worked. It didn't take a country boy to figure out fancy apps were useless here in the cove. It was a simple fix. Get a landline to the house. If she didn't want that, then get a sat phone like the one he had.

Guilt nipped at him. He should have stopped by the first day after he didn't make it to dinner. Each day he waited made it harder to drop by. Now, here it was, four days later. He supposed she could argue that she had every right to toss him off the front porch. However, technically, half of that porch was his.

He gripped the steering wheel and stared at the lake, drawing strength from the memories he'd shared with Mags. The old woman had a way with her, digging into his secrets while she plied him with the best cooking he had ever eaten. And that included his mom's. In her digging, Mags made him look at what she had unearthed. She poked him, made him admit the dream was still alive. He may have given up on himself, his skill, but she would not. Even when she began to slip away. She said that the stories of the past shaped him as they had shaped her. She made him look at himself, the person he was now.

The broken man who left Chicago five years ago no longer lived. He wasn't that same man. He wasn't whole yet. Not by a long shot. The nightmares made sure of that. Mags kept pointing out there was a piece missing, and he had better find it before she left this earthly plane.

He knew he didn't have all the time in the world, but he sure thought he had enough. Mags knew different. His jaw tightened. The burning, squeezing in his throat choked him. He had planned on taking over the cottage, remodel it, groom the garden and honor Mags. Make it a showplace. He never realized Mags was so late in her mortgage payments. Nor did he believe the bank would foreclose before he got the money together. He had a plan. And so did Mags.

That someone Mags worked into his life walked around the corner of the house. Victoria had her earphones plugged in. Her steps bounced along with the music. Her pink tank top, announcing peace and love in rhinestones, stretched around her full breasts. The V cut deep into her cleavage. Her rounded hips trimmed in jean shorts, capped off a pair of tanned legs.

Barrett grinned. He'd never seen a sexier pair of scuffed, sensible work boots. She had her hair pulled up in a ponytail. It swung in time with her steps. The sun caught it and pulled out auburn threads. She stopped in the shade and set the wheelbarrow down. Her hands smoothed the arms of a chair. Arching her back, she stretched up to the sky. A satisfied smile gentled her face.

He shifted in his seat. His pulse quickened. Despite the air-conditioning on full blast, the heat in the cab seemed to grow with every breath.

Barrett unsnapped his seat belt and turned off the ignition. He felt like he was back in high school. Pausing, he gripped the door handle and braced for the shovel that might come sailing past his head.

CHAPTER 15

Barrett stepped cautiously toward the shade tree. He couldn't help the grin. Victoria was dancing and swaying, doing some interpretive steps to the music in her ears. He stumbled when she added the twist to the dance moves. Her hips wiggled, making her jean shorts hop, rising toward the crease of her cheeks. The smudges of dirt on both of her dimpled knees were his undoing.

He swiped his mouth, checking to make sure he wasn't salivating. Who was he kidding? He was. He just didn't want her to know it. *Keep it in control, Barrett.*

Victoria spun in a pirouette. Letting out a yelp, she froze. She yanked out the earpieces. The rock music blared from the little bits of plastic. Barrett grimaced and made a note to lecture her on unsafe decibels. Later.

"What are you doing here?" Her voice had an edge to it that brooked no crap from him.

"Wanted to stop by. Check on you."

"I see."

No hand tools in sight. The shovel was out of easy reach. Things looked better and better. He needed to see what lay behind the oversized sunglasses hiding her emotions.

"Do you?" Needing to know what she was really thinking, he gently lifted the sunglasses from her face. Brown eyes widened under the arch of raised brows. A glitter of hurt registered just below the surface. It pained him to know he had put that wariness in her eyes.

Barrett touched the smooth skin that covered her cheek, down the column of her neck, the edge of her collarbone peeking out of the pink tank top. He nudged her chin up, stroking the pad of his thumb across her lips.

"I'm sorry," he whispered.

Victoria placed her palm on his chest. He felt her fingers tremble through his denim shirt. It was like placing a brand on his heart.

"I know you are. But I can't do this." She let her hand drop to her side. "I have to protect me."

He shoved his hands through his hair. "Look, I know I should have stopped by sooner. I did stop." The flicker of doubt in her eyes made him rush in. "That first night. But it was too late."

Victoria folded her arms across her chest. "How late?"

"I don't know. After midnight."

"What were you working on that took so long?"

"I can't really talk about it. Not yet."

Victoria stepped away until her thighs touched the back of a chair. Her eyes rounded in horror. "Oh my gosh, you're married."

"No!" Barrett felt his chest squeeze. He didn't want to have to relive why he left medicine. He'd left it all behind. How could he explain his absence and not include the hospital visit with Chief Graham?

She narrowed her eyes, her nose flared as if she'd stepped in a dog's mess. "Then you have a girlfriend. Tilly, right?"

"Tilly is not my girlfriend. She's my—."

"I don't want to hear it." Victoria spun around on her heel. Jerking the wheelbarrow handles up she gave him her back. "Get off my property. And don't think you need to come around for any handyman work."

"Our property. Right, Partner?"

She looked over her shoulder, her glare slicing him in two. She drawled out the last word. "Nev…er."

Barrett stood rooted under the shade tree. He glanced at the mound of stones he and Mags had built together. Ironically, she'd had him working on his present and now he was about to take what he'd learned and try to reach past the deep walls Victoria had erected. He had to get her to listen and get past what drove her to Honeybrooke Cove. Visiting a distant aunt was not the complete truth.

—————

F or all Victoria cared, the man could take his hip-slung tool belt and drive his pickup into the lake. Course that would mean Barrett had received her message to leave. Instead, he seemed lost in studying the toes of his boots. Judging by the fact that he hadn't budged from the spot under the shade tree, she bet he had the male affliction every man she'd ever met had. He didn't know how to listen.

She hunched her shoulders and dug into the earth, attacking it with vigorous strokes. She had work to do. In the earth. In her life. She did not have time to waste on the idiotic man who just did not get her. She was done with secrets. They hurt her. They cut her deeper than her own secrets.

His shadow expanded over her shoulder and blocked the sun. Sniffing, she twisted the trowel in the baked dirt. She needed the shovel, but that required her to stand up and take the chance of meeting his gaze. Maybe, just maybe, he would go away. Gritting her teeth, she muzzled the snarl that was on the edge. She wanted to rip into him, teeth and claws. She sniffed back an annoying tear. Darn allergies.

"I'm sorry," he whispered. Remorse threaded its way around the simple words.

Seriously? She hacked at the ground. *That is supposed to make it better?*

"Victoria?" The warmth of his hand radiating through the tank top.

She swallowed the cotton patch that had grown in her mouth. "I told you to get off my...our property." As soon as the command was out, she wished she could gobble the words out of the air. They were still co-owners of Mags's cottage. But not for long.

She waited, her mouth as dry as the Nevada desert she drove through a few weeks ago. Why was he being kind? What did he want? The house? The chance that he wanted her, well, that was ridiculous.

Her shoulders bunched closer to her ears, fighting against the pressure of his fingers. A traitorous sigh slipped past her pressed lips. God, it felt good. How does one stay mad when his slightest touch felt so good?

The urge to beg him to rub every square inch of her body, jumped up like a bad dog. She clamped her lips tight and pushed the desire down. The steel, razor-edged trowel skipped off a stone and struck her leg. Victoria bit off a gasp when the metal cut into her knee. Her grip tightened. There were just too many distractions. Could the man not receive the message she was sending out? Go. A. Way.

Barrett knelt down to examine the cut. Curling tendrils had slipped out from his baseball cap. Strong bands of tendons and muscle led from his black t-shirt. His thick palms cupped the tender skin behind her knee. She shivered. Heat radiated from his touch. It slid up her legs, her hips.

His brows furrowed in concentration. "Doesn't require stitches." He whipped out a neatly folded bandana from his back pocket and pressed it to the cut, his fingers brushing the back of her knee. "But you need to get it cleaned up."

Victoria nodded. "I'll take care of it when you leave." She didn't make a move to get up. It felt too darn good. God, was she that desperate for attention?

He tilted his head. "I can do it." The cast of his eyes put her on alert. Threads of gray had altered the azure blue. "If you want me too."

"I can manage on my own," she said, her voice harsher than intended.

"So I've heard. Loud and clear." Barrett rose, dusting his jeans off, and handed Victoria the bandana. "You'll want to keep pressure on it for a little while."

Silence stretched between them. Closing her eyes, she ducked her head and nodded. Yes, her behavior was childish in a temper tantrum sort of way, but she couldn't bear to watch him walk away. Not yet. She listened for the sound of his footsteps, leading him back to his truck. The apology for growling at him tapped against her lips. Inhaling, she swiped the back of her over her dampened cheek.

"I can't leave us like this," he whispered beside her ear. "Will you please accept help when it's offered? At least once in a while?"

Her eyes snapped open. How did he get there beside her? Victoria tensed. The adrenaline washed over her in a wave. It withdrew, pulling any energy she had left with it. The trowel dangled in her hand. The other hand continued to press her knee. "I'm so tired," she whispered.

"I know." Barrett squatted down beside her. He propped her leg in his lap and pushed her hand away from the bandana. He waited, silently.

The space between them closed. A fragile truce formed, and peace began to bloom.

Calloused fingers gently braced her leg. The back of his tanned hand, curling sun-bleached hair from the wrist up, was a stark contrast to her slender knee. Victoria stuffed the chuckle, and it came out a snort. "Really? What do you know?"

Barrett had the male version of the deer-in-the-headlights look. His eyes widened. The pressure of his hands went into massage mode. Not that she didn't love the shiver that ran through her body, but she knew he was putting on a front. He was the walking embodiment of having no clue what she was going through. She sniffed. She had to give him credit. He was trying and hadn't run away in terror of female emotions. Tears, otherwise known as kryptonite to any breathing male.

"Hey," he caught a tear sliding down her cheek. "Don't cry."

"I'm fine," Victoria announced stoically.

Barrett had the good grace to grimace with her pronouncement. "Yeah, my sister would say that right before she kicked my butt."

The smile that tweaked the corner of her mouth overcame her resolve to freeze him out of her life. "Okay, maybe not fine." She glanced over her shoulder. Why did he have to be so darn tall even when he was sitting? It put a crick in her already cramped neck. "But I'm getting better every day."

"You know," he said, pointing to the mound of stones. "Mags made me help her carry all those stones from the lake shore." He shook his head. "She was a crafty one. Coerced me with home-made meatloaf and mashed potatoes."

Victoria's eyebrows rose. "Hefty price for basic labor."

"Hey, I'm not cheap, but I can be had."

"I'll remember that next time I need some muscle."

"Anytime, sweetheart." His eyes sparkled back at her. "Does that mean I can come back and work for you?"

Victoria laughed. It caught in her throat, like it didn't know whether to come out or hide. "You haven't left yet."

His grin lit up. "You noticed that, did you?"

She scrunched her nose. "Maybe we can work something out."

"Like I said, I can be had."

Heat began to build, scorching a path up her neck. Clearing her throat, she reached out to stroke the pile of memory stones. "Why'd she have you build it?"

"It was Mags's way." Barrett touched the stone with his fingertip. "Kind of awkward. A little eccentric." The wistful smile that lifted his lips was almost angelic. Almost. His eyes twinkled. "The base happened the first night I drove into town. She said we had to commemorate the event."

Victoria leaned back on one elbow and watched the sun play over the ridges of Barrett's cheekbones. The tender flesh under his eyes was deeper, darker than she remembered. If they were in a race for exhaustion, they would be in a dead heat. She bit off the questions and let him talk if he willed it.

Barrett pointed to the next layer of stones. "Those, she had me dig up out of a hole a mile away and haul them back here. It took me nearly a day." He tilted his head. "The trek sure gave me plenty of time to think. Mags said it was the perfect time to contemplate my navel." He took a deep breath. "She was right. That trip into the woods. The quiet. Gave me some clarity."

He looked down where Victoria had slipped her hand into his. "The last stones were placed there right before she passed. She said I needed to move on, and the peak was to guide me on the new path. Like a lighthouse." He paused, closing his eyes. He covered her hand. Their fingers entwined over the alabaster stone, moving, bending, as one.

Victoria squeezed his fingers. "I won't move them. I'll work around them." She searched his face. "I swear."

Barrett gave a quick nod, acknowledging her promise.

Reluctant to leave the little space of peace in the garden, Victoria rose slowly from the memorial pile of stone. She bent her neck, praying the stiffness would work its way out of her joints. She grimaced when Barrett popped up like an Olympic gymnast.

His palms ran over her shoulders, pressing and stretching the muscles. A deep sigh escaped.

"Too many nights sleeping on the overstuffed couch," she muttered.

"Harold doesn't have any connections to get a mattress delivered?"

"Not for another two weeks." She grimaced. "I think I'll be dead by then."

She shivered when his fingers slid down her back.

"Do you feel like going for a drive with me?"

"Right now?"

"Sure! Why not? I'll even feed you."

Victoria hesitated. Her to-do list had grown instead of shortened. It would be the ultimate in stupidity to leave everything undone.

But how could she resist? He had that eager little boy look in his eyes again. Although next time, she vowed she'd be more resistant to his cajoling.

CHAPTER 16

The stand of trees began to thin and the rolling hills stretched out in front. Cows dotted the green meadows shared with the spinning wind turbines. Barrett's pickup bounced over the basement-sized ruts in the road.

Victoria bit her lip. How did he persuade her to let him take her mattress shopping? It was bound to be as awkward as having your dad and boyfriend there when you chose the perfect mattress with just the right bounce.

She glanced at the bandage and faded stains on her knees. At least he gave her time to wash her hands. She peeked over at the speedometer. The man was on a mission. Either that or he was having second thoughts and planned to take them off the grid. A huge pothole caught the tires and suspended the pickup for a fraction of a second.

They sped out of Honeybrooke Cove and over the hill. When her cell phone caught the elusive signal, it started buzzing like a hive of bees.

Victoria shimmied to one hip and yanked the phone out of her pocket. She gripped the phone and stared at the climbing number of messages. The red light blinked as fast as a Morse Code Decoder Ring.

Barrett glanced from his intent concentration on the road. "Popular lady." He pointed with the tilt of his chin. "Don't you want to listen to your messages? Aren't you a little curious?"

"No." It was like watching a traffic accident. She couldn't tear her eyes from the messages flowing in. She flinched when the ringtone took over the vibrations and Jennifer Hudson sang Where You At.

Connor's name and number streamed across the screen. Wonderful. Victoria heard a snarl and realized it came from her. She flipped the ringer to silence. Butterflies and spiders fought for space, twisting her stomach in knots. She shoved the phone in her pocket, happy to have it out of sight. But that didn't mean it was out of mind.

Billboards lined the street, announcing they were nearly to their destination. The mattress store was just a mile down the road.

"We really don't have to do this," Victoria gritted out through clenched teeth.

Barrett shot her a quizzical look before braking. Tires squealing, he pulled into the mattress mart. "We're here now. Might as well check it out."

Hopping out, he jogged over to her door and had it open before she could get the seatbelt unlatched. He opened the door and held out his hand. "My lady, your new mattress awaits." He waggled his eyebrows. "Let's try it out."

His ball cap plastered down all but his bangs and the curling ends sticking out at the bottom. Long, dark lashes encircled his blue eyes. Victoria swore they were constantly changing nuances of color with every swing of his mood. Right that minute they were a deep azure and they sparkled. If she didn't know any better, she would have to believe that he was enjoying himself.

She swallowed the lump that had started to form a half-mile

down the road. She had this sinking feeling that bouncing on a bed in front of Barrett would rank right up there with having to buy tampons on your first date.

"Course, if you don't think you can handle it…"

Victoria grabbed her purse and slid out of the cab. She pushed him out of the way with the flat of her hand against his chest. "Just watch me, handsome."

––––––––

B arrett stayed back a distance, admiring the way her hips swung with each step. He knew she was a little uncomfortable shopping with him. She had twisted the hem of the shirt she'd thrown over her tank top during the whole thirty-minute drive to the mattress store. Even the phone vibrating across their seats hadn't given the shirt a break.

Her avoidance of the phone was a mystery that he couldn't help following. He'd never had that many messages even when he was on call for ER duty on a New Year's Eve. He realized she'd had a life before she moved from California. Probably a lot of friends. Who wouldn't miss her radiant face? But her nerves had amped up, fingers twisting, trembling when the phone rang. Her face had drained of all color until he started teasing her about giving the new bed a little test run. The pink in her cheeks had bloomed prettily. Real nice. He'd like to see her skin flushed, glistening and rosy from his kisses.

Victoria stopped at the door, turned to wave him on and gave him a toothy grin. Barrett swallowed. He suddenly felt like he was looking at a she-wolf. And he was dinner.

He shivered despite the heat waves shimmering off the parking lot pavement. Tipping his cap back on his head, he strolled toward her, letting her eyes get their fill. She never let her gaze waver. By the time he joined her at the door his knees felt rubbery.

He grabbed her hand and they pushed through the doorway. Barrett grinned.

Game on.

———

The salespeople met them as soon as they walked in. It took a few minutes of convincing the store manager that they would holler when they were ready. Victoria and Barrett wandered the showroom, hand in hand, acting like a couple.

Victoria pretended to focus on the purchase of a bed, but the phone in her back pocket felt like a ticking time bomb. It was hot, and she needed some time to gather the messages, and then respond to them as fast as she read them. She sucked in her bottom lip, catching it with her teeth. She'd have to deal with Connor's messages too. Chances were they weren't love notes. Those she would happily delete in one click of the key. There was also the slight chance that there was a response to one of the hundred resumes and applications she'd filled out and sent before heading to Wisconsin. Maybe they'd allow her to work from home. If that were the case, she definitely needed to figure out phones and internet. With reality pressing in, Victoria concentrated on finding a bed.

She wove her way through the store, scanning for the answer to sleepless nights and aching muscles. She had a list of things she wanted and would know the perfect specifications when she saw it. The highest priority was that she didn't sway from getting a queen bed for one. The empty space where the other head of the couple should press into the pillow would be less noticeable. Lying spread out like an eagle, she could take up the entire bed and never feel lonely.

Barrett skirted the kids and baby section. He slid his wide shoulders and narrow waist to the other side of the walkway. The way he acted, you'd think it held the plague.

He led her with precision to the row of mattresses. His forehead crinkled, his ball cap tipped back. Shooting her a challenge, he sat down on the king-sized pillow-mattress and bounced. Fascinated, Victoria watched. His pace slowed to a gentle rocking. "Come on," he whispered, patting the place beside him.

"This isn't right." She cleared her throat. "It's too big."

He kicked back, stretching his full length across the bed. "Give it a try."

Victoria looked down. Barrett's shirt pulled up to reveal a nest of coiled inky hair, tempting her to trace it with her finger. Although his tool belt was absent from his gunslinger-hips, she could still see it dipping low to one side. Tanned satin stretched over rock hard abs. He clasped his hands and made a pillow with his forearms. He closed his eyes and sighed. A satisfied smile tempted her to give the bed a chance.

She poked the pillow-top with a tentative fingertip. It was luxuriant and firm. Hesitant, one eye on Barrett and one eye out for the store manager, she perched on the edge of the mattress. It felt good. No. It was wonderful. Sighing, she braced her hands and gave the bed a bounce.

Barrett's arm locked around her. The air in her lungs rushed out in a surprised whoosh. He pulled her close, tucking her next to his side.

Wide-eyed, Victoria pushed against his ribs. "The managers—"

"Will be thrilled to sell a bed." He rolled to his side. His chest almost touched her shoulder. Barrett smoothed back her hair, his touch gentle and careful. He studied her face, starting at the top of her head and stopping at her mouth.

Their lips joined; a tentative kiss, testing, remembering, wanting more.

Victoria gasped when his fingertips slid up her jaw. Their kiss deepened, tasting each other. The mint. The sweet. Combined as one.

"Ahem." The voice over their head interrupted, jerking Victoria from the dream.

"Oh no," Victoria squeaked. Pushing and shoving her hand against Barrett's chest, she sat up.

A groan emanated from behind her. She whipped around, ready to take Barrett to task. The terse words melted when she saw the shock registered on his face.

The manager smiled, the hand-held computer ready for an order. "Is this the one you'll be wanting?"

She stroked the mattress wistfully and stole a glance at Barrett. It may be too big for one person, but she'd have the memory of the hottest kiss on record. Flinging the list of specifications out of her head, Victoria nodded. "Can you deliver it by tonight?"

CHAPTER 17

True to his promise, Barrett pulled into the roadside restaurant, Clyde's Der Hey Café. Despite its name, they had an excellent reputation for their fish fry. Their burgers weren't too bad either. He owed her at least that much for embarrassing her. After that steamy kiss back on the bed, he could use a cold drink himself. Too bad he was driving. An ice-cold beer would taste great and wet his parched throat.

His hands had finally stopped shaking. The heat thrumming in his blood had finally slowed to a simmer. It waited just below the surface, ready to ignite at a moment's notice. As long as he didn't have to look at Victoria, he could manage it. The fact that she sat next to him, and he could smell the scent of the shampoo she used, the lotion she smoothed over her body? Yeah, his attraction would be harder to manage than keeping mosquitoes away on a humid Wisconsin night.

He gripped the steering wheel, focusing on things that might turn off the heat. *Resetting broken bones. Open-heart surgery.*

"Barrett?"

"Hmm?"

"Are we getting out here? Or what?"

Barrett glanced up. Lord, she was beautiful. Tendrils of auburn stuck to her cheek. Silk. He'd felt it. Her hair was as soft as silk.

She sucked in her lower lip, catching it with her teeth. "Are you all right?"

He shook his head to clear it. "Yeah. Sure." He offered her his best confident grin. The one he used with patients. Only this time, he was the patient and in need of a distraction. STAT. "I'm starving."

"Me too."

They looked up into the rearview mirror. A tour bus headed for the local casino pulled in behind them.

"Hurry," Victoria said. "Let's get a table before they get them all."

They raced out of the truck and walk-sprinted to the hostess stand. A horde of women and a handful of men crowded in behind them.

The young hostess, her hair pulled back in a ponytail, stood barring the café. "We'll seat you just as fast as we can."

She led Victoria and Barrett to the large back booth. Dealing the menus out, she took their drink orders. "Shannon will be back in a short bit to take your order."

Victoria slid over the faux-leather bench. The forgotten cell phone poked into her hip, reminding her she still had quite a few tasks on her to-do list to complete. But the day was successful. She had a new bed coming by evening, and she'd had a really-hot kiss from a really-hot man.

Lifting her hip, she slipped the phone out of her pocket and laid it on the table. Now that the onslaught of messages was over, she figured she could turn the ring tones back on.

She looked up. Barrett was watching her. The threads in his irises were darker, more azure than gray. He motioned toward the offending bit of technology on the table. "I don't get it. What's on there that makes you as nervous as a cat in a room full of rocking chairs?"

Victoria spun the plastic case with her finger. "I guess I've started getting used to being without." She scrunched her nose. "It's been kinda nice. I have a built-in excuse and don't have to take any calls I don't want to take."

Barrett leaned forward, his hands folded over the table's smooth surface. "You don't have to answer me, but are you hiding from someone?"

"No," The phone slid back and forth in her hands. She searched his face. The crease between his brows deepened. What answer was he looking for? "I've been busy. I just haven't had the chance to hook things up. You know. A house. Gardens. Things that go bump in the night."

Barrett flashed a grin, dissipating the frown in one motion. "And buying a bed." He wiggled his brows. "It was like being with Goldilocks. The first too hard, the second too soft." He reached out, rubbing his thumb over her sensitive bottom lip.

She nipped his thumb, warning him off, and then licked the tender flesh. "And the last one was just right."

"Hey there," the voice beside their elbows bubbled with sweetness. Their waitress, Shannon, showed up with an order pad and pen at the ready. Her eyes widened.

Victoria cringed. The heat she'd been trying to keep down and avoid swooped in with a hawk's precision.

She had to give Shannon credit. The young woman did her best not to ogle Barrett. However, with her mind on something other than their order, she kept dropping the pen. The latest maneuver landed in Barrett's lap and rolled onto the floor. "Oops. Sorry. Clumsy."

Shannon bent to retrieve it. Barrett followed suit. Their heads narrowly missed colliding. He jerked to a stop, his nose perilously close to diving into the woman's cleavage.

Victoria's eyes narrowed. Sweet little Shannon wrapped her fingers around Barrett's forearm, leveraging herself from the floor.

They got a full view of Shannon's tip-maker. Was that her belly button ring? "Yay, dinner and a show," Victoria muttered.

She wiped her lips with the paper napkin and folded it neatly beside her glass of iced tea. "I think we're ready to order." Victoria blinked. Did that hideous growling sound come from her? Why did she want to defend her space with everything within her? She flexed her fingers, wrapping them around the glass instead of the woman's neck.

"Two green salads. Two brats and a side of fries to share."

Barrett swept up the menus and handed them to their server without taking his eyes from Victoria. The blue orbs, wide-eyed and innocent, twinkled back at her. "Well, that was interesting," he said.

The sinking feeling that he was a cheat like Connor began the whispers inside her head. "You liked that, did you?"

He had the good grace to hide his enjoyment and reared back in the booth. His palm smoothed his shirt down. "Well. Yeah. Didn't you?"

The snort she had been doing her best to diffuse erupted. "Yeah, awesome. When she comes back, maybe you can get her number."

Barrett's mouth drew down. He rocked forward, forearms on the table. "Hey, V, what's that all about?" He grabbed her fingers. "I'm here with you. Remember?"

Reclaiming her hand, she shook her head. "Don't call me that."

Settling against the booth, he folded his arms across his chest. "V? Okay."

"And don't call me Vic or Vicky. Plain and simple. Keep it to Victoria," she snapped out.

"Note taken." His nostrils flared. "Look, what's really eating you?"

"What's eating me?" Victoria slid the straw into her glass and tried to ignore the thick icky wave of jealousy. "You mean like watching the man I'm with ready to lick whipped cream off the next easy woman he sees?"

"That's not fair." Barrett rubbed his hands over his jean-clad thighs. "You don't know her story. Maybe she's lonely. Or has low self-esteem and needs to push her attributes out for attention since her daddy didn't give her any. Attention, I mean."

Victoria snorted, and mid-drink narrowly missed choking on her tea. She twisted the empty straw wrapper between her fingers. Daddy issues? Maybe she had them too.

She glanced up at Barrett. Would she ever be able to put Connor's betrayal behind her? Barrett watched her with the wariness of a cornered animal. Maybe she was overreacting. She much preferred the man whose smile reached his eyes and drew her in.

"Here we go," the waitress warbled. Her free hand draped over Barrett's shoulder, she placed the plates on the table. "Pardon my reach," she whispered.

Victoria's stomach twisted, shutting off the hunger pangs with one turn. Grabbing her purse, she slid out of the booth. The server's eyes widened, and she snatched her hand back with the silent threat of broken fingers.

Victoria knew what the hussy feared. She had visions of doing it. She locked eyes with the woman. "Excuse me," she snarled. "I'm going to the ladies."

She spun on her heel and squeezed into the throng of women waiting in line.

"Hey, Doc Collins, how's Chief Graham doin'?"

Victoria rose on tiptoe to look over the sea of gray hair. An elderly gentleman, balding and leaning on a cane, caught Barrett's hand, pumping it with enthusiasm. The recipient of the priming handshake looked uncomfortable. And extremely guilty.

Doc? As in, the handyman is a doctor? That was a nickname he never told her about. She couldn't wait to get back to the table and press him for details.

Barrett sat back and made a steeple with his fingers, pressing the bridge of his nose. What the hell just happened? He tapped the fork's tines on the plate and waited for Victoria to return.

He glanced in the direction she had taken. Maybe she was in enough of her own personal snit that she didn't notice Mr. Schneider had come to their table. He could only hope.

He wasn't a criminal on the run. Or ashamed he had been a doctor in his previous life. He had built a life outside that world for the last couple of years. Five, to be exact. And then Mags had to tell Chief Graham. Basically, that meant telling the whole cove and all four surrounding counties. The old lawman should have kept his mouth shut.

Barrett stretched his legs out under the booth. The restaurant's customers were filtering out. Judging by the volume of excited mavens, the casino had been good to the bus passengers.

Victoria's cell phone went off, announcing another phone call. The ringtone had an annoying habit of asking, Where You At? The restaurant's clientele turned to glare in his direction. He shrugged helplessly and glanced at the phone number lighting up the screen. Connor.

Mercifully the phone calls stopped. With a quick glance over his shoulder, Barrett nudged the phone closer. The phone call count registered dozens of missed calls. He grunted, the low sound surprising him. For whatever reason she wasn't ready to share, she had made it clear that she did not want to talk to Connor.

The thing vibrated against the Formica table. It made a jack-legged dance, threatening to fall over the edge. He picked the cell phone up, cradling it in his hand, his fingers covering the offense against privacy and thumbed the screen to the text message app. The window popped open. A new message from Connor.

Barrett's appetite spun out as he read on, text after text, threat upon threat. His heart pumped adrenaline flowing to his brain. His muscles twitched. The scumbag was about to find out what it was like to come against someone who wasn't afraid of hurting his feelings. Just his bones.

"Barrett, what do you think you're doing?" Victoria snatched the phone out from his hand. "Or should I call you Dr. Collins?"

"Sit down." He scrubbed his palms over his jeans. He needed antibacterial soap to wash off the violence that leached out from the text messages. When she didn't budge, but looked like she was looking for the nearest exit, he added, "Please. Sit down."

Victoria gave a long-suffering sigh and scooted into the booth. "That wasn't right. You have no right to invade my privacy."

He held up his hand, seeking peace. "I know. Sorry. It just sort of happened."

Barrett cringed. Whatever the reason that last sentence caused her eyes to flare. Searching for a way to smooth things over, he shifted in his seat. "I'll tell you mine, if you'll tell me yours."

God, he felt like he had been called into the family room for sharing his sister's diaries with the peewee football team. That little stunt had caused him a serious butt kicking from his sister. He swore Tricia enjoyed the full power-ride over big brother. She had punished him for weeks. In the end, she eventually forgave him. Too bad she hadn't kicked her ex-husband's butt as hard as she had his. But by then, the jerk had worn her down.

Barrett looked down at the fork in his hands. The long stainless steel shaft bent out of shape. He tucked the utensil beside his plate and pushed his napkin beside it.

Victoria sat across from him. Her guarded brown eyes watched him. She reminded him of Tilly when he'd first found the dog hiding under the porch. Sweet, but unable to give up the trust that he wanted so badly. It had taken some time. Real trust builds in time.

He pointed toward the untouched food. "Better eat something."

Victoria moved in slow motion. She nodded and took a small bite of the sandwich to appease him.

Barrett swallowed and searched for a way to avoid the guilt that reared up with its dragon breath ready to burn through him. "Her name was Jessica. And I lost her."

CHAPTER 18

Victoria reached out, covering Barrett's hands. He didn't realize until she squeezed, that he had clenched his hands. He relaxed his fingers, stretching and flexing them. They were sturdy hands. Yet, they trembled like they were amped with five cups of espresso.

"You don't have to do this," Victoria said. The restaurant was still a buzz with clientele. "Not here."

Barrett stretched the tension from his neck. Reprieve. Or just more torture? All it did was prolonged the wait of seeing the pain register on her face, condemning him with her judgment. He really had lost his spine in Chicago.

Victoria spun the phone on the table. She held it up, showing him the screen. Connor's name reflected back. "This was my mistake. I thought I loved him."

A shuddering breath followed that announcement. Barrett didn't know if it came from her or his own lungs.

"And I thought he loved me." She looked up. Pain etched her face, her mouth, her eyes. "I was wrong about that, too." She thumbed the screen. "I stopped responding to his messages on the drive to Wisconsin. I figured he'd get my message we were done. I enjoyed having that bit of peace. No cell phone was inconvenient, but it brought some sense of rightness. Gave me a chance to heal." She froze as she read the last text messages. Her throat worked to get the words out. Her voice shook. "Looks like I was wrong again."

Barrett nudged his way onto Victoria's side of the booth. He wrapped his arm around her, offering himself as a shield. He put his hand over hers. Gripping the phone, she trembled under his palm. Gently, he pried her fingers away. The phone slid across the slick surface. It sat beside her glass of tea but could not wield any more pain until she was ready to face the demon on the other side. And if he had any say about it, Connor would never make good on his threats.

"Sweetheart, do you have a gun?"

Victoria reared back. Shock and the dawning reality of the danger bleached her face. She searched him, looking for a telltale sign of a pistol in his pocket. "No. I wouldn't know what to do with one anyway."

He held his hands up, proving he was defenseless against her argument. He'd seen enough patients in the ER with self-inflicted wounds. There were also times when a person needed to know how to protect themselves.

He might not persuade her to get a gun, but there had to be something he could do to offer protection. In the meantime, he sure wasn't leaving her side until they got this resolved.

———

Victoria gazed at the blurred images of small towns and villages as they zipped past. The bed would be there in a few hours. Thanks to Connor's messages, she doubted if she would find sleep for several more nights. His rage-filled words burned a hole in Victoria's memory. His threats replayed until she couldn't shut them off. She closed her eyes and listened to the hum of the tires on hot pavement.

The truck downshifted, the motion slowed to a halt.

Victoria scooted upright. "Where are we?"

"If you plan on refusing a gun, you at least need some way to contact the outside world." He pointed to the storefront. "This is it."

An hour later, Victoria was the proud owner of a satellite phone. Armed with the promise of never having a connection dropped and the privacy of a new phone number, she walked out of the store with a bounce in her step. The landline connecting her cottage to the outside world was on their schedule. Someday. The disappointing news that the internet connected to the cottage wasn't possible for the next couple of months, maybe years, did not bode well for a home office, but she would figure things out. She still had Mr. Tewilliger's offer to use their office if she needed a Wi-Fi connection.

Barrett slid into the pickup and Victoria leaned over. She grasped the back of his neck, pulling him close. She slipped her tongue along the crease, tasting, her mouth covering his. The center armrest stood between them, the only thing preventing her from climbing into his lap. He shifted, restless, trying to pry the console out of the way. His elbow connected with the horn, sending the neighboring dogs to barking. They jumped, breaking apart like a couple of teens deep in a make-out session.

Breathless, she sat back and looked straight ahead. Curious, the shop owner had stepped out onto the porch. He waved. Victoria waved back. She shared a glance with Barrett. His lips were bee stung. His impossibly long lashes shadowed his cheekbones. She touched a dark curl escaping from the bottom edge of his baseball hat. "Thank you."

Barrett caught her hand and kissed the inside of her wrist. The regrowth of afternoon whiskers scraped the delicate skin.

"Sweetheart, if this is how excited you get with a sat phone what are you gonna do when they deliver that mattress?"

She half-rose in the cab and stretched out to reach his ear. "Wouldn't you like to know?"

He chuckled and put the truck into gear.

Still in range of service, the phone rang in Victoria's purse. It was a different ring tone. One that announced the ominous moment coming in an afternoon soap opera. *Bwah-hah-hah.*

Victoria supposed it was the reruns of Dark Shadows that made her buy the tone for her dear old dad. It matched his dramatic, brief entrances and swift exits out of her life.

"Who's that?"

She scrunched her nose at Barrett. "No one special." She pointed ahead. "Eyes on the road."

Silence stretched out, separated by the occasional incessant ringing.

Barrett cleared his throat. "Avoidance isn't going to work on this one, is it?"

"Actually," she sniffed, "yes, it will." She folded her arms across her chest. "He can leave a message. I'll decide when and where I want to listen to it. Then I delete it, and he doesn't contact me for another year or so. I know he's still alive, and he thinks he's done the fatherly duty to check on his daughter." Her rant over, she caught her sour-faced reflection in the side mirror. "Cripes' sake. I'm horrible, aren't I?"

She locked on Barrett's face, wishing she could read his mind. He licked his lip, chewing on the lower edge. "Well, doctor? What's your verdict? Am I forever going to be a mess?"

"Nah." He swung the truck to the side of the road and braked. Reaching out, he unbuckled the seat belt and tugged her over. Once the center belt was in place, he set off down the road. "You're justifiably cranky and tired of the head games."

Her shoulder tucked near his rib cage, she braced her palm against his chest. His breaths came in slow and deep, reassuring her of his protection. The sleeve stretched over his bicep. "When are you going to tell me a bedtime story of how the handsome doctor turned away from medicine?"

"Soon." He bent, brushing a kiss, capturing her knuckles. "If you are a good girl and get some rest."

A few moments later, Victoria snuggled deeper into his side, with his chuckle vibrating under her ear. "Handsome, huh?"

She bit her tongue. A sassy comeback would just make the man realize how delicious he was.

———

Barrett shifted, allowing Victoria's head to rest on his shoulder. It felt good. Having her pressed next to him made him feel whole. He dipped his head, kissing the top of her head. The corner of her mouth lifted. A soft sigh ruffled the hair near his ear.

The miles stretched before them and gave him a little time to work through the best way to reason with Victoria when she woke up. Whether she liked it or not, they still had a lot of ground to cover to make sure that scumbag Connor didn't figure out where she lived.

He hated to think about the pain it would cause Victoria, but they needed to listen to the voice mails and read the messages together. She might not like the idea, but she needed to lodge a complaint and have everything documented. The legal threat might not work to keep the creep away, but then again Connor was a lawyer. Maybe the threat of exposure to his law firm would.

Protecting secrets was something Barrett had perfected. Exposing them was a whole new game.

———

Victoria awoke when Barrett pulled into the driveway. Gravel popped under the turning tires. A flock of bobwhites scattered to the row of shrubs by the shade trees.

She scanned the rock garden. Everything looked like she'd left it. All the tasks were waiting for her to finish. The piles of rocks loomed in front of her. The wheelbarrow stood next to the rocks and half-dug holes.

Squinting up at the sky, she figured there were several hours left of daylight. Maybe she could get the roses planted before the roots dried and the loose dirt baked into a brick. She shifted in the cab. Somewhere along the road to Honeybrooke Cove, the growing camaraderie between her and Barrett had faded. An edge about him set his jaw tight. Definitely stubborn.

Victoria slid out of the cab. Barrett was around the pickup before she could reach in and get her things. He grabbed her arm.

"Wait," he said.

"What the…" She jerked out of his hand.

"Let me check it out. Okay?"

She squinted at the door. Did it look different from when they left in a hurry? Actually, Barrett had been all fired up to get her to a mattress store. Did she remember to lock the door?

A chill ran up her arms. Instead of scaring her, it made her furious and ready to fight back. Temporary or not, this was her house and she would not be run off because she was too scared to live alone. She wasn't stupid though. "Go on." She nodded, waving the new sat phone. "I've got your back."

Barrett grinned. "That's my girl."

He trotted to the front porch and tried the door. Victoria's stomach pitched and rolled when he walked in without a key. She dialed in the emergency number, her finger ready to jab it at the first sign of big trouble. Breathing became harder, pulling one breath in, remembering to release it.

A clatter, followed by a string of curses, drew Victoria from her hiding place. Her plan to stay put forgotten, she careened toward the back door. "Barrett?" she hissed. Skidding to a halt, she narrowly missed tromping on his chest.

He lay on the ground, staring up at the hazy summer sky. Rolling his head, he worked to focus on her face. His lashes fluttered.

"Oh, my god." She knelt down beside him. Gathering him close, she shielded him with her body. "Are you hurt? What happened? Where are they?" Her hands shaking, she attempted to hit send. "No. No," she muttered.

He wrapped his fingers around her hand. "Shh. I'm fine." He gave her a gentle squeeze. "Stand down. No need to call for reinforcements. We're fine."

Victoria blinked like a barn owl. "But you're hurt."

He struggled to rise, stopping when his nose buried deep into her cleavage. A steamy breath tickled her breasts. Victoria jerked back. Groaning, Barrett caught himself before he hit the ground again. He propped up on one elbow and glowered at the small wildlife traps scattered over the porch steps.

"Some careless idiot put them just out of sight. I caught my foot on one and it started a chain reaction." He rubbed the back of his head. "Just about jumped out of my skin when I thought a critter had already been trapped."

Her eyes wide, Victoria bit her lip to keep from laughing. The sparkling stainless boxes still had their tags and wrapped in the instructions for the wild creature's demise. "What made you think that?"

"I swore I heard something hiss when I stepped down." He pushed up to kneel on the ground and muffled a groan.

"Poor baby," she said. Smoothing his shoulder, she dusted the dirt from his back. "If anything was there, I bet it's long gone now."

"I bet," he muttered.

Victoria jumped up, holding out her hand. "Come on. The

coast is clear, and the delivery truck is bound to be here soon. If you can manage it, I need help moving some things to make room for that bed."

Barrett scrunched his face. "When did you order those traps?"

Victoria eyed the metal contraptions. They looked like medieval weapons meant to torture poor innocent souls. "I didn't. I thought Mr. T intended to wait until he talked it over with you."

He nudged a larger steel apparatus. It didn't have a warning label. The razor-sharp teeth were warning enough to stay away.

"I sure as heck didn't order a bear trap."

"Bear?" she squeaked.

CHAPTER 19

Doing her best to banish the traps from her thoughts, Victoria squinted, trying to visualize how her bedroom would look once it had furniture in it. What it needed? Enlarging.

Barrett stood at the window, staring out at the lake. He had that little-boy-lost look to him. She gave his shoulder a vigorous rub. Maybe, if she rubbed long enough, she would erase the wild animal traps from their minds. "Hey, how hard would it be to knock out the wall between the two bedrooms?"

Ignoring her question, he wrapped his arms around her waist. Encased in his protective cocoon, she would have been happy to stay there. But those darn traps. The what-if scenarios buzzed in her head. What if she had stepped into the big-ugly one? What if she had been alone? What if Barrett hadn't insisted on her getting a sat phone? One big nasty trap, crushed leg, alone, and without help. If not for Barrett, she would be heading for that long nap in the sky.

She rested her forehead on his solid chest, grateful he was there to lean on.

He took a deep breath. "You're okay." His voice rumbled near her ear. Tilting her chin, he lifted her hair from her face. "We're okay."

Veronica didn't know if he was reassuring her or himself. Maybe both. That was fine by her.

She nodded and offered a smile that would have made her dad proud. "I know." Prodding him in the ribs, she pressed her earlier question. "So, what do you think? Can we blow it out?"

"You're going to keep pestering me about a little demolition, aren't you?" He held up a hand. "Don't need to answer. I already know."

"Good. Saves me time that way." She nudged him toward the wall. "See, we get rid of this and stretch the floor plan into the other room. Create a master bedroom *en suite*. Add a walk-in closet. We can fix this place up. Make it a solid investment."

"Hold on. Before you start any demo jobs, let me take a look in the other room. See if it's a load-bearing wall." He shook his head and muttered. "Just like your aunt. Bouncing from one idea to the next. Makes me dizzy."

Victoria rocked on the balls of her feet. The possibilities made her toes tingle. She glanced out the window, envisioning an addition. She would eventually need office space. Of course, that was if she extended her stay. She really couldn't, could she? At least until they sold the place.

Sunlight bounced off the lake behind the cottage and caught her attention. Pinks and reds, azure and hits of gold, all swirled over the water.

A fishing boat bobbed near the dock. Its poles were up. She was certain it was her imagination playing tricks, but it sure looked like the angler was watching the house. Sunlight reflected back in her eyes. She blinked. Were those binoculars?

"What the heck?" Barrett's voice roared from the other room.

Victoria spun away from the window, plastering her back against the wall. Wild panic made her dig in her back pocket for her phone. It was empty. She inched slowly along the wall. Tears burned her lids as she drew in a slow, calming breath. Letting it out, she scrambled out the door and ran down the hallway.

She collided against a jeans and t-shirt barrier made of bone and muscle. "What?" she cried. "What is it?"

Horrified, Barrett stood ramrod straight. The beam of his flashlight cut past the clothes he had shoved over in the closet. The light danced over Mags's notes posted to the wall.

"You knew about this? No. Of course you did. You would have seen it when you hung up your clothes."

"Sure. I saw them. But I didn't have time to remove all of them."

Victoria didn't know why, but she felt she had to defend Mags. Thankful she had removed most of the notes and tucked them out of sight, she slipped over to shut the closet door. The notes regarding Barrett were tucked securely in her suitcase. "I'm sure they're probably nothing."

He opened the door again, walked deeper into the closet, and whistled. "What were you up to, Mags?"

"Maybe she was playing out a fantasy," Victoria said. She traced one of the poems that caught his attention. "Just innocent fun for an old lady."

"Or maybe she was sicker than she let on." He clicked off his flashlight. "I should have paid better attention."

Victoria tugged on his hand. "What were you doing in there?"

"Hmm?" He shook his head, clearing the new information about his close friend. "I needed to see how deep the space is between the walls. The owner of the cottage before Mags was quirky." He caught her eye. "Quirkier than Mags."

"That's saying a lot." Judging by Mags's endless notes stuck to walls, inside cookbooks, and memory stones, Victoria admitted, that her great aunt's behavior went beyond quirky. She shoved her hands deep into her back pockets before she gave into the temptation of gnawing on her nails. "Add the noises during the night and I might reconsider putting the house up for sale."

Barrett grunted beside her and folded his arms over his chest.

"I said might. Not for sure." She craned her neck to peek out the window and avoid his stare. "And then there's the man in the boat that might convince me to move."

"What man?" Barrett joined her side.

"Looks like he's gone." She rubbed her temples. Maybe her imagination was making her see things. "I hear there's a corner on Wilshire Boulevard that's available."

His long arm draped over her shoulder, turning her gently away from the window. "Nope, I won't let you give up that easy."

"Really? What makes you think that? I ran away from Connor and L.A., remember?" She took a shuddering breath.

"That ex of yours doesn't know anything. Maybe you weren't running away. Maybe you were running to someone." He kissed the top of her head. "You just didn't know it."

A horn tooted at the front of the house. A large delivery truck pulled in. Its air brakes let off a loud hiss.

He gave her a quick hug, anticipation brightening his eyes. "Besides, you're not a quitter. Nor am I. We're fixing this place up. Remember?"

Victoria nodded, her gaze soaking in the view of his sexy backside. "And then what?" she whispered under her breath.

The crawling feeling of being watched made her turn toward the lake. The water was like glass. Not even a ripple to signal the trail of movement. Shivering, she squashed the urge to search for the man in the boat and headed out to give direction to the men.

———

Victoria stood in the bedroom doorway, her hand covering her quivering lips. Once the snort released, the giggles began. It was as if someone had turned on a faucet. Before she knew it, the giggles turned into some type of weird cackle and up until that moment she was unaware she could produce that sound.

The price on the king-size bed had stretched her bank account and now it stretched the house. They had squeezed the monster through the door, determined to make it work. It was the veritable ugly stepsister, doing her best to make the glass slipper fit. On the upside, they'd obliterated the fear of falling out of bed and hitting the floor. And created a new one. A few inches rolled too far, and she'd be caught between the mattress and the wall.

She snorted again. Good thing she had a phone that worked. *Help! I've fallen and I can't get up!* She could see the headlines. Woman Eaten by Her Bed. News at eleven.

She looked over her shoulder. Barrett kept his distance. He had already apologized for convincing her to go against her better judgment and get the bigger bed. She crooked her finger at him.

"I promise to blow out that wall for you," he said, moving cautiously toward her. "Soon."

"Well, you are my resident handyman."

"It'll be great." He grimaced. "If you want, I'll start on it tomorrow."

"Um, hmm." When he was close enough to grab, she hooked his t-shirt. "Waiting until tomorrow is highly overrated."

"Yeah?" He arched his brow, his questioning gaze never leaving her face. She pressed her head into his hands as he tunneled them into her hair.

"Oh, yeah." She could not let this opportunity pass her by. Not this time. Biting back a purr of pleasure building at the back of her throat, she tucked her foot behind his ankle and flipped him down. They didn't have far to fall. The king-sized bed stopped just short of the door.

Their legs entangled, they toppled over together. The pillow-top caught them as the space between them narrowed. Their lips brushed, tenderly testing.

Barrett gazed down at her. The blue of his irises had shifted to a dark azure. "Victoria."

The way he said her name, gruff with barely contained emotion, was her undoing. She caught her lip with her teeth.

Barrett's sat phone vibrated on the side table in the living room.

Victoria clutched the back of his head, her fingers forking through the curls. Her lips moved against his. "Ignore it."

The phone rang again. Then stopped.

She drew circles over his shoulder blades.

The phone began again.

Her hand stilled. "Go, check that thing." She grabbed his fore-arm, stalling his departure. "Then hurry back to me."

Barrett pressed his forehead to hers. "Thanks." Kneeling, he caged her with arms and legs. "Wait for me." Capturing her mouth, he made her toes curl before dashing off to the living room.

Victoria blew out a breath, whistling as the sight of his strong, broad, shoulders sliding out of view. She listened to the sound of his feet padding down the hall while she touched her lips. The kiss-swollen flesh, still sensitive where his late afternoon whiskers brushed her skin was a fresh reminder of their shared passion. She glanced out the window. The sky showed signs of the day ending. How had she allowed the day to get past her? Time with her handyman never seemed to hold the same sixty minutes in an hour.

The deep timber of his voice carried from the other room. Evidently, the plan to return to her had shifted. Frowning, she flipped her legs over the foot of the bed. Eavesdropping on one-sided conversations never served anyone any good. Was that one of Mags's quote that she recently read? She tiptoed to the bathroom.

Her reflection in the mirror questioned where she just about took this new...what was it? Friendship? Whatever it was, she didn't know where it was going. That didn't settle well with her. She liked things listed in columns. Orderly. That's what makes sense to her. Friends with benefits didn't.

She smoothed the tangles from her hair. Dark eyes, wide and glistening, stared back at her. "Victoria, sweetheart," Barrett called through the door. "I have to go."

Victoria gripped the sink and leaned in to its ceramic edge. "Saved by the bell?" she whispered to her image. If that was fate's way of saving her, why did she feel so empty? Clearing her throat, she tossed her hair over her shoulder and opened the door.

Barrett met her in the hallway. "I'm sorry." His large hands wrapped around her waist. "It's an emergency. Otherwise, nothing could drag me away."

She hooked her thumbs through his belt loops. "That bad?"

He kissed her forehead, leaving her wanting so much more. What happened to the fiery kisses that melted her down to liquid?

He turned to rescue his boots from the floor. He was already pulling away, his mind as busy as his hands. She bit her lip. The questions swirled in her head.

"I shouldn't be gone that long." He grimaced. "I hope. Look, I'll need to swing by and check on Tilly while I'm out...working."

Victoria's heart squeezed with a pinch of jealousy. No way was she going to let him see she cared. "Do what you have to do, Barrett."

He stopped lacing up his boots and looked up, searching her face. "We never listened to the messages on your cell."

"No biggie." Her hands retraced where the bruises on her arms had been. "I'm sure they are nothing. Just Connor letting off...steam."

His foot dropped to the floor. He snatched the other boot and shoved it on. The nylon strings flipped and snapped as he laced it up. "The jerk left over fifty messages and hasn't stopped." Barrett rose and cupped Victoria's cheek. "We have to deal with him, or he'll keep harassing you."

We? "I'll handle it." She stroked the back of his hands. "I promise."

Worry continued to darken his gaze. "I wanted to be here with you when you do." He tunneled his fingers through her hair, drawing a shiver from the top of her head to the tips of her toes. "You shouldn't have to do this alone."

She blinked back the offending tear and forced the smile she really didn't feel. "If the messages get to be too much, I'll call you."

"I can come back after I defuse the emergency."

"No. You need to go home afterward." She swallowed the lump that had formed in her throat. "Take care of the emergency. Besides, Tilly will be waiting up for you. Right?"

"You could come with me," he said.

She sucked in a deep breath, fortifying her confidence, and shook her head. "I have too much to do around here. I want to feel like I've moved in. Make this place mine while I'm here."

"But—" His phone vibrated against her hip.

"I'm a big girl and can tell the jerk to get lost all by myself. I've done it before, remember?" Victoria stood on tiptoe and silenced his suggestions by covering his mouth with her lips. She lingered, taking great satisfaction in knowing that the heart beating under her palm had increased its tempo. Dreading his departure, she drew away first. "Go."

"I'll call you later. Okay?" He paused at the door. "Victoria, for the record, Tilly's my dog."

A smile tugged at her heart as she watched the taillights trail off down the road. Beaten out for a guy's attention by a dog. She shrugged as she locked the door. Not the first time.

Taking a deep breath, she steeled her back and stared at the dreaded task that waited for her. *Connor.*

———

Victoria glanced up at the clock on the wall. She had given her ex-boyfriend nearly an hour of her life. Resolved to never do that again, she opened her hand and let the cell phone drop onto the kitchen table. There were so many nasty things left on her voicemail. She should be wearing a hazmat suit. Rising on shaky legs, she began checking all the locks.

Connor was beyond furious and she couldn't figure out why. He was the lying, cheating jerk. Not her.

She stared out the kitchen window. Connor's threats echoed in her thoughts. How did she make the mistake of thinking that man once loved her? Tears slid down her cheeks.

Shimmering, the lake moved under the setting sun, the colors shifting like a mood ring. The towers of stone in the barren rock garden called to her. The wheelbarrow and shovel lay where she'd left them earlier in the day.

Fingers trembling, she filled up a drinking glass with water and drained it gunslinger-style. The empty glass clattered against the counter. This was her home. Maybe even her new life. She wasn't about to be bullied by that jerk or anyone else.

Watchful of more traps set by someone who wanted her to give up and leave, she headed for the garden. An hour later, sweating, caked in mud and exhausted from muscling wheelbarrow after wheelbarrow of rocks, Victoria stepped back to admire her accomplishment. Her heart swelled with pride.

Two new magnolia trees now stood at the entrance of the garden gate. Come the following spring, they would be in full bloom. Their cupped flowers, pale lavender petals and yellow stamens, would fill the air with perfume. She took a deep breath, envisioning the scent.

The five David Austin rosebushes were exactly where they needed to be. Their shiny leather leaves glistened in the sun. The rocks she'd moved to give the roses the perfect amount of sun was dumped to the side. Maybe she'd repurpose them and build a wall or hardscape with them.

She scrunched her nose. Whether it was out of respect or not, she had kept each spire separate when she dumped the rocks in the back corner. Moving them again would wait for another day.

Her muscles sore and well-used, she trudged up the steps. Surely now that she'd abused her body with manual labor, she would find sleep and not hear Connor's venom repeating in her head. She should have asked Barrett to come back over. He would know how to take her mind off her troubles.

After rechecking the locks, she toed off her boots and headed down the hall. There was a bath with her name on it.

———

Victoria awoke with a start. The cookbook she'd been reading had slid off her chest and landed on the floor. She bent to pick it up and looked at the living room clock. It was after midnight. She checked her phone. Barrett hadn't tried to call or leave a message.

Scrunching her hair out of the way, she tilted her head against the high-backed chair. "What is it with men?" she asked the ceiling.

Eyes closed, she listened to the rhythmic ticking of the clock and willed her aching muscles to relax. Tick, tick. Drag. Drag.

Something was outside her door. Again.

CHAPTER 20

By morning, Victoria's knuckles ached from gripping the phone in one hand and the fire poker in the other. She could have called Barrett, but there was that small matter of pride. The man said he'd call and check on her and he didn't. Instead, she'd spent the rest of the night huddled in the chair. Alone.

Her back stiff from gardening, she stumbled to the kitchen. Staring out the window while she filled up the glass carafe for life saving coffee, her eyes watered from the sunlight shooting through the window.

Stretching out the kinks, she reached for the ceiling, then doubled over to touch her toes and rose to offer a sun salutation. She grinned. Daylight brought everything into focus. Nothing broke through the door. She had survived the night.

Probably as they thought, some kind of animal had made a nest under the porch. The carafe filled, she pushed the power button and watched the LED light glow. Sunlight reflected on the stainless strips on the machine. When the water hit the ground coffee, the rich aroma filled the air.

Snagging a mug from the cupboard, she waited for the coffee to finish brewing. Heat radiated through the ceramic and warmed her fingers. She leaned over the steam and worshiped the life-giving caffeine that would soon rush through her veins and inhaled. The first sip brought a rush of energy to her brain, melting away the fog. A new day. A new dawn. *Bring it on.*

Her attention returned to the view outside her window. Something was different.

"What the—" The coffee cup clattered against the granite. Victoria gripped the countertop. It could not be happening. The stones she'd moved yesterday were back. They stood in almost the same spot.

Muttering under her breath, she yanked on her work boots. Still in her Hello Kitty pajama set, she marched out to the garden. Who was she kidding? She might as well admit defeat and call it a memorial rock garden. It appeared she had no say in the matter.

She kicked at the spire of rocks. Satisfaction swept through her when the first one toppled over. Spinning on her heel, she found her next target.

"Hey there," Mrs. T called. She waved from her back patio. "Watcha doing there? You need a hand?"

Victoria caught her breath. Her lungs burned. So did her big toe from that last kick. She hopped on one foot and plastered a smile on her face. The laugh bubbled up. "Don't you worry, Mrs. T. I'm just doing a little gardening."

Judging by Mrs. T's immediate departure into the house, Victoria wondered if it resembled The Joker's cackle.

———

Victoria sped down the country road in her red BMW. The top down, wind whipped her hair and cut through her scrambled thoughts. By the time she reached the market, she didn't have to check the rearview mirror to know her hair looked like she had combed it with a wire whisk.

The tires squealed to a stop. Her hands still shaking, she

climbed out of the convertible. Despite the early hour of the day, the two elderly men were already sitting at the checkers table.

"Hey there, Miss Victoria. Aren't you a sight for old eyes?"

George wore another golf shirt. This time it was bright orange. He tugged at the waist of his plaid pleated pants. It rose above his navel, narrowly missing his chest.

His checkers partner, Fred, ducked his head and focused on the board game.

"Hi, guys. You're up early." Victoria couldn't help herself. She had to try. "How are you, Fred?"

His blue-veined hand paused, the checker piece wavering over the red square. He tugged his golf cap down farther on his balding head and made his move. "Fine."

George hopped two spaces and took Fred's piece.

"Awful hard to concentrate with your yammering." Fred glared, the bloodshot whites surrounding his pale gray eyes glistened with the signs of age. "Don't you have somewhere to go?"

"Don't you hurry off, Miss Victoria. He's already mad cause I kicked his a..., uh, beat him at golf this morning." George hooked a chair leg and nudged it toward her. "Grab a seat."

Fred reared back, folding his tanned arms across his chest. "Bet she has more important things to do besides sitting here with a couple of old farts like us." He snorted. "I sure would."

"Yeah?" George thumbed toward the parking lot. "Don't see a car with your name on it. Do you?" He made a show of searching. "Nope. Just mine. You're stuck." He turned to Victoria, an eyebrow rose over a mischievous twinkle. "He lost his license 'cause he's too old to drive. Got a citation for driving his John Deere lawnmower while under the influence."

"And I'm telling you I was on the sidewalk and I had taken me a dose of cough medicine. Chief Graham is just peeved because I quit dating his momma."

George rolled his eyes. "So you say." He motioned to the

empty seat. "Sit down pretty lady. I thought young people liked to sleep late. Tell us why you're up and about so early."

Swallowing the sigh, Victoria joined the men. What could it hurt? She could use some friendly chatter. Maybe it would help her make sense of her new home. Might as well jump in with both feet. They probably already thought she was a nut since she came from California. "George. What do you know about ghosts?"

"Shoot." A smile almost broke through Fred's stony visage. "Girl. He don't know nothing." He took a sip of coffee from a Styrofoam to-go-cup. "But me, I'm the one you want to talk to. I've seen 'em all around the cove."

George leaned forward. A serious frown pursed his mouth. "Ignore the old fool. Why are you asking such a thing?"

Victoria stared down at the hands clutching the purse straps. She let out a deep breath. "There're these sounds. At night."

"Rodents," George said. "Maybe raccoons."

"That's what Barrett thought."

"There you go. Get some traps. Catch 'em. All done," George confirmed.

"Wrong," Fred said. "It's ghosts. For sure."

"Now, Fred," George began. "You know there is no such thing as ghosts."

"Do not. You best start rethinking life on the other side. You don't have that much time left."

"Aw, now, that is a downright mean thing to say," George sputtered.

Fred harrumphed. "Not mean. Truthful. Me, I got it locked down. Been donating money to the church for the last couple of years."

The men showed all signs of taking off on a tangent, driving a John Deere lawnmower down the road, and leaving her behind. And she had thought it was a brilliant idea to ask them for advice.

"Bought the traps, even one big enough to scare off a bear," she said, shuddering at the thought. "Barrett already checked it out. It's not rodents. Not unless they've grown opposable thumbs."

"Raccoons," the knowledgeable George offered. "They like the lake. Got one nearby, don't ya? Need to watch 'em. They'll tear down stuff and make a mess."

Victoria shook her head. "These stack things. In the night." Now she had their full attention. "Rocks."

"You mean Mags's rocks? You moved them?" George leaned forward, his peppered brows forming a V. "She put a lot of store in them. Said memories were built into each tower. Made one for me when my wife passed. She was the best woman I ever met in my life."

"Your wife?" Victoria whispered, her heart melting for the love carried through centuries.

"No." He swatted at the air. "My wife was mean as a badger. Mags built the tower to remind me that life was short, and I had better not stay with a mean ol' battle-ax just because I was holding onto legal vows. We built it in celebration of my divorce."

"Poltergeists or ghosts," Fred leaned back in satisfaction. He shoved his hat back on his head and scratched his thinning hair. "Told you so."

"Mags was a good-hearted woman. She wouldn't be malicious against the new owner of her cottage. Especially since she's a relative," George argued.

"Your wife would."

Victoria could not believe their nonsense. "Look, there is more to it than raccoons, rodents or your garden variety ghost. They wouldn't lay out traps to scare me away."

"Barrett—"

"—is too busy to call." Victoria snapped. "These vandals have taken enough of my time and sleep." She rose, resolute in her decision. "You're right, George, my aunt Mags wouldn't resent me. You get the word out. I've decided to stay and I'm not going anywhere until I'm good and ready."

———

G rinning, Victoria wove her way to the market's back office. "Step Three: Stand your ground," she whispered under her breath.

She didn't know where her sudden decision came from, but she was now more determined than ever to stake her claim in Honeybrooke Cove. First chance she got, she intended to speak with Barrett and buy out his portion of the cottage.

Harold stood behind the counter. His ruddy face was a study of concentration. She cleared her throat before he raised his head.

"Hello, neighbor," he said. "What can I do for you?"

"Hi. I need to ask a favor."

He paused in what he was doing and pushed the reading glasses on top of his head. "Sure."

"Can I use your internet? I need to check some emails. I have my laptop with me." She started to dig in her bag to show him. "They're important. I know it's an imposition and I—"

"Stop. Of course, you can." He motioned her around the counter. "Desk is back here. Don't mind the paperwork. If it's in your way, just move it to the side or on the floor."

Victoria's heart clutched. Her unsettled world tilted off its axis. To say the back office was a mess was like saying the atomic bomb made a little noise. Sweat beaded over her lip. Her palms itched to sort through the stacks of papers. "Has your accountant been on vacation long?"

"Sorry, Victoria, I haven't had a bookkeeper or a vacation in years. Been so long, I quit counting. Mrs. T, she does her best, but I know her heart isn't into it. Truth be told, she hasn't really been into anything since our Tommy left us." He shuffled his large feet. "Listen. It's not fit to work in, give me a few minutes and I'll clear it for you."

Victoria placed her hand on his forearm. "It's fine." She forced the smile she didn't feel at all. "All I need is a place to sit down and connect to the internet."

Harold motioned to the desk chair. "Have at it."

The connection hit quickly. That was a blessing. Who knew you could get a strong connection in the cove? Victoria watched the emails drop into her mailbox. A few responses to her job search. A string of unpaid bills she never knew existed. She flinched when Connor's emails streamed in. Then systematically put them in a special folder that she would send to the cloud for added security.

Victoria closed the laptop and imagined a safe place where she no longer felt threatened. Smoothing her jean shorts, she rose from the surrounding chaos. This was something she knew how to deal with.

"Harold," she called out.

He popped his head around the corner. "Victoria."

"I think you need my help." She pointed to the desk. It looked like it had a mountain on it and was about to erupt.

"Oh, now, I know it looks bad. But I'll get to it."

"Harold, I'm really good at this." She read the questions on his face. "Really, really good at this." Seeing his hesitation, she added, "Tell you what. Think of it as payment for the use of your internet."

Relief warred with nervousness. "Helen doesn't need to know. Right? It might hurt her feelings."

Victoria bet that Mrs. T would be relieved to have it taken out of her hands and off her shoulders. She grinned and held out her hand. In one tentative handshake, a new partnership was formed.

It was a win-win situation. By making her presence known, whoever was trying to scare her would get the message she was here to stay.

She looked down at the first stack. The top invoice addressed to the Cove Market was for a set of bear traps. No name. Just an order that someone picked up.

The invoice crushed in her hand, Victoria walked out to the counter. "Harold, who ordered this?"

He spread the paper out and frowned as he searched his memory. "Don't know. A stranger traveling through. Called it in, prepaid, and had it on hold for pickup here. Happens a lot. Hunters come up north for a weekend. Buy something last minute. Have it waiting for them here. Why?"

Victoria twisted the hem of her shirt. "I had a bear trap delivered to Aunt Mags's place. Wondered if it was left there by mistake."

"Not by us, that's for sure." Harold straightened his spine, his cheeks pinked. "Your aunt never ordered a trap like that in all the time I've known her."

"I thought it kind of odd." She searched his kind face. "I doubt it will happen again. Don't you?"

CHAPTER 21

Victoria pulled her BMW into her driveway. The last four days had been heavenly. Putting the Cove Market's office and books in order gave satisfaction. It brought a sense of balance into her world. She was giddy with joy. She knew she'd sleep well tonight. Finally.

The whippoorwills scooted out of the way, lecturing her all the way as they ran for safety under the shrubs. She sat in the car and let the sun beat down on her head, warming her bones.

The last couple of nights she hadn't slept, but she'd finally wised up. Yesterday, she didn't knock down the stone spires. She let them stand. Once she quit trying to move the rocks, the dragging sounds in the night stopped.

Whatever or whoever wanted those stones to remain was appeased.

She stepped out of the car and went to the front yard to check the mail. Her steps paused. The yard was unusually quiet. Her gut twisted, winding like the deadly curves on Mulholland Drive.

Boxes were stacked on the front porch from floor to ceiling. She crept closer and snagged the envelope taped to a box.

She read the scrawled note. The Meat Master Moving

Company had delivered her few meager belongings. Too bad she wasn't there, but since she never responded to their attempted contact, they felt the need to drop the load and move on. That's what she gets for hiring a couple of hungry looking college kids.

Victoria crumpled the note and closed her eyes. She'd forgotten to listen to all the messages. Actually, she was a coward. It was purposeful procrastination. Good thing she had paid them in full. She might have never seen her piddling amount of possessions.

Resolved to finish by nightfall, she began unpacking. Each opened box revealed a portion of the life she had left behind. Her treasured accounting books were stacked neatly in the room that would someday become her office.

Pictures of her and her mother, together, BC-before cancer, covered the side tables next to the couch. They stood arm-and-arm, laughing at something ridiculous. The sun glistened off their hair. It was at an adventure park. Victoria stroked the glass protecting her mother's face. It was her 8th grade graduation. Two years later, Mom was gone. They'd all forgotten to laugh by that time. Their little family of three had fractured.

Victoria found a frame for the photo of her mom and Aunt Mags. Somehow, it felt like life had created a complete circle.

Smiling and humming a tune from her childhood, she carried the box of winter clothing into the spare bedroom. Fall was nearing. Plenty of time to pull them out later. They probably wouldn't get cold weather for a few more months. Maybe by Christmas there'd be snow.

Relieved to finish unloading the last box, she tossed the flattened empty boxes out the back door. Sitting down at the kitchen table, her elbows resting on the edge, she tipped the tall glass of iced tea and drank it in one long swallow.

She glanced at the satellite phone. Barrett still hadn't called and no one at the market seemed to know where he was. Countless numbers of his clients were a little perturbed that he'd taken off without notice.

She would have liked to know what was going on with him too. He still hadn't started blowing out the bedroom wall. She could call him, ask what his plans were. To, um, start work on the house.

The phone stared back at her, urging her to pick it up. "I don't think so." She sat on her hands to keep them from disobeying her command.

A truck door slammed outside her window. She looked up. A long shadow danced across the yard. She'd recognize that walk anywhere. His name released in a whispered breath. "Barrett."

Victoria slowly set the glass down. She didn't want anything in her hand when she saw him. No flying missiles at his head. She'd be polite. Ask about his day. Then show him the door and let-it-hit-him-where-the-good-Lord-split-him.

Even though she knew he was on the way, she still jumped when he knocked. She drew her hands into her lap, squeezing the trembling appendages into fists. Darned if she was going to greet him with open arms. He'd have to come to her this time. She was sitting right where she was. "Come on in."

Her dad's command reverberated in her head. *'Smile!'* "I already am," she muttered.

Only this time it was true. She couldn't help it. Her heart leaped in anticipation, galloping with each step he took toward her.

"Hey there, sweetheart." Barrett opened the door and swept off his baseball cap. Victoria tried to play it cool but she couldn't help noticing he didn't wear his usual attire. A royal blue polo replaced the t-shirt. His biceps still stretched the cuff. Although his jeans hugged his thighs and hips, he'd exchanged work boots for flip-flops. His feet were big. How'd she miss that little bit of knowledge? The high school rule comparing shoe size to penis ran though her head. *Really big.* No wonder he kept them protected with his work boots. That was a lot of flesh to step on. His toes curled under her scrutiny.

"Hi," she squeaked out. Suddenly conscious of her trashed makeup, long rubbed off from sweating while moving boxes around, she ducked her head.

His large flip-flops padded close. Tiny black hair sprinkled the tops of his toes. "Hey." He squatted in front of her chair and lifted her chin to meet his gaze. "There was an emergency thing and then I just...I didn't know where we stood. I was afraid I'd make it too easy on you if I called."

"Too easy?" Victoria's blood started to heat.

"You'd tell me to get lost and I wouldn't be able to get you to listen. Or give me another chance to do this." He leaned in, cupping her head in his hands, and met her lips with his.

Victoria slid her hands up his forearms, elbows, biceps, and shoulders. God, he felt good under her hands.

He broke away from her mouth to kiss her forehead, each eyelid and the tip of her nose. She opened her eyes to stare into his. They were the color of the Caribbean Sea; deep blue, sparkling, full of excitement. "I'd ask you to wait here, but I don't think you'd believe me when I say I'll be right back."

The mischievous boy had returned. What did he bring this time? A bag of worms? A frog? Maybe a puppy? Who was she kidding? The warmth washing into her stomach proved she was weak and would accept anything this man had to offer. But she wasn't the old man's daughter for nothing. He'd taught her to play hardball and not give in so easily.

"You've got that right, mister." She grabbed the points of Barrett's collar. "I haven't decided if I forgive you."

He turned his jaw, brushing her knuckles with his lips. "Guess I'll have to keep trying."

Rising, he lifted her hands and led her outside. He spun her around, leading her backward by the shoulders. "Lean into me. I won't lead you astray."

"You want me to trust you?" Victoria shook her head. "I don't think so, Mr. Handyman. Not yet."

His deep groan vibrated through her shirt and into her chest. "Come on now. Maybe this will tip the scale." He danced her around and pointed to the truck. A shiny stainless grill stood in the bed.

She blinked. Men were so confusing to her. Why would she forgive him if he brought her a grill?

"Before you start talking, you need to stop and think what I can do with Man's Best Friend."

"I thought dogs are man's best friend."

"Hush. Am I going to have to silence you again?"

"Promises. Promises," she muttered, biting back a smile.

"Challenge accepted."

He twirled her like they were doing the Texas Two Step. Wrapped in his arms, he planted a deep, probing kiss. He nipped hungrily at her neck. His tongue followed, licking where his teeth had skimmed over her skin.

Victoria grabbed his hips, certain if she didn't, she'd be in a puddle at his feet. God, his feet. She squeezed her eyes closed.

Barrett whispered. "Steaks. Grilled to perfection." His breath tickled the hair by her ear. "Ribs. Dry rubbed or barbequed." He tongued the outer shell, making her shiver. "Roasted chicken. Racks of lamb." Lifting her hair off her neck, he burrowed his fingers into her nape. "And that's just a taste of the heaven I can provide you." He paused, a hint of worry deepened the crease above his nose. "If you let me stay."

Victoria leaned her cheek against his chest. She wasn't about to let him run off again. At least not yet. "You had me at steaks."

———

Barrett sang a lonesome song about being left behind in Atlanta while he set up the grill. He liked Alison Krauss. Her voice cut through the crap in his head. He had liked to listen to bluegrass when he was in the operating theater and had avoided it the last several years. It brought back too many memories. It was funny how the recent trip to Chicago brought them back so fast. Some songs stick with you no matter how hard you try to push them out of your head.

Victoria had pleaded to needing a shower. He would have welcomed an invitation to help scrub her back, or front. Hell, just about anywhere she asked. With a little more encouragement, he might have earned a little playtime. But he didn't dare push his luck.

Weary smudges darkened the delicate area under her eyes. If he guessed right, she hadn't been getting much sleep. Probably hadn't been eating properly either.

Judging by the stack of flattened boxes, she'd been working all day. He'd heard about her new position at the market via the cove's personalized telephone system. Tell-a-George-Tell-a-Fred-Tell-a-Friend. Harold must have been desperate. The man took a huge chance taking Victoria on. There'd be a price to pay when Mrs. T found out. Given the size of this small and very tight community, she'd find out real fast. It amazed him that the secret had lasted the four days he was away.

He looked up. Victoria strolled toward him, wearing jean shorts and a tank top. It didn't cover a lot of skin and that was fine by him. She glistened. Like there was a light shining around her. His breath locked in his lungs. All the blood left his brain and headed for points south. He shook his head and licked his lips. Mainly to clear his head, but also to making sure his tongue didn't hang out, panting like a wild-eyed puppy.

She carried a tray loaded with the steaks he'd brought. Veggies on the side must have been her addition to their feast. She set the tray down on the grill shelf. Her damp hair, coiled up in a clip, exposed the column of neck that he couldn't get enough of. He could smell her citrus shampoo, the coconut beach scent of her lotion. She stood, hands on hips, surveying his work. Her posture lifted her breasts, stretching her top. Barrett lost his grip on the tongs. It clanged against the grill grate.

"Easy there, my handsome grill master." Tilting her head, she eyed him, letting her gaze travel slowly from head to toe. She nodded as if coming to a conclusion. "Want a glass of wine?" Rising on tiptoe, she grabbed his ass and kissed his jaw. "I'm buying."

The steaks forgotten, Barrett leaned toward her as she slid out of reach.

She shook her finger. "Not this time. I'm hungry and you're going to feed me."

"Baby, you're gonna not only forgive me, you're gonna want me, too."

"Yeah? We'll see." She sauntered back to the house. Her hips swinging to a slow jazzy beat nearly brought him to his knees.

Victoria returned with a bottle of pinot noir and popped the cork. Barrett took the offered wine glass. He couldn't help noticing that her hands trembled as she poured the red liquid into his glass. He took a sip, letting it swirl on his tongue.

"This is great."

"Arrived today. Central Coast California. Thank goodness, the movers didn't break any bottles. Or run off with the cases."

Barrett pulled the steaks and veggies from the grill and plated them. Victoria led him to the bent willow chairs. She had added a low table and cushions. A low hanging citronella candle burned to chase off the mosquitoes that were bound to show up at any moment.

"Movers, huh? Saw the boxes. You should have waited until I could help."

Victoria paused. Her fork hung in mid-air. "How was I to know when you were returning? Someone," she said, drawing out the word. "...was supposed to call me."

Barrett carefully set his glass on the table. "I had things I had to take care of."

"I see." She lifted her glass in a toast. "As did I."

———

V ictoria wanted to poke him with her fork. Or maybe pour the wine over his head. But the steak was too tender, the wine too good, and she wasn't about to waste either on a stubborn, hardheaded man.

Only the scrape of the knife or the clink of the glass broke the silence.

Barrett cleared his throat. "I'm sorry I wasn't there to sit with you during the message session. Did you file the complaint with the authorities?"

"Oh, that. I, um, listened to some of them." She twirled her napkin under her fingers. "I haven't talked to the sheriff. I started a project for...someone, and I haven't had the time."

"Victoria, you have to protect yourself from that jerk."

"I don't know. I mean, what good will it really do? Connor's over two-thousand miles away. What harm can he do now?"

Barrett pushed his plate to the side. He made a steeple of his fingers. "Talk to Graham. Please. You ex is a problem you can't ignore."

"Don't be upset with me." She touched Barrett's wrist. "It really has been a busy couple of days."

He bent to kiss her hand. "I'm not upset with you, Victoria. I don't want you hurt."

"Then stay with me. Tuck me in at night. Share the morning with me." She bit her lip. Oh no, she said what she'd been thinking. Blame it on the wine.

CHAPTER 22

"Baby, I would love nothing more." He cupped Victoria's jaw. Gentle fingers massaged her nape. "But...."

She groaned. There was a "but," and she bet it wouldn't lead them to the bedroom. No begging. Right. Time to slap on that fake smile and move on. "Yeah?"

He leaned in, slowly. His blue eyes, flecks of cobalt and gray, searched her face. Capturing her hands, he extracted the mangled napkin from her fingers. "You need a break. Let's go to the Bluegrass Saturday Nights show."

She scrunched her nose. "Bluegrass? That's the twangy stuff, right?"

"Some of it. Not so much anymore." His thumb grazed her lower lip. He stroked her cheek. She leaned into his palm, as if she was a cat starving for attention. "Come on," he whispered. "It'll be a real date."

"Tonight?" She reared back, letting him know that she had her doubts. "Does that mean your phone stays off and you won't take off on a mission to save all of Honeybrooke Cove? Or forget to return?"

Barrett had the good sense to look contrite. He held up his fingers in a Boy Scout salute. "I swear."

Peeking up through his ridiculously long eyelashes, he penetrated her thoughts with bedroom eyes. If she were still in high school, she would have pulled him behind the garden shed, right then and there, and had her way with him. Besides, a part of her would have enjoyed the thrill of annoying her dad and breaking all his freaking rules. That was before she really thought about the consequences or knew real heartache. Too many broken hearts left on the trail to maturity. She didn't know if she had anything left to break.

Barrett lifted her hands in his and rose. His eager smile stretched his kissable lips. "Say yes."

Victoria found her head bobbing in rhythm with his. "Okay."

———

B arrett's truck shredded the country road. The lakeshore sped past them. They were going the opposite direction of town. "Where are we going?" Victoria said.

"Detour. I want you to meet someone." He glanced at her. "And no one should go to a concert while wearing flip-flops."

"Why's that?"

"You get the urge to dance, and someone's liable to dance you right out of them."

She gave him the one-raised-eyebrow.

"I swear. I've seen it happen."

Victoria laughed. "Oh, all right." The sun was slowly setting. Maybe the show would be half over by the time they arrived. It would save her from possible eardrum damage. "So, who's this mystery person you want me to meet?"

Barrett braked and turned into a long, steep driveway. Tall trees towered over the road, offering shade in a sweeping arch. They wound down the drive toward the lake.

At the bottom of the hill, a log cabin stood along the shoreline. Pale chinking accented the rows of logs. Bay windows reflected slashes of yellow and pinks. The covered entryway showcased the wide stained glass door.

Barrett was at her side before she could unbuckle the seatbelt. He grabbed her hand, leading her away from the front of the cabin. "This way."

Victoria craned her neck. Correction. Cabin? Not in her lifetime. Was this one of Barrett's worksites?

They followed a wide path of flagstones that took them beside a water feature complete with stones and a bench. Her eyes shot to the windows. "Don't you think we should let the owners know we're here?"

"No need," he said.

They rounded a rose-covered gazebo. Their canes twisted along the columns, draping seductively over the entrances. The owner had positioned the benches to catch the 360-degree view. Victoria dragged her feet, wanting to sit on the bench and inhale the perfumed air.

Sensing her hesitation, he looked over his shoulder. His smile stretched. "Pretty, isn't it?"

She shook her head. "No. It's gorgeous."

His grin grew. "Come on."

They turned to a fenced yard. Shade trees surrounded it, offering several cool corners to escape the heat.

"Tilly," he called.

A woof, click, and a smack came from the back of the house. A golden retriever shot her head through the doggie door and ran to the fence.

"There's my girl."

"She's beautiful!"

Barrett opened the side gate. "Victoria, meet Tilly."

The golden sat primly at her feet, waiting for permission to greet her. Her tail swept the ground. Her haunches trembled as she held her position.

Victoria reached out her hand for Tilly to sniff hello. "Such a beauty. Yes, you are," she crooned. The dog nudged her hand, offering her the privilege to scratch behind her ears.

"Tilly," he scolded. "Where are your manners?"

Victoria pried her attention away from the golden head. "Is Tilly yours?"

Barrett joined Victoria and scrunched the fur around Tilly's collar. "It's mutual." He kept his head down. "We come as a set."

"Of course. I would protect my fur baby too." She gulped the emotions of inadequacies and wonder. "I'm just putting the clues together here, but am I to assume that you are the owner of this...palace?"

He turned, the sunset skirting over his cheekbones. "Not a palace. But yeah. It's my home. Mine and Tilly's."

"But, but you're a handyman." As soon as the words were out, she wanted to eat them. Instead, they hung there like faded laundry on a clothesline. "I didn't mean it like that."

He watched her. His gaze slid over her hands. Up her arms. To her face. "I was a decent surgeon in another life. Used to come up here every few years when the powers-that-be forced me to take a vacation. When I escaped that life," he shrugged his shoulders, "it just seemed a natural place to land."

"Why'd you leave it all behind?" She bit her lip. Maybe tonight he would open up. It was the only way to make the haunted look fade to dark.

His face closed down. "I had my reasons."

She cringed. Too soon to push into his secrets? If not now, then when would she draw the line and demand to know about Jessica? Perhaps some time digging through the internet would give her the answers. Hadn't she vowed never to tangle her heart up with a man who carried around secrets?

He straightened. "We better get a move on. Come girl." He patted his leg for Tilly to join him.

Victoria looked back at the lake, then at the cabin. Cabin. That was an understatement. More like a candidate for the cover of those log home magazines. So why did he want Mags's little cottage? He sure couldn't call it an upgrade.

"Here." Barrett held out a check. "This will cover my portion of Mags's back-payments."

"How...how did you know I paid it off?" Victoria felt the heat rise up her neck. "You didn't need to pay me back all at once."

The check fluttered between them. She hesitated, reading his emotional scale. Since the thought of him mad at her hadn't set well, she'd simply chosen not to mention that little thing about calling off the foreclosure.

Barrett rocked on his heels looking pleased with himself. "I stopped in at Jack's office to do some work. He mentioned you'd been there to see him."

"I just, you know, wanted to get that taken care of." She caught her lower lip with her teeth. "So sue me. It's a personal flaw."

Barrett laid the check in her palm. "I get it. Just next time. Talk to me. Okay? We're supposed to be partners. Remember?"

She should have taken that moment to mention buying him out, but to be honest, she liked being in a partnership with him.

He paused, holding open the door to the house. "Victoria? You coming?"

She hurried to catch up with Barrett and Tilly, following their backsides into the garage. Counting the bays, there was room for three vehicles. Instead, stacks of wood and tools stuffed over half the building. A set of unstained rocking chairs stood on a work-bench. Old furniture leaned against the walls. All were in different stages of repair. The man was still trying to fix things.

———

The Tewilligers had turned the Cove Market into a concert hall. They had moved several racks out of the way and set up tables and chairs for the crowd. The families traveling with the musicians sat in groups. They helped tune the instruments before they took the stage.

A smoker grill stood in the corner. George worked the grill zone, offering brats, and various mustards, onions and peppers. He twirled his tongs like a majorette, keeping time to the music. Fred concentrated on the all-important task of keeping the keg tapped and ready for the next draw on the arm.

Barrett worked his way through the throng waiting to hear the next set of songs. Victoria accepted the beer he held out to her. He dropped into the chair beside her. Nodding toward the stage, he began tutoring her on the nuances that separated bluegrass music from the rest of the world.

Victoria braced for an evening of torture. Instead, after the first lines of the song, her feet and fingers began to tap out the rhythm. The lyrics pulled at her heartstrings. They sang of love found and lost to the grave.

Barrett tugged her chair closer. "True bluegrass music is all acoustic."

Impressed with the talent, the speed in which their fingers danced across the strings, she lost herself in the beauty of the songs. "Do they come here every week?"

"Some do. Mostly locals. Some come from all over the state. Depends on the time of year. Right now, it's what's called a jam session. During tourist season, they'll put on concerts at the church."

An elderly gray-haired woman in a wheelchair came toward them. Zeroed in on her target, she bumped unprotected knees and wheeled over the occasional toes. Barrett shifted his legs to avoid being her next victim.

"Mrs. Eldridge. Out for the evening?"

"Hmph. Looks like I'm outta that place, don't it?" She placed her veined hand on his arm. "Where've you been?" She peered at him with rheumy eyes. "Let me tell ya, we need those rockers. You promised them to the Friendship House. Said they'd be ready a few weeks ago." Shifting her attention off him, she turned it on Victoria. "Who's this? She the one that's been keeping you from delivering on your promises?"

Barrett had the good sense to shift uncomfortably. He cleared his throat. "Mrs. Hetty Eldridge, this is Ms. Banning."

"It's a pleasure," Victoria held out her hand. "Call me Victoria."

Mrs. Eldridge moved stiffly, her arthritic fingers wrapped Victoria's in a surprisingly, firm handshake. "You plannin' on a long stay, Ms. Banning?"

Victoria smiled. "That's the plan."

"Hetty, she recently inherited Mags's place," Barrett added.

"As did he," Victoria added. "Right, Partner?"

"Hmph," Hetty snorted. "Figures, Margaret Ellington never had good sense. Shouldn't expect her to find it on her deathbed." She angled the wheelchair, giving her back to Victoria and jabbed her gnarled finger on the chair arm. "Barrett, when are you bringing those rockers?"

Barrett's eyes narrowed. He folded his arms across his chest and chuckled. "Now, Mrs. Eldridge, I do believe you are forgetting. Good workmanship requires time and attention. They'll arrive when I say they're ready." He cast a glance over the room and stood. "Where are your friends?"

"Now let me tell ya, Barrett Collins. I don't forget a thing. Not one dad-blamed thing."

"Nice to meet you, Mrs. Eldridge," Victoria called out. "I'll make sure he gets right on those chairs."

Mrs. Eldridge jerked the wheel on the wheelchair as he pushed her. She gripped his wrist. "That one looks like trouble. You put that woman out of your life. You'll thank me for it. You'll see. She'll destroy you just like Mags—"

"Here you go, Mrs. Eldridge." Barrett delivered her to her friends and escaped. He made a mental note to put in a call to the nursing home. The staff doctor may want to reevaluate Hetty's meds.

He reclaimed the seat beside Victoria and took a deep breath. After enduring four long days without seeing Victoria, he knew that putting her out of his life was the last thing he intended to do. Did she really mean it when she told Hetty she intended to stay? Did he dare ask for how long?

"Welcome back." She nudged him with her arm. "Making rocking chairs for senior citizens?" She wrapped her fingers around his. "You're full of surprises."

A new set of musicians stepped forward. The audience quieted. They waited, their anticipation palpable.

Barrett tensed. "See that guy there, thumping the upright bass?"

"The tall, skinny guy with the frown?" she said.

"That's Teresa's son, Jackson." Barrett's hand shifted, resting protectively on her shoulder.

"She owns the We Aim to Bloom, right?"

Barrett nodded. "He's a good kid. Took it hard when his dad ran off and left his mom with the garden shop bills." He took a deep breath. "Jackson has talent. I'd hate to see it go to waste."

The young man had slicked back his hair, plastering it to his head in ridged comb-rows. He took a solo and fell into the song. The deeper he got, slapping the strings, pouring his soul into the rhythm, the looser his combed-back style became. Coated in a layer of pomade, his bangs bounced above his eyes, shielding him from the audience. The mandolin and fiddle kept up with speeds that threatened to set the market on fire. A hank of hair fell in front of Jackson's face. The trio ended in unison.

The people erupted in cheers and hoots. Victoria was part of the crowd, standing and cheering. Goosebumps danced over her arms.

Barrett was beside her, hip to hip. "Good to see him back on his feet again."

She cast a quick search across the room. Teresa stood in the corner. Tears streamed down her cheeks. She clapped, pride and joy lighting up her face.

Jackson called his mom up. Teresa hesitated, and then urged along by the crowd, she walked to the center of the stage. She took a turn with her son. Her voice lifted up to the rafters. They spun a slow song that had couples separating off into a vacant space on the wooden floorboards.

Barrett nudged Victoria toward the couples on the dance floor. He pulled her close, his hands around her waist. His hands branded her hips. Liquid fire slid over her limbs. She lifted her arms, draping them around his neck. Their steps floated across the floor. Over and over, they moved, one-step up, and one-step back. The music swirled around them, the edges of the crowd dissolved until it was just the two of them. Alone.

Victoria lifted her chin, offering her lips, wanting, oh, so much more.

———

Barrett and Victoria pushed through the front door. They tripped over a box she'd forgotten to put away. Pausing to catch their breaths, they silently questioned each other.

Victoria nipped his lower lip with her teeth. She ran her tongue over his mouth. Barrett captured her head, sliding his fingers into her hair. He sprinkled kisses over her face, covering her nose and cheeks.

Victoria caught the loops on his waistband, walking him backward to the living room. Her hands ran over his broad chest, pausing only to feel his heart thundering under her palm. The knowledge that it nearly matched her erratic heartbeat made the corner of her mouth kick up. With the slightest tug on his jeans, they were tumbling onto the overstuffed chair.

His gaze locked on hers. Time slowed. She tugged her lower lip under her teeth and heard him groan as he redirected his attention on her mouth. What did he see when he looked at her that way? "Barrett," she whispered.

"Shh." He kissed the tip of her nose. "I'll sleep out on the couch. Promise not to wake you when I leave in the morning."

CHAPTER 23

Barrett scrunched the pillow under his arms and listened to the morning. It was early. The birds were singing, announcing the beginning of the day. He stretched his legs and arms, cramped from the too short couch. He could have made his excuses and slipped out earlier. There was a comfy bed waiting for him at home. Better yet, knowing there was a woman sleeping down the hall enhanced his aches with stupidity in taking the couch instead of carrying her off to the bedroom. But he chose not to take advantage of the offer. His body was making him pay dearly for that decision. How would he explain his restlessness, waking in a drenching sweat, or worse, fighting the demons that would not let him sleep in peace? No. He made the right decision to bed down on the couch. Knowing Victoria was safe made a little discomfort worthwhile.

He covered his eyes, rubbing them as if to erase the remnants of the all too familiar dream interrupting his sleep. The darkness had slipped in again. He had hoped it would dissipate with time. His last trip to Chicago had stirred his brain, triggering memories and heartache. He had no right to whine and complain about a few lost hours of sleep. Jessica Day's parents had lost their child. For five years, they've lived with that loss every day of their lives.

He ducked his head, burying it into the pillow. The scent of Victoria's perfumed body lingered, soothing his heavy heart.

"Ready to tell me who Jessica is?"

Barrett couldn't move. He was like a deer, caught in a hunter's sites.

"You called out her name in your sleep." Victoria padded closer.

She must have showered. The smell of her shampoo filled the room. Like sunshine and warm tropical breezes.

"Talk to me," she said, shaking his shoulder.

Barrett rolled onto his back. He threw his wrist over his eyes. The breath he took stuck in his chest. Would the sterile smell of the surgical suite forever be associated with the loss of a seven-year-old little girl with flashing blue eyes? He could feel her little fingers squeeze his. Her frail voice. Although she'd been so ill, she had encouraged him as they began to administer anesthesia. "It'll be okay," she said. "I'm ready, Dr. Collins."

Only it wasn't okay. And Jessica never woke up.

Victoria pulled his arm away from his face. Tempted to resist, his muscles tensed. She bent and kissed the crease by his eye, then the other. With her fingertip, she gently traced his cheek, his jaw. "I promise not to judge."

Tears. He didn't even know he'd cried. Maybe he should have listened to his father and had another visit with a counselor. But it wasn't as if he'd never lost a patient. As a doctor, particularly a surgeon, you practiced medicine. Even though there were times you wished you could have it otherwise, life had a way of reminding you that you are not a god.

Victoria bit her lip. Her warm brown eyes darkened with concern. She waited, silent, determined to wait him out.

"Jessica was a patient of mine." He swallowed the ache that always formed. "My last one."

Her eyes sparkled with unshed tears. They pooled, filling until they spilled out and ran down her cheek. "You cared for her."

"Patient confidentiality." He caught a tear. "I'm sorry."

Victoria nodded. She kissed the inside of his wrist. "I see." Taking a deep breath, she rose from the couch. "I thought maybe…Never mind."

Barrett caught her fingers, willing her to come back to him. So much for no judgement. A barrier had formed, and he didn't know how to take it down without telling her every step of the day he had quit medicine. He didn't want to lose her in the process.

A wan smile lifted the corner of her mouth. "Hungry?"

He let go of the breath he didn't realize he'd been holding. His muscles relaxed. She wasn't tossing him out on his rear end right away. For now. "Starved."

Victoria let her fingers slip from his hand and walked away. "Towels are in the bathroom. Watch out for the closet."

"Yeah, it'll snap your finger off."

She paused at the door and cocked her head. "That's right. I almost forgot you have firsthand knowledge of it."

―――――

While apple-smoked bacon sizzled in the skillet, Victoria furiously whisked the eggs and milk together and poured it into the pan. The stainless bowl and wire whisk clattered together.

She might not be a great cook, but she could manage an omelet for two. Mags's cookbook lay beside her elbow as a safety net.

Barrett's pain-riddled sleep had awakened her after she'd drifted off in a state of relaxed bliss. And now he built the stone walls as fast as she tried to tear them down.

The bathroom door, just a few feet down the hall, opened and closed. He would be slick and steaming. All she had to do was walk toward him, demand he kiss her senseless again. Erase the pain from his eyes. Perhaps even ease the bruises of her heart in the process.

She wanted...Victoria shook her head. Yes, she wanted him. But she wanted all of him. He shielded too many sections of his life. He'd used the patient confidentiality clause. She understood some of his reasons for keeping it. However, there were ways to talk about an issue without revealing a patient's private life. After living through Connor's many lies, she couldn't let it go.

Barrett caged her shoulders. His long fingers wrapped over her fingers pressed into the countertop. He kissed her nape.

God, he smelled soapy clean. So good. She leaned her back into his chest and let him cradle her in his arms. Her hands relaxed, releasing the fists.

Her eyes popped open. "Shoot, the bacon is burning."

Twisting the knob to off, she pulled the omelet pan and skillet from the stove. The grease splattered, dotting her forearm. "Ow!"

"Oh, baby. Here, let me see." He pulled her to the sink and ran cold water over the stinging skin. His brows furrowed. "Not too bad. It should feel better in a few seconds." He looked up, his frown deepened. "Is the pain increasing?"

"No." She wiped her cheeks with the back of her hand. "I was sure I could manage a decent breakfast."

"Sweetheart." He hooked her waist with one arm. "I like crispy." He leaned in, the open cookbook catching his eye.

Barrett drew back, releasing Victoria's waist. "Keep the water running," he ordered. Flipping the book in his hand, he examined the pages with Mags's scribbled notes. "Hey, what is this?"

———

Mags's books, scattered over the kitchen table, lay open for their scrutiny.

He flicked a finger over a recipe. "I remember that meal. Mrs. Eldridge was there," he said.

"Hetty?" Victoria scrunched her face. "So that's where I thought I recalled that name."

"Her husband had passed. Hetty's." He jabbed the page. "Angriest widow I'd ever met."

They moved closer to read the scrawled handwriting.

"What do you suppose Mags meant when she said she ate crow that night?"

The kitchen chair creaked under Barrett when he leaned back. "Don't know. Hetty sure was bent out of shape when Hank passed." His eyes dancing, he bit the inside of his mouth and fought back the grin. "Course, it could have been because Hank's passing happened with Mags."

"With Mags? Like, with, with Mags?" She toweled off her arm and angled a hip against the counter.

Barrett ducked his head and rocked forward. He scratched his chin, pretending to concentrate on the page. He hadn't intended on spilling that bit of gossip. Mags would have had his hide for that one. Maybe Victoria would let it go and move on to something else, like knitting or shopping, or whatever. He'd settle for anything but discussing the love life of a couple of senior citizens.

Barrett flipped through the cookbook, searching for a recipe to draw her off the scent. "Ever made devil's food cake?"

"No. And don't try to change the subject, Barrett Collins." She tapped her fingers over her lips. "Mags involved in a love triangle. That sure puts the perfect paragon in a whole new light."

Victoria's eyes sparkled with mischief. She showed all the signs of holding onto the scent with the attention of a bulldog and a bone. She reminded him of his sister Tricia when she was onto something juicy. There was no winning this one. Resolved to his fate, he set aside the book.

Her eyes widened, a frown dipped low. "She was the other woman."

"No one ever said Mags was angelic. Far from it. She said she'd rather live life with the right kind of regrets, than to be too afraid to take a chance."

Barrett scooted the chair back and stood. He held out his hand. Victoria eased away from the counter and followed him.

They walked out to the rock garden, stopping in front of the largest one of the five towers of rock. The stone memorials stood in defiance of the elements and Victoria's efforts to relocate them.

"This one," he said, "Mags erected the day after Hank passed."

"I can't believe it." Victoria's brows winged up. "I thought about moving them, but they were too heavy. How'd she do it in the first place?"

"Grit, determination, and a lot of guilt. Almost killed her." He warmed his palm on the top stone. "She told me that one day I'd understand what it meant to take a chance on something I wanted real bad."

Victoria cupped her elbows and shook her head. "He was someone else's to love. Not hers. Poor Hetty."

"Hold on. Hetty is a hard-hearted sour puss."

"Yeah? A broken heart can cause a person's heart to harden. Or didn't Mags teach you that one?" She turned, taking account of each pile of rocks. "Maybe if I started with this one, whoever keeps rebuilding them would decide it was too much work and let it go."

"Right or wrong, Mags and Hank aren't here to explain their choices." Barrett grabbed her hand. "Hold it. What do you mean moving them? I thought you gave up on that idea." He squinted at them, trying to see the change. "The memorials sure look like they're where Mags left them."

"I did. I have," she corrected. "It only took about four days of hard labor and sleepless nights to get me to see the light. You know that old adage of the definition of insanity. Repeating the same thing and expecting a different outcome. When I admitted defeat and stopped, *voila*! No more creeping sounds in the night. And, no more rebuilding stone towers." Her frown deepened. "That and I told George and Fred to get the word out that I'm here to stay. Next time my work is vandalized I'm filing a complaint with the authorities."

Barrett hooked his thumbs in his pockets. "I still don't like it. Vandals rarely creep around at night and rebuild memorials." He took a cautious step back. "I'm just saying."

"I know." Victoria looked out across the rock garden toward the lake. "Add those traps on the porch and it doesn't add up, does it?" She swept her hand over the yard. "Why does someone want me to leave so badly?"

He surprised himself when he said, "I don't want you to leave."

"Why? It'd make life easier for you if I did. Wouldn't it, Partner?" She turned on him, hands fisted on her hips. The tank top rose and fell as she blew out a deep breath. "Sorry. I've barely unpacked. I'm exhausted. I haven't even had time to chase the guy off the lake."

"What guy?" Things like this did not happen in Honeybrooke Cove. Their big news is an affair with the dairy farmer and the mayor's wife. Or a tornado touched down.

She waved toward the shore. "That same creeper in a boat who likes to focus his binoculars on shore. I've only seen him a couple of times." She rubbed her arms. "As far as I can tell, he doesn't do anything. Just surveys the houses."

Barrett had his own personal mini tornado spinning in his gut. Either he convinced Victoria to stay with him, or, she had better get used to the idea that he was spending the night with her until they knew who was tormenting her.

CHAPTER 24

B arrett went to the garden shed and pulled out the two
fishing poles and a tackle box. "Mags and I used to do a
little fishing along the bank. That was before her health took a
turn. I almost forgot I left these here. I figured I'd be back to
retrieve them."

"Once you owned the place?" It was obvious he didn't need
another place. Not when he had a log home that you could fit five
cottages inside. So what made Mags think they needed to share
the inheritance?

"Come on!" He held a pole out to Victoria. "It's time to go
fishing."

"I don't think so." She shook her head. It might as well be a
hot poker. "Besides, we don't have any bait."

"City girls. Bet we'll find some worms within ten feet of where
you're standing." He set to work, determined to prove he knew
what he was talking about.

City girl? The man came from Chicago. That was not exactly
Podunk City. The city boy was trying hard to prove he belonged in
the cove. Well given enough time, she'd prove she belonged just
as much as he did.

Barrett returned, satisfaction gleaming from his face. The bucket of worms and poles in hand, he grinned. "Let's go."

She bit her lip. There was more keeping her from the lake than Mr. Creeper. Bad memories built a wall across the path to the dock. Right after her mom passed, she and her dad tried to create a vacation without the primary figure of their family. It was like trying to steer a boat with your feet. You were bound to hit a breaker eventually. The trip had ended in a shouting match. Each one blaming the other. Him shouting at her to '*Smile!*' Her, yelling that she wanted her mom back. He was a workaholic who smoked and drank too much. It should have been him that died.

Victoria winced. She knew now that none of it was anyone's fault. Life and death happened. They would never be the same again. They had been a three-legged stool and had lost a leg. They just kept falling down until both of them splintered and went on their way. God, she was a horrible teenager. No wonder he never tried to spend time with her after that.

"Victoria?"

Barrett waggled the fishing pole in front of her. Maybe Mags had it right after all. It was time Victoria built a stone memorial of her own. Let the heartache stay with the stones and not in her heart.

———

B arrett and Victoria sat on the bank. The fish they caught for dinner hung on a stringer in the lake. They shaded their eyes and watched the fishing boat bobbing on the waves.

"Is that him?" The tone in Barrett's voice had an edge she'd never heard before.

"Maybe." She twisted the bottom edge of her t-shirt. "Hard to tell."

He began to pack up their things, reeling in the fishing line, pulling up the fish. Helping her to her feet, he followed behind her until they reached the house. His mouth drew down into a frown, a deep V formed between his brows. "I need to go take care of Tilly. Why don't you come with me?"

"Why? I'm fine."

"I don't like you being alone here."

"It's Sunday. It's daylight. I have Mr. and Mrs. T next door. And, I have my sat phone, remember?"

Barrett cupped the back of her head in his palms. He kissed her deeply. His teeth brushed her lips, then nibbled on the shell of her ear. "Come with me," he whispered.

She stood her ground. "Not happening. If that man in the boat wants to scare me, he's about to get a strong message of NO. Even if it means I have to stand on the dock, screaming 'We Shall Overcome' and flipping him a three-fingered wave."

Groaning, he pressed his forehead to hers. "Do me a favor and don't."

"Not the best plan, huh?" She scrunched her face, doing her best to make light of Barrett's concern. "It's the best one that comes to mind."

The other plan was to hide at Barrett's place forever. Or, he tired of her and kicked her out. That last one she didn't plan to implement any time soon.

"Anybody ever tell you, you're stubborn?" Barrett tucked her closer. "Let me do some checking around the cove. If there's a stranger in town, we'll know." He smoothed her hair from her face. "Do you have a picture of Connor on your cell phone?"

"Yes. I think." She bit her lip, searching. Had the man been close enough to see? Did he look like Connor? Tall, yes, but that's all. Not much to go on. "Barrett, you don't really think it's Connor, do you? For cripes' sakes! He'd never travel over two thousand miles to stalk me. He's more than likely hanging out with the latest new-hire from the courtroom."

"I wish you would have filed a complaint."

"I told you, they were empty threats."

Barrett tried again. "Come with me. Until I know who that is out on the boat, I don't want you to be alone."

"I have a better idea. We both have work to do. So you go do what you've gotta do. Take care of your dog. Play investigator, and then…," Victoria stood on tiptoe, wrapping her arms around his neck. She dipped her tongue in his mouth, kissing him deeply, ensuring that he wouldn't even be able to think of distracting phone calls or mysterious trips out of town. "Drop by and check on me."

Barrett dragged in a shuddering breath. He gripped her hips, hauling her close enough that she felt his heartbeat through their clothes. "Keep this up and I'm bringing Tilly and my toothbrush when I come back."

"What's stopping you?" she whispered. "We are co-owners of Mags's cottage, remember?"

———

Barrett sat in his office and scanned the computer screen after downloading the photos from Victoria's cell phone. Connor Hemming, Esq. gazed back at him with an indifferent smile. His smirk left you feeling like he knew something you didn't. You could almost smell the swamp coming off the man's bad karma.

What did Victoria ever see in that sewer rat?

Okay, tall, athletic build, blond, blue eyes. Connor didn't physically fit Barrett's profile of a monster who likes to leave phone threats. He punched in the phrase, Psychology of a Stalker. His shoulders bunched. Simple Obsession Stalkers. That was an oxymoron if he ever heard one. How can those three words strung together not make you consider registering for a gun? Simple obsession stalkers had a personal or romantic relationship before their stalking behavior began and they represent 70-80% of all stalking cases. Statistically speaking, there was a good chance Victoria's ex-lover boy had gone off the deep end.

Taking a deep breath, Barrett gripped the chair arms, memorizing the details of Connor's face. He keyed in Connor's name and began the search. News clips began popping in. Academic awards. Court hearings.

He dug a little deeper. His gut rolled.

Lover Boy, make that Ex-lover Boy, had been busy after Victoria left California. He now had a police record. And apparently left a trail of destruction wherever he went.

Bolting from his chair, Barrett grabbed an overnight bag. Remembering the hot goodbye kiss, he tossed his toothbrush on top of a shirt.

He glanced at the clock. An hour had already passed. He didn't like leaving Victoria alone for another minute. After slipping Connor's printed photo in his jacket, he locked up and headed out. "Tilly girl, up!"

Deliriously happy to be going, Tilly jumped into the cab, her golden tail waving like a flag. Barrett set her supplies and his bag next to the ten-pound sledgehammer in the truck bed.

He swung his pickup by Chief Graham's place. The office in front of the house looked buttoned up. He tried the back door that represented the sheriff's home. "Graham?" he called, knocking on the door.

"Hey." The screen door swung open. Graham's color was less gray and pasty since the last time Barrett saw him. "Whatcha doing here?"

"I have a favor. If you're up to it." Barrett stepped in, doing the quick home check. The place was clean and uncluttered. His patient was indeed on the mend.

"Course I am." His hand fluttered over his chest before he yanked it down and scowled. "I'm waiting on that worthless doctor you shoved me off on. Need a quick checkup before he releases me back to duty."

"You know I had to. I don't have any connections to the hospitals here."

Graham deepened his scowl, pinning him with a glare. "I heard you. But I don't have to like it."

"I understand." Barrett clapped him on his shoulder. The muscles were firm. He might not have had complete control over his medical case, but it appeared Graham's health was nearly restored. "Came to give you a heads-up."

"Oh? Does this mean I have to take more medicine? You can stop right there, if it does."

"Nope. This is of a police nature."

The old man's eyes sparkled with anticipation. "Go on. I'm listening."

Barrett filled him in as fast as he could. "I'll swing by the Duck Blind. See if Lyle has noticed anyone new hanging around."

"Until this Connor does anything significant, I can't do anything official." Graham tapped the stack of papers on his desk. "Victoria needs to file a complaint. You tell her that I'll come by and start the paperwork just as soon as she gives me the green light."

Barrett shook his head. "I understand the protocol, but it doesn't mean I have to like it."

Graham nodded. "Gimme whatcha got and I'll do what I can."

Barrett left the photo and details with the sheriff and headed for his truck. Tilly barked, announcing her joy that he had returned so quickly.

Pushing the recent call button, he tried Victoria's satellite phone. He let it ring, then hung up and tried again. Still no answer. He slammed the phone down on the seat. His muscles bunched. "Hold tight, Tilly. We are going on a ride."

The tires squealed, marking up the driveway. He caught Graham's reflection in his rearview mirror. Great. He'd probably get another safe driving lecture.

CHAPTER 25

Victoria took a long swallow of iced tea. The tall glass wavered on its path from her mouth. She should have gone with Barrett. At least until he had calmed down and realized that Connor couldn't do anything major to her as long as he was still in California. It was a relief, actually, knowing that he'd destroyed what she thought they had. She would have hated being another Hetty, being screwed by the situation and not the man.

She spun her cell phone on the kitchen table, digging up the nerve to listen to Connor's messages, trying to get a handle on the ridiculous notion that he meant to harm her. Their relationship was over. It died the moment he got the idea to stick his tongue where it didn't belong. His betrayal proved he wouldn't have any reason to come out to Wisconsin.

So why did her skin feel like it had been in an acid peel?

She looked up. Her heartbeat sped until it pounded in her ears. A car door banged shut. Twice.

The knife block was within arm's reach. She tensed, ready to pounce, and hated the shiver of fear running up her back.

Toenails skittered across wooden planks, doing their best to gain purchase. Tilly poked her regal, strawberry-blond head around the corner and barked. Her brown eyes dancing, she ruined the grande dame act by wiggling her butt until she turned in a full circle of joy.

Victoria scrambled from the table. "My lady! What a wonderful surprise." She opened the door and the golden swept in. Standing on tiptoe, she scanned the yard. "Where's your handsome master?"

Barrett turned the corner. Her brows rose. Loaded down, he carried his phone in his mouth, a beach bag and an overnight bag under each arm. His usual blue eyes were an icy gray. She'd been with him long enough to recognize the color of his eyes reflected his mood. Whatever it was, this was a new level of emotions, but she didn't care. Tensing, her nerves already coiled and ready to explode, she leaped into his arms, burying her face into his chest.

The bags and phone hit the floor. Barking, the dog scrambled out of the way.

"Baby." He gathered her close, shielding her body. Her chin tilted, he searched her face. "What's happened? Are you okay?"

She worked to hold the hated smile in place like a shield. It wobbled and slid when her lips trembled. Relief and fear rolled together, creating a tumbleweed of emotion. Realizing she was overreacting, Victoria gathered herself and nodded.

His breath rushed out. He squeezed her close. "Shh. I'm here. It's gonna be all right."

"I know. I'm just a little nervy."

He ran his hands up and down her back. They settled around her hips. "Tilly and I are here now."

———

B arrett stretched his legs out on the ottoman. The comforter bunched under his head for a pillow. He ran his fingers over Victoria's shoulder blade. The tactile contact warmed his hand.

The pleasure of the satiny skin under his palm reminded him of their differences.

Glints of gold and fire highlighted her hair. The silken strands shimmered through his fingers.

He took a breath, filling his lungs with her sweet scent. She lifted her head from his chest. A rare, contented smile reached her eyes.

Rare and beautiful. It broke his heart to be the bearer of his suspicions. To wipe away the smile.

Shifting, she ran a finger over his brow. "That's a very serious V forming there."

Barrett closed his eyes. What was he to do? Problems and nightmares belonged to another life. An ex-boyfriend didn't send threatening messages. They were content. At least they were for now. He didn't know what was developing between them. And he didn't want to let it go.

The cushions moved under their weight. Her lips, warm and soft, pecked him on his mouth. His skin cooled when she drew away. He snapped open his eyes to see her cross into the living room. Shoving his hand into his hair, he scrubbed his scalp, brushing aside the edginess that burned through his blood. He had to talk to her about Connor.

He paused in the hallway. Victoria stood by the kitchen table, offering a sumptuous view of her lean back. Focused on what she held in her hand, she didn't hear him approach.

"What's wrong?" He nipped the delicate area along her neck that made her shiver. Instead of melting under his touch, she stiffened.

She turned. Her face drained of color, she searched him for answers. "What is this?"

"A photo." He couldn't help frowning. The photo was tucked in a pocket. Not that he meant to hide it. He just wanted to present what he found about ex-lover-boy when things were a little less...passionate.

She shook the paper under his nose. "I know it's a photo, Barrett. Why do you have a picture of Connor? And these?" She slid out the forms and identity reports underneath it. "What are these?"

Barrett rubbed the back of his neck. Why was she so annoyed? Did she still have emotions wrapped up in Connor?

"Research." He caught her hands and pulled her to him. Victoria's pupils flared. Aware that he meant to distract her, she stepped back.

"It isn't your responsibility." Her arms crossed over her stomach.

Barrett tore his gaze from her stern frown and flipped a throw blanket off the couch. He gently settled it over her shoulders. "We have to talk."

Victoria tucked the blanket closer. "That was a police report. Wasn't it?"

Taking a chance that she wouldn't rip his head off, he closed the distance between them. Gently, he cupped her jaw and desperately wanted to kiss all the care and worry lines from her brow.

"I'll make us coffee." God help him, he couldn't stop his arms from wrapping around her. He kissed her forehead. "After we talk, you can decide if you're still mad at me or not."

She plucked at the blanket's fringe. Tears drained down her cheeks. "I don't want secrets between us, Barrett. Next time, you talk it over with me. Okay?"

He did his best not to stiffen under her declaration. There were some things he wasn't ready to discuss. Jessica Day's death was off limits.

He nodded. "Got it. I'm sorry."

"You're forgiven." Satisfied with his response, she kissed the corner of his mouth and slipped into the bathroom.

―――――

The coffee set, Barrett waited at the kitchen table. In times past, even from his childhood, the kitchen table filled the role of round table, boardroom, and the trial and punishment center.

The plaque on the wall caught his attention. In Mags's last days, she liked to point out that worry never changed a thing, except make you sick. She had gazed up at the wisdom printed on the piece of wood and say, 'You have to know what's in your power to change and have the guts to let go of what you can't. Once you figure that out, Barrett, you better get off your rear end and fix it.'

Victoria couldn't remove the impact Connor had made in her past, but she could do something about keeping the scumbag out of her present. Barrett was determined to protect her, even from herself.

She sat down. Her cheeks, pale under red-rimmed eyes. Resolute in hearing what he had to say she drew her shoulders back, ready to carry the burden of truth against the man she once loved. Barrett's gut twisted. If she still loved the prick, he'd do his best to change her mind.

Tilly came up, bumping Victoria's hand with her black nose. The dog scooted her golden head under her hand, resting her chin on Victoria's thigh. They let out a simultaneous sigh.

Barrett stood and filled two coffee mugs and set them on the table. He spread out the documents for them to view. "I'm sorry you're mad at me but I don't want you hurt."

Her eyes flashed. "I told you, Connor doesn't care where I am. He has his life and I have mine."

"Sweetheart, Connor has been busy while you've been away."

He dropped into the chair beside her and pushed the brief police report that he'd scrounged from the internet toward her. Headlines announcing the allegation of misconduct and the disbarment of an up-and-coming attorney shouted across the page. Hesitating while she read the document, he slid the additional grisly information Graham had pulled. The photo of a young woman, battered and abused, looked back at them through swollen eyes.

Victoria smothered her mouth with the back of her hand. Her eyes wide, she shook her head, silently begging him to tell her it was a lie. She dropped her hand to the table. The papers stayed out of reach, far enough they could not cut her deeper than they already had. Tears streamed down her face and dripped onto her lap.

Barrett pumped a reassuring squeeze to her cold fingers. "Baby, I'm sorry. Please don't cry."

He fought back disappointment. Now was not the time for him to get emotionally involved. His heart didn't matter. Her safety did. "I know you still love him." He swallowed the bile creeping up his throat. "But you have to protect yourself."

She shook her head violently, "No."

———

Victoria rose on legs that felt like the bones had shattered, liquefied by disgust and anger. Fear; a byproduct of the unknown. Where was Connor? How could he commit an act of violence against that woman?

Despite the bruises and swelling, Victoria recognized the face. She would never forget the surprise and anger that crossed Connor's Adonis-face before he'd unwrapped his arms from the other woman. "V. You know I need you. I still love you." He'd grabbed her wrist. "V. We need to talk."

Appalled and disgusted, Victoria screamed at him. She couldn't recall what she said. Throwing anything within reach, she had pushed them both out of the condo and into the hall. Aroused, Connor's face red with rage, his nostrils flared, he had vowed to get back what was his.

The cottage kitchen swam in front of Victoria's eyes. The coffee mug clattered when it hit the table. Dark, burning air, filled her lungs. The pain scorched her chest. She ran to the bathroom, her bare feet padding over the oak flooring.

"Sweetheart? Baby?" Barrett called.

The bathroom door slammed open, bouncing against the wall.

Victoria turned. Her hair tumbled around her face, sticking to her cheeks. "I'm a fool."

"No, you're not." He gripped her shoulders, forcing her chin up. "We will work through this. Together."

He pressed her head to his chest and rocked. Fragile. Easily broken. And wary. A barrier formed that hadn't been there an hour earlier. She wanted to turn back the clock. Return to the passion they built between them. How could he believe she still felt something for Connor?

She gripped his biceps, forcing his embrace to open. Walking on ancient legs that felt petrified, shriveled, and dead, she headed for the living room. Her fingers tightened around Barrett's.

Together. She didn't have to face this alone. Barrett stood at her side, waiting for her to make the next move.

The cell phone lay on the table, waiting for them to hear everything Connor had to say.

CHAPTER 26

Victoria wearily sat down on one of the bent willow chairs Barrett had made for her. She sank into the pillows and propped her feet up on the ottoman. Connor's threats had sucked out all her energy. The levels had dropped to an all-time low. They were lower than the day she found him with someone else.

Although a month had passed since Victoria had filed the complaint against Connor, she soon discovered the restraining order was slow in coming. And no one knew where he was hiding.

Her fingers grazed over her jeans. She could no longer carry rage against the other woman. They both had stupidly bought into Connor's lies.

Secrets. She had really come to dislike them. It stung that Barrett still held his close to his chest. She wanted to push him, but frankly, it would be so much better if he would trust her enough to talk to her about Jessica Day.

She tucked the throw blanket around her shoulders. The leaves spinning in the breeze had begun to change, lighting up the trees with the fiery colors of autumn.

Barrett held out a mug of coffee. Looking up, she accepted it and breathed in the pungent aroma.

"Mmm, thanks," she said.

He watched her closely. "Are you okay? You look a little tired."

Victoria forced a smile. Things had been different between them ever since the day he'd made her accept that Connor was a real threat. Barrett worried about her and treated her as if she was made of spun glass. Instead, she wanted him to pick her up and kiss her until her toes curled.

Tilly rested her regal head on Victoria's lap. The golden silk teased her fingers as she scrunched the area behind the dog's ears.

"Any news from Chief Graham?" she said.

"No. Everyone is keeping an eye out for him." He glanced over at her, his smile weak. "You know how Honeybrooke Cove is. We watch out for our own."

Victoria's heart warmed. "I'm part of the community?"

"Well, yeah. You already have quite the following. The seniors can't crow your praises loud enough. Especially Mrs. T."

Victoria chuckled. "Once she got over the shock and annoyance, she admitted she was glad to no longer have to crunch the numbers."

"Bet Harold is relieved to stop jumping through hoops to keep his secret. Imagine his financial windfall from the investments you steered him to didn't hurt either."

"Sure didn't hurt Helen's feelings. She's been hinting about a vacation. The other day, I nearly tripped over one of her travel magazines. Harold's oblivious to it. She's going to have to come out and tell him she wants to move to warmer winters."

"Can't picture him giving in to that idea," Barrett said. He blew on his coffee. "The lake will start freezing soon. Maybe start to tonight. Won't be long, you won't have to worry about anyone watching you from a boat. Only your neighbors to keep an eye out for unwanted visitors."

Victoria's brows rose, her stomach twisted, rebelling against the coffee. "Guess you won't have to sleep on that lumpy couch anymore." She carefully set the mug on the table. "What with everyone watching out for me."

"It's not that. I need to make a trip and will feel better knowing that access is cut off. At least until it freezes over solid enough for ice fishing." He scooted forward, his hands hanging between his knees. "I'll be back before that."

"I see." Why did her jaw feel like it was made of ice?

"Victoria, I have something I need to ask you."

Her breath caught. Her heart pounded in her chest, tapping out a staccato beat. "Yes?"

"Will you…will you keep Tilly for me while I'm gone?" He ducked his head. His knit beanie bounced when he scratched the back of his neck. "I might be gone for an extended length of time."

"Of course." Her senses heightened, she gripped his forearm. "What's this about, Barrett?"

"It's nothing. Just some personal business in Chicago that I've needed to handle for a while. I'd take Tilly, but she doesn't do well with strange places."

Victoria cocked her head, looking for cracks and holes in his story. He was leaving something important out. "Barrett, are you in some kind of trouble?"

"What?" He rose from the chair, nearly knocking over the coffee table. "No. Jesus." His fists shoved deep in his front pockets. "Look, if you don't want to be bothered with the dog, I'll ask someone else."

"You will not." She'd certainly struck a sour chord. Too bad, all she knew was it sounded off key and didn't know why. Stiff and tired, wanting desperately to have a good cry, Victoria pushed up. She gripped his sleeves to keep him from stomping off and partly to keep her from tipping over.

His eyes were a thunderous blue, stormy and full of pent-up emotions. "You sure?"

"Tilly will keep me company while you're away. Maybe by the time you get back, we'll have run off," she teased. His frown deepened. The muscle in his chiseled jaw clenched. Well, at least he wasn't neutral about that. "Or," she added, "given enough reasons, we'll stick around for you."

The first snowflakes began to fall. They dusted his dark hair. Victoria licked her lips and blinked the snow from her eyelashes.

"You need reasons?" Barrett dipped in, drawing her to his chest. He tilted her chin, giving him access to her mouth. Hot tears seared her eyelids. His silence scared her, made her worry for his safety. Shivering, she welcomed the warmth of his embrace and ached for him to let her in. Why didn't he understand? Whether he liked it or not, she was his ally.

"When do you leave?" Victoria hated the answer before she heard it. Any time away would be too soon. She hadn't seen or heard of any travel arrangements, noticed any suitcases lying about. At least they would have another week or so. She swatted the snow from her face. Maybe they'd be snowed in and he would have to postpone his trip until spring. Please God, she wanted to whisper the desperate prayer.

Barrett lifted her hand, kissing her wind-chilled fingers. His breath caressed her flesh. "Tomorrow morning."

She shivered, this time, but not from the early winter winds.

B arrett propped his back against the bedroom doorframe and watched the rise and fall of Victoria's slender shoulder. Her golden tan from the summer had faded into a soft ivory. Brown, silken hair feathered her cheek, framed her face. He ached to let it shimmer through his fingers. Long eyelashes fluttered over her downy cheeks. Soft lips, full and lush, invited him to kiss her forever.

He shifted, gaining control of his thoughts. He owed her an explanation for his trip. Who was he kidding? He owed her for putting up with his frequent nightmares. She didn't push. In her quiet way, she waited for him. He knew she wanted him to trust her. He owed her that much. Didn't he?

The wind pushed around the trees forcing their limbs to scrape against the roof. He had intended on trimming them before he left. He wanted to postpone his trip, wait until the sun came out. But this was northern Wisconsin. Although the calendar hadn't officially called fall off, Mother Nature had.

He glanced out the window. Snow already accumulated on the windowsill. Shoot, he had planned to check out Victoria's little red convertible before he left. He prayed she had snow tires and knew immediately that she wouldn't.

Barrett flinched. The floorboards thumped under his feet, then a blast of heat came from the outdated radiator. He closed his eyes. He'd also intended to teach her how to make that cantankerous furnace run despite its efforts to die.

But he couldn't postpone what he'd already set aside for five years. Five years of life-changing heartache couldn't be ignored. The anniversary of Jessica's death was in a few days. He'd have enough time to get down there and pay his respects. By then, the proceedings against his onetime friend and colleague, Tim St. James, would start.

Although the lawyers expected Barrett to stand up as a character witness, he intended to put the record straight. After reading the affidavit, and doing some research of his own, Barrett had to stop this medical monster before St. James's actions caused another death.

He had punished himself long enough. That's what Mags had tried so hard to make him see. It was time to quit rolling over as the bad guy and end his silence.

He tucked the comforter around Victoria's shoulders. Smiling in her sleep, she wiggled deeper under the blankets. A soft purr escaped; making him want to stay with her, find a way to stall a little longer. Would she want him after he told her about the night his life had changed so drastically and another life had stopped?

Talking about it was like ripping open a wound. All punish-
ments come with a price tag. His was his practice. But he now
knew that it had allowed him to hide. He had told himself that he
was being noble, removing himself from the medical scene. In
reality, he had been a coward. He should have taken Tim St. James
with him.

He bent over, stroking her velvet cheek. His throat tightened.
"Baby," he whispered. The morning sun played hide-and-seek with
the clouds, illuminating Victoria's face, then throwing it into
shadows. He prayed he was doing the right thing. "We need to
talk."

CHAPTER 27

V ictoria looked up sleepily and squinted at Barrett's distorted face. She brushed her fingers over the morning growth of beard. Concern marred his soft gaze. Confused, she stiffened, and began that death march into self-doubt. What had he said when he woke her up? He hadn't said good morning. Her stomach did a belly flop, pain shooting to her lungs. They needed to talk. Never a wonderful way to start the day.

She turned to roll away. Did he feel smothered? What that it? She untangled her legs from the comforter and bounced her bottom over the mattress to get away. If she could have managed an aerial tuck and roll, she would have done one just to avoid contact.

"Victoria. Sweetheart," he said. His fingers streaked over her arm as she slipped free.

Avoiding eye contact, she ducked down the hall and slammed the bathroom door shut. Cranking the faucet wide open, steam swirled in the shower. Hot needles pelted her back, scrubbing the ache from her body. If only it would wash it away from her heart.

She slid into her comfy housecoat and tied off the belt. Bracing her hands on the cool tile, she let the tears fall as she gathered the pieces of her broken self-esteem. The last hours spun through her thoughts. Was he breaking it off? *It. What were they?* Even friends with benefits shared something other than their bodies. They shared secrets. He wanted to talk, did he? Well, he better put his helmet on, because she was done getting run over.

Readying for a fight, her hands curled into fists at her side. She marched down the hallway in search of Barrett.

"Babe—"

She smacked his chest. Stunned that she had actually struck him, her jaw unhinged.

"Ouch." Barrett rubbed his chest. "What's going on with you?" Wide-eyed, he stepped toward her with all the trepidation of a lion-tamer stepping into a cage.

"I thought you were leaving?"

"I'd have to be certifiable to take off on a trip right now."

"You want to talk? Or what?" Victoria hugged her waist and tried to shimmy past him to the safety zone of lots of space.

He wiggled in closer. Smoothing back her hair, he tilted her chin. Gazing into her eyes, the corners of his mouth ratcheted down. "Hey, no tears. Please." One corner dipped up. "Can we 'or what' now?"

"We will talk." She gripped his forearms firmly. "I mean it Barrett Collins."

Their bodies collided with all the passion they had been holding back. Hungrily, their lips and hands traveled over each other, dancing and swirling until both were unable to put two words together.

———

An hour later, as much as they had tried to avoid it, the time to talk had come.

Victoria hunched over the cup of coffee and flexed her fingers around the heat. Barrett's walls had returned.

She took a deep breath. So this was goodbye? It was torture. Maybe shoving Connor out the door had been easier. She liked the quick, yank-the-Band-Aid-off method, instead of the long-prolonged pain of one-thousand-cuts. She didn't know how she would make it through this. *'Smile!'* echoed in her ears. Instead, she lifted the mug and took a long sip of coffee. It left a scorched path down her throat, bringing tears to her eyes. Of course, it was the coffee. *Right?*

Barrett sat down beside her on the couch. Warily, she braced for the, 'It's not you, babe. It's me.'

He lifted her hand, pressing kisses over her wrist. "I—" He struggled, searching for words. "Listen, I need to go back to Chicago. I have some stuff that I've put off for too long." He swallowed, sweat beaded on his forehead. "Jessica. Her family. I don't—"

"Want to be with me anymore," she finished. "I get it." She closed her fingers over his hand. "Look. We can be friends. Besides, we're still co-owners of the cottage. You'll be nice when you see me, and I'll do the same. I'll be able to buy out your share by spring. If you can wait that long."

"That's not what I was going to say." He sat back. Stunned, his dark blue eyes stormed back at her under raised brows. "Is that what you want?"

Victoria stood on shaking legs. Her knees defied her commands and kept her locked into position.

His jaw ticked under the strain of gritted teeth. "I would have thought you'd listen. Given me a chance to explain."

"Explain." She rubbed her temple, shoving her fingers through her hair. Her mouth pursed, she forced the best smile forward. "Yes. Do explain how you are leaving me for Jessica. The woman you dream about and call out to during the night. The one you protect and keep buried with silence." Her hands flapped the air, coming close to knocking over a lamp. "I just love a happy-ever-after-story that doesn't include me."

"That's not how it is." He scrubbed the back of his head. "If you'd just listen."

"Fine." She snapped up the high-backed chair and sat down. Crossing her legs, fingers wrapped tight around her kneecaps, she waited. Her white knuckles betrayed how hard she squeezed to maintain control.

Barrett bent his head. He leaned forward, elbows braced, his hands hung between his legs. "Jessica was a little girl," he growled. "Notice, I said, was." He looked up, his eyes searching her face. "I killed her." At her gasp, he finished. "On the operating table. I should have called someone else in. But I didn't."

He rose, slowly, as if every bone in his body was exhausted. "There were some details that no one, but me and another colleague, are aware of. It's been five years, but I have to take care of this, Victoria." Tears glittered in his ever-changing, ice-blue eyes. "There. Now you know my secret." He took a deep breath. "I get it if you can't stand the thought of someone like me touching you."

"Oh, Barrett," she whispered. "I'm sorry. I didn't..." Tugging on his fingers, she led him back to the couch. "I know it's hard but why don't you start at the beginning?" Clasping his hands, she added, "I'm here. Not going anywhere. I thought that's what you wanted. That you were tired of me."

He gave a snort. "Not in a million years. But you might want to break off our partnership once you hear the whole story."

She glanced up, met his gaze and held it. "Try me."

He smoothed a strand of hair from her cheek. "Five years ago, I made the decision to help my friend, Tim St. James. Stupidest thing I've ever agreed to."

"Does this have to do with the nightmares?"

"Yeah. I can't get her face out of my head. Her delicate fingers wrapped around mine." His voiced cracked. "She told me that everything was going to be okay." He cleared his throat filled with emotion. "But it wasn't. She never made it through.

The review board stated it was natural causes. But I know different."

"What happened?"

He scrubbed the back of his neck. The scene replayed again in his mind. It was still fresh. "It had been a long weekend. I'd been in ER, pulling extra shifts. I was supposed to have ended the day. My friend, Tim St. James, cardiology is his specialty, was to start his next shift. I was going to observe. Learn from the best. Be the best.

"Tim came in, unsteady on his feet. I'd been pulling over thirty hours straight and was still steadier than he was."

Barrett gritted his teeth. *Inhale, exhale. That's how we get through this.* "I'm pretty sure he'd been drinking. I could smell it on him as he washed up. Heard rumors of his popping pills, later. From what I know now, it might have been both.

"Instead of reporting him, stopping the procedure, I took the case. We convinced the surgical team that it was planned earlier. I don't know what went wrong." He glared at his long fingers. "The scene replays in my dreams. My hands shaking with exhaustion. Jessica and her family had placed their trust in me. Their faces, raw with the shock of losing their little girl. Her momma screaming for Jessica."

He gripped his ankles, rocking back in the couch. "I should have waited. I should have reported him. But I was the bright, up and coming new doctor."

He felt Victoria watching him, wary and concerned. "Would you believe it never fazed him?" Barrett shook his head in his own disbelief. "Tim went on to become the head surgeon at another hospital. And I moved north to hide from the bitter memory of a promise I couldn't keep."

Piercing her with determination, he sat up. The time to go was drawing near. The snow was coming down, and he needed to get this battle started.

"The man is still screwing up. I read the recent stats. His death

206 C C WILEY

rate is off the charts and his lawyers want me to be a character witness to save his butt. Instead, I intend to go to Chicago and make Dr. Tim St. James's life miserable. I can't hide up here and let him destroy any more lives."

"What do you intend to do?" Victoria still claimed hold of his hand.

"I'm going to tell the truth. However long it takes."

Barrett closed his eyes. He sat, waiting for Victoria's judgment and he feared the verdict. He lay bare, stripped of his secrets, stripped of his pride. He might as well have honey dripped on him and staked to an anthill. He itched to get going.

Victoria soothed her hand over his. "We all make poor decisions."

He couldn't control the snort. "Really? Does yours involve having someone's life in your hands? No? How about having a mother and father entrusting their child's life in your hands? Not that one either? Guess that's where I have you beat, babe."

Victoria's brows arched over emotion-filled, dark brown eyes. "What do you want from me? Do you want support? Do you want me to condemn you?" She squeezed his arm. "I'm doing my best here. I care about you. But if you don't tell me what you intend to do now, I can't help you."

Barrett stood, ready to shoot out the door like a horse breaking through the gates at The Kentucky Derby. "I'm going to fix things. Okay?"

"I can go with you. It'll take me two minutes to pack my bag."

"Sorry. I'm on my own with this one." He wrapped his arms around her, inhaling her tropical scent of coconut and citrus. "And what are you going to do for yourself, Victoria? When are you going to stop allowing Connor to change who you are?"

CHAPTER 28

"Goodbye, October," Victoria muttered. She flipped the kitchen wall calendar, ripping off the Wild Woman Sisterhood quote of the month, 'This too shall pass.' The next page held a group of women dancing around a fire, the caption taunting her to action. 'Most of us live with our song unsung—sing it!'

"Hello, November," she whispered and made a red X over the first day. Her pen paused as she read, 'May your holiday feasts be resplendent and your family dynamics peaceful.'

The coffee spewed across the table at that last saccharin statement.

The holidays. There was an excellent reason Halloween masks, chainsaw-wielding killers, and candied corn, ushered in the holidays. It foreshadowed the torture promised by the next three holidays.

"Ah, childhood memories that stay until you erect your own," she said to the dog lying at her feet.

Thanksgiving, where families gathered around the table, barely civil, choking on dust-bowl-stuffing and bits of hardened breast meat. The bird and its accomplice, the chef of the day, should earn a place on the post office wall as wanted serial killers. Thank God for cranberry sauce. Even the kind that slid out of the can, the lines imprinted in its cylindrical shape. That red lube saved the lives of many. And that was the easy part. After her mother passed, the conversations with her dad were minimal. That day of gratitude was torture.

Mags's cookbook lay on the counter. Each page chock full of notes and advice. It called to her, chastising and challenging her to find some guts and cook an actual meal for someone other than herself. No frozen meals of turkey nuggets and yellow bullets of corn served this year.

Victoria bit her lip. Maybe Barrett would be back from fixing his past. How long had it been? She glanced at the calendar, counting. "Three weeks. One week of checking-in phone calls. Two weeks of silence," she said. "Three more to go."

Circling Thanksgiving Day with the bright red marker, she wrote gobble-gobble over the square. Her brain automatically started composing the Gratitude List. Number one on the list; no creepy sounds at night. They'd stopped the night Barrett began sleeping over and she'd quit trying to move the memorial rocks.

Steeling herself, she geared up the nerve to flip the calendar page to the second holiday of torture. Christmas. Panic started to build. What was she supposed to do? The weight of loneliness crashed down on her like an anvil. Wylie Coyote, eat your heart out. She absolutely hated the emptiness and silence of spending Christmas alone. A good time to get out of the frozen tundra, work on a tan.

She sighed, turning to the golden retriever that apparently Barrett had abandoned, too. Who was she kidding? Tilly needed her. Besides, her bank account had taken a few death hits in recent months. She might as well figure out how to make the best of winter in Wisconsin.

Her toe tapped out Jingle Bells as she dreaded the white Christmas coming. "The Grim Reaper cometh," she whispered under her breath. Turning to Tilly, she added, *"Mwah-hah-hah-hah."*

The thirteenth month included in the calendar gaped at her. Its maw wide open, cajoling her to step into the darkest part of the year. Victoria shivered despite the sun beaming through the windows.

New Year's Eve is the night that pokes you. It shouts, 'Everyone, look at the single woman, party of one, standing in the corner with no one to kiss.' For the last two years, even though she and Connor had been a couple, they hadn't shared that date. He'd been traveling on business. She snorted. "Yeah, right."

Finished punishing herself with the promises of anguish and ridicule, she grabbed her mug of coffee and cookbook. Nestled on the couch, she perused Mags's cookbook and dreamed of the perfect turkey. Maybe, if she followed every bit of advice, she would cook a meal worthy of a Thanksgiving feast.

She scrunched her nose and whipped out her notebook to jot down the possible guest list. "All to keep you busy, my dear."

Tilly pressed her muzzle into Victoria's thigh, signaling to go outside. "Okay, pretty lady. Message delivered."

They padded to the kitchen door. The wind whipped the bare tree limbs as the snow swirled out of the gunmetal skies. Victoria clutched the collar of her cardigan tight against her chest. Her fingers stiffened in the chilled air. The numbers on the outside thermometer had dropped below thirty. Today's forecast promised this was supposed to be the warmest part of the day.

Tilly made short, efficient work, and trotted back in. She left a trail of miniature snowballs in her wake and curled up on her special pillow. Her brown eyes followed Victoria, watchful for any sudden morsel that might rain down from the heavens.

"Not this time, girl. Your master will probably scold me for the extra rations I've been giving you." She shivered again, mindful of her cold feet and fingers. Frowning, she checked the thermostat. No wonder the cottage had seemed so quiet. The furnace had quit working. The numbers had dropped almost as fast as they had outside.

After pulling on the boots and the cashmere fingerless mittens she'd thought were so darling, she headed to the basement. Armed with a flashlight and Barrett's list of how to keep the furnace going, she felt her way down the dark stairway. Until now, she'd been able to avoid the basement. Shadows ebbed and flowed, stretching over the two-foot thick fieldstone walls. They looked like they should be able to withstand a bomb or a tornado.

She pulled the cord. The bare light bulb lit up the low ceiling and the cantankerous octopus monstrosity Barrett had the audacity to call a furnace.

The beast was stone cold.

———

Victoria wrapped the comforter over the knit beanie on her head. She threw another log on the fire and warmed her hands. Stomping her feet in front of the hearth, she cursed the furnace and gave thanks for the fireplace.

A pot of hot tea would warm her up. She shuffled to the kitchen in her makeshift cocoon.

Frost coated the windows over the sink. Scrubbing the glass with her sleeve, she peeked out. The skies had darkened early. Flashes of sleet and snow tapped the window. Grabbing the teapot, she opened the tap over the sink and waited. Nothing.

Barrett had warned her to keep at least a trickle of water flowing in one of the faucets. Was it that cold to freeze the pipes? She turned, kicking the dog's water bowl. A skim of ice clicked against the stainless steel sides. How could this be happening?

She glared over her shoulder at the calendar. "For cripes' sake! It's still fall," she said, blinking away the tears. A shiver of fear forced her to look at the thermostat.

Tilly looked up from her coiled position hunkered down in the pillow. The only thing she agreed to raise was an inquisitive brow.

Victoria was certain the dog curled tighter, stuck to the warm spot like a bur in a blanket.

"Smart girl."

She had to get help. After relinquishing the comforter for her down parka, she pulled on insulated mittens and headed for the white hell raging outside. Tilly barked when Victoria opened the door and the storm slammed in, threatening to knock her back from the porch.

Her flashlight cut through the dark, illuminating the snowflakes in front of her. It rode the wind, coming in horizontally. Barrett's house, complete with water and heat, tempted her to make the drive. The light flashed toward her little car. A snowdrift buried the hood, and that didn't count the five-foot drifts behind it.

The insane idea to drive in this mess was out.

"Okay," she muttered into the scarf wrapped around her face. "As long as I don't take a blind turn and fall through the ice on the lake, I should be at the Tewilligers's house in five minutes."

Victoria hesitated. Was it smarter to stay inside where it was an icebox? Or step out into the freezer? She hoped Harold would know what to do with the freakin' furnace.

"Barrett Collins, if you're on a beach working on your tan, I will personally kick your butt."

———

B arrett sat in the conference room, lawyers flanking him on both sides. The members of the medical advisory board filled the remaining seats.

Sitting still for hours, day in and day out, had stretched his patience until it was ready to snap. When it did, he hoped he would have enough control to keep from hurting anyone, especially the butcher sitting across from him.

Doctor Tim St. James, now head of the cardiac unit, leaned on his elbows and tapped his silver pen on the walnut table. The icy stare he'd been trying to hold for the last week had begun to waver.

"Mr. Collins," said St. James's lawyer. Barrett couldn't recall his name. Smith-something?

"Doctor," Barrett said.

"Excuse me?" Smith-something looked up from his paperwork. He widened his eyes for effect. "Didn't you leave your medical license five years ago?"

"I left the hospital on the night in question. Not my license." He leaned in. "And you know that." He cast his attention on everyone at the table. "You all do."

The condescending smile, the one used for idiots and toddlers having a meltdown, was back in place. "I see. Doctor. It says here, you walked away after the surgical procedure on your patient, Jessica Day. The reasons you stated at the time were that you were burned out. Why is that, Doctor Collins? What shut your system down?"

"What?" Barrett's jaws ached. He had a feeling Smith-something and his crew intended to go in for the kill and portray him as the screw-up. Yes, he probably shouldn't have left so soon after Jessica's passing. But she was the one that made him walk out the door and head north. To tranquility. He was ready to go back there, back to Victoria. His fingers rolled over the pencil in his hand. He leaned forward, scanning the men and women. "How about back-to-back 12-hour shifts in the ER? Hours where I was supposed to be relieved, but never was. And how about the constant stream of head traumas, shootings, and stabbings?"

He stared into St. James's face, boring into the man who once was his friend. Filling with painful memories, his voice lowered. "Car accidents involving little children. Kids and drug addicts OD'ing on their chemical of choice. How's that for starters?"

Barrett's lawyer, Mark Brandon, stilled him with a slight nudge of his foot.

"Yes," St. James's lawyer said. "Every Emergency Room's resources are taxed from time to time. I'm sure everyone here has that same story to tell, Mr. Collins." He paused before correcting, "Sorry, I forgot. Doctor." The readers dipped low on the bridge of Smith-something's nose. His pale eyes stared back at Barrett. "But I still have to ask. Why come forward with drug and alcohol allegations against Dr. St. James now? Where have you been all this time, doctor? Rehab, perhaps?" He tipped back in his chair, hands resting on his paunch, sated by his recent meal of Barrett-on-a-stick. "It is our belief that you had something to hide, and you ran."

Barrett's grip squeezed the chair arms. He lurched forward. If he were a panther, he would have been all over the lawyer, ripping his throat out. He pushed back the desire to maim the idiots in front of him. His purpose was to stop St. James from harming another patient.

St. James's pen tapping came in rapid-fire. "Barrett." He turned to his lawyer and the advisory board sitting around the table. "Doctor Barrett Collins is a fine doctor and surgeon. It's obvious there's some misunderstanding. Give us a minute, will you?"

Waving off Smith-something's rabid complaints, St. James confirmed he was safe and wanted some privacy with an old friend

"Barrett," Mark whispered. "As your attorney, I advise you to listen to what he has to say but agree and admit to nothing."

Barrett watched his ally walk out the door. His empty stomach ached. God, how he wished he had never opened this door. He had never wanted to go home so badly.

CHAPTER 29

Victoria hunkered over at the table, warming her hands around the bowl of stew. She dipped her spoon into the savory mixture and let the flavors coat her tongue. God bless Mrs. T! The stubborn woman wouldn't take no for an answer and forced the thermos of stew into Victoria's hands.

Tilly pressed into her leg. Whether it was for warmth or comfort, Victoria didn't know. Their developing companionship felt too good to send her to her dog pillow.

Harold stuck his head up the stairway and hollered, "You ready to come down here and let me give you a lesson?"

She set her bowl down and rose on stiff legs. "You betcha!"

The metal monstrosity hummed beside Harold. The basement holding the aging furnace had begun to heat up.

He hitched his snow bibs and tipped his head toward the furnace. "Can't imagine Barrett left without leaving instructions. Been limpin' this thing along for the last several years."

Victoria shoved her hands into the plaid flannel jacket she liked to wear indoors and felt Barrett's crumpled directions. She'd gone over everything on that page. "He must have forgotten something."

Harold's gray brows rose over his tortoiseshell reading glasses. "Lemme see whatcha got."

"I've been through every step. Each one at least four times." Withdrawing the paper from her pocket, she spread it on his outstretched hand.

His eyes widened and narrowed. "Pretty thorough. Can't imagine why he didn't write down one of the first things I'd do if the furnace doesn't start."

"He was in a rush to get on the road." She didn't feel the need to add that Barrett was irritated with her. When he left, she was hard-pressed to decide whether the weather outside was colder and stormier than the storm brewing between them. All she'd wanted to do was be there for him. But she couldn't do that if he wouldn't let her past the wall he'd built. It was clear, she wanted to pinch his head off when he tossed out the challenge before he left. Had she allowed Connor to change who she was?

"Well, here it is," Harold chuckled. He showed her the message written on the backside of the directions. "Looky here." He shook the paper under her nose. "It says, 'Check the pilot light.' Yup. That's what was wrong. Fire blew out."

"Well, so it does." Victoria's cheeks flared. The warmth shot up to circle her ears. She knew if she looked in the mirror that they'd be bright red.

"I got it going and was gonna walk you through it, but he does a pretty good job of explaining it. You want me to do it anyhow?"

Feeling contrite and wanting to climb into bed and pull the covers over her head, she said. "I'm sorry I dragged you out in the middle of a blizzard."

"Blizzard," he chuckled and shook his head. "Victoria, this is just a little squall. Betcha it'll blow itself out by the time I walk up these basement steps."

He shuffled his way past Mags's old boxes and barrels that Victoria hadn't had a chance to go through. They tipped as he crab-walked around them. Victoria steadied their rocking before they hit the floor. She had hoped Barrett or someone from town would step up and lay claim to them. That hadn't happened. It looked like it would make it onto her to-do list.

"Looky here." He grinned and pointed to the sun shining through the kitchen window. The snow had stopped, and the drifts glistened like piled diamonds. "Looks like I win that bet." He pulled open the cabinet under the sink. "In a little while, once the house warms up, if the pipes don't thaw out, you bring in your hairdryer. It'll heat the pipes up real fast."

Harold stood in the center of the kitchen, studying the cookbook spread out on the table. He glanced over his shoulder at her. "You planning on making one of Mags's feasts?"

"Thought about it. Don't know how good it'd be. Never cooked most of those recipes. Not too many have lived to tell about it."

He snorted his disbelief.

Tempted to reveal her losses, she sealed the food disasters behind her lips. He actually thought she was kidding. She hated to disappoint him.

"Helen quit cooking Thanksgiving dinner a couple of years back. Said it didn't matter because there weren't enough people sitting at the table." His fingers caressed the pages. "Oh, but I dearly loved it when Mags had her neighborly feasts."

Victoria swore she saw an unshed tear threatening to steal his manhood. Was he crying over missed turkey and stuffing? She shook her head. She bet Mrs. T cooked him a homemade meal every day of the week. Harold whipped a multi-colored hanky from his large pocket and wiped his eyes.

"I thought I'd have some friends over and wanted to ask you and Helen over for Thanksgiving a la Mags."

"Really? Now wouldn't that be nice."

She swallowed, unsure what got over her, but the words came out while the rest of her brain was trying to back-peddle and stuff them back in. She could barely boil pasta and an egg or two. Maybe she'd been huffing furnace gas fumes.

"I'll let Helen know. I bet she'd like that. Might even get her to bake a pie."

Despite the shining sun, the temperature outside was still below freezing. They pulled on their winter gear together.

"Where you going?" Harold asked. "No sense in both of us freezing our…noses off." The tips of his ears reddened.

His near curse made Victoria smile. The whole time she'd known him, he hadn't raised his voice or laid out a string of curses.

"Tell you what, Harold. I'll walk back halfway. Tilly needs to run around anyway." Tired of tripping over Barrett's sledgehammer, she carried it to the door. "Might as well move this thing while I'm at it."

"Gimme that ten-pounder," Harold said, holding out his hand. He swung it up on his shoulder with ease. "Tell me where to put it."

"I suppose the garden shed will do." She looked up at the clouds building in the distance. "I should probably bring in more wood. How long until we get another storm?"

"Now don't go fretting over the weather. A little snow is part of our Wisconsin buildup to winter in January."

They stepped off the back porch and stomped through the shin-high drifts. Other areas of the garden barely had snow. Patches of lawn peeked through the thin layer.

"Except for the cold and wind. And shoveling white stuff till you can't take it no more." He patted her mitten. "You just wait until tornado season. That's when you learn to bug out and sprint to the root cellar."

Victoria scrunched her nose. None of the real-estate documents mentioned anything about a root cellar. Nor had Barrett. "Do I have one of those?"

"Root cellar?" Harold paused, rubbing his chin. "Course you do. Let me think on where Mags kept hers." His eyes lit up and he smacked his thigh. "Come on, I'll show you."

He led the way to the garden shed and held open the door. The winter wind had picked up and tried to rip the handle out of his hand. "It's a ways away from the cottage. But Mags wanted it that way. She had a keen fear of being trapped in the basement."

Victoria nodded. She'd seen the movie *Twister* and didn't want to think about tornadoes. There was a season for them? How did she miss that in her pros and cons list?

Harold leaned the sledgehammer near the trapdoor. "You hear the sirens go off, you hightail it to the root cellar. Keep your emergency kit sealed nice and secure so that mice and spiders don't get into it. And have an extra pair of shoes nearby. Comes in handy when you run barefoot in the middle of the night."

They bent down to pull the lead ring on the trapdoor built into the floor. How would she ever lift it by herself? The door creaked on its hinges, revealing its dark gaping maw. How would she ever go down there alone, already terrified, and hide from a monster wind?

Oblivious of the panic building beside him, he continued with his tutorial of surviving a tornado and the beauty of the cellar. Victoria caught bits and pieces, but most of it was "*Mwa-mwa-mwa.*"

Harold lit a lamp tucked inside a cubbyhole. Victoria followed, every step she took, she wished Barrett were there to hold her hand. She prayed that if she ever had to run to the cellar that he'd be right there by her side.

"Mags said if she had to stay down here for hours at a time, she wanted safety and comfort." He lifted the lantern to shine over the room. "Looks like she has you well-stocked."

Canning jars lined the shelves. Some were empty, others were filled with the previous year's harvest of beets, pickles, green beans, corn, and tomatoes.

He swung the light and froze. "We best get out of here."

"What is it?" She pushed her way past his arm. Paper plates and empty to-go cups stained with old coffee littered the camp table. Someone had ripped open one of the sealed containers and scattered the supplies over the little bed built into the side of the wall. Rumpled blankets were tossed to the side.

"How...how long do you think it's been since someone was last here?"

Harold rubbed his thumb through a ridge of dust. "A couple months. More or less."

Victoria did the mental math in her head. "About the time Barrett started to..." Her gut tightened. That would make it about the time he started spending the night.

"Must have run the trespasser off," Harold said.

She swallowed the lump of fear wedged in her throat. This was not L.A. They didn't have homeless people looking for a place to crash for the night. What if he's still here? Hiding somewhere. She spun around, grabbing Harold's sleeve, she tugged him up the stairs.

"Oh, now, I think you're safe. I didn't notice any footsteps in the snow. And nothing was disturbed outside."

"Were you looking? I sure wasn't." She bent double, pressing her palms on her knees. Who would feel comfortable enough, desperate even, to sleep in a root cellar?

Harold's face was pale. The frown, creasing his forehead deepened in a V. "Let's make a call to Chief Graham."

———

Victoria clung to the pillow and waited in the chair by the fireplace while Chief Graham completed his search of the property.

Harold and Helen hovered around the living room to keep her

company. They held hands, talking quietly, trying not to get in the way.

Chief Graham came in and placed a comforting hand on Victoria's shoulder. "When does Barrett say he'll be back?"

"He didn't. Hasn't." She cleared her throat. "Haven't talked to him in at least a week or more." She looked up. "Can't you dust for fingerprints? Find some DNA?" She knew it was a long shot. Law enforcement in the country was not like they show on CSI. Chief Graham knew it, too.

"Victoria," Graham shifted and swung into the chair across from her. "We pulled the trash and bagged it in case something breaks. But you and I know those chances are slim. I've searched your property. And we put in a call, trying to get the latest on Connor Hemming."

No one knew where Connor had run. Every day the news of his past deeds became darker. Victoria couldn't imagine him settling into the earthen room. Then again, there was a time she would never have believed him capable of violence and twisted thinking.

She stood, wrapping the collar of her coat close to her chin. "I know."

Graham followed suit. His thumbs tucked into his gun belt. It reminded her of Barrett and his sexy tool belt, always dipped low on one hip. She blinked back the tears.

"You have your sat phone?" At her nod, he added. "You keep it charged and at your side. Mr. and Mrs. T are here for you if you need to holler out." He paused before leaving. "Keep Tilly next to you. She doesn't look too scary, but I have a feeling she's become one of your devoted fans."

Victoria watched his headlights swing out of the drive. It took a little doing, but Mr. and Mrs. T finally agreed to head home for the night. They were just a scream away.

She shut the door and slid the bolt home. The cottage was deathly silent, and she was alone.

Tilly bumped her hand. "Almost alone. Right, girl?" She scrubbed the golden retriever's head. "Where the heck is your daddy?"

CHAPTER 30

After weeks of studying the cookbook, Victoria finally felt like she was ready. She stared up at the bedroom ceiling and repeated the affirmation. "I can do this."

Tomorrow she would recreate Mags's Thanksgiving Dinner. The organic, farm-raised turkey waited for her at the Cove Market. The list of ingredients she needed for the other dishes was ready and tucked inside her purse. The extra items might put a pinch in the budget, but she had to have them to make it according to Mags's notations. If everything went as planned, there would be enough food for eight, possibly nine guests, if Barrett made it back from Chicago.

Pictures of burned bread and raw turkey danced in her head.

Her stomach quivered. What made her think she could pull this off? Until she'd moved to Wisconsin, she could barely boil water. Emboldened by Mags and her cookbook, she sent out the invitations, and to her horror, everyone accepted.

She trailed her fingers over Tilly's silky, golden coat. They had taken to sleeping together since the day she'd discovered the signs of a trespasser in her root cellar. Sometime during the night, the dog had tucked into her side, creating dead weight across the comforter, trapping Victoria. She wiggled her legs until she loosened the blankets and angled her position.

Tilly acknowledged her efforts, rolling one chocolate brown eye in her direction. She closed it and relaxed her body, settling deeper into the mattress.

"Come on," Victoria said. "I have a turkey that needs to go into the oven tomorrow. If you're a good girl, I'll let you supervise." Puffing, she shoved and rolled to her side. Her feet hit the floor, the chill stealing her breath. She grabbed her slippers and slid her icy toes inside.

Shuffling to the window, she pulled back the curtain. Her heart squeezed. Gunmetal gray skies threatened to pour out the latest storm. When was the last time she checked the weather?

Without an internet connection at home, her only source was to drive to the market office. Thankfully, she no longer had to hide using the store's internet ever since Harold admitted to Helen that he was getting Victoria's accounting help. The paycheck had come in handy and gave her a cushion to rebuild her bank account. The successful investments she and the seniors enjoyed had helped smooth the way. But, on days like this, when it looked like a storm was brewing, she didn't relish the drive to town. She'd rather stay inside, sip a cup of hot chocolate and warm her feet by the fire.

The open cookbook laying on the countertop beckoned her attention. A corner of the spreadsheet she'd been working on the night before peeked out from the pages. The hours to Thanksgiving were ticking down. No matter what she wanted to do with a cup of cocoa and bunny slippers, she had to make the drive into town. Guests were coming.

———

Victoria clutched the steering wheel in a white-knuckle grip. Snow floated down, innocently swirling through the air, unaware of the terror it caused when the convertible's back end slid to the right. The tires gained purchase when they dropped below the pavement, spraying the frozen dirt by the side of the road. She bounced back, trying to keep the car between the blurred yellow lines.

Barrett was right. Her little red beauty handled the winter like a bear on skates. She should have listened and found the money for snow tires. "Where are you?" she whispered between gritted teeth. "I need you."

Tears burned her lids. She blinked, too afraid to let go of the wheel to wipe them from her eyes. Her heart tapped her rib cage. It pushed the blood through her veins, racing to her ears.

Victoria pulled into the store parking lot eerily empty of cars. Unaided by visible white lines, snowmobiles, and four-wheelers angled in some semblance of organization.

She clambered out of the car, gripping the door to steady herself. Standing on shaking legs, she hugged her purse to her chest. She ducked her head and pushed against the blowing wind and icy needles.

Two men, bundled head to toe in insulated gear, stood side-by-side. They held the railing like it was a lifeline and cautiously stepped down on the first step. The wind caught the scarves wrapped around their faces. One of the men trapped the knitted yarn whipping the air.

His face lit up, his eyes sparkling over a hunter orange scarf. His gray brows rose, "Hey there, Victoria. Are we still on for dinner?"

In the last two weeks, that man had talked to her about each delectable item Mags had ever served. Victoria had some huge shoes to fill.

"I don't know why not, George." She grinned up at him, gritting her teeth against the cold. "I'm here to pick up the bird."

Fred stopped beside him. His muffled voice piped in, "Winter's coming early."

She shifted, ready to move them out of the way. "Unless something happened with the order, we should have that feast we've been talking about."

"Good to hear," Fred said. "Thought maybe the snow would scare you off." He shook his head, his scarf and fur hat moving in unison. "Can't postpone Thanksgiving. Then it would just be a big ol' meal."

Victoria glanced up at the heavy sky. Storm clouds boiled in the distance. It looked a lot like the squall they had a few weeks back. She had thought it was a blizzard and Mr. T made sure to tell everyone in the cove that she'd feared a few inches of snow.

"George, are you still bringing the pumpkin pie?"

"Got it right here." He held up the grocery bag. "Pecan, too."

Fred grunted. "I'm bringing beer."

His contribution did not surprise her. "Sounds good." She nodded, mentally ticking the items off her list. "Then gentlemen, it looks like dinner is on. Be there at six o'clock."

"Gentlemen." Fred snorted. "Is that fancy talk for you're expecting me to dress up? Cause if you are, you're gonna be disappointed."

"You guys come as you like."

The men parted for her like the red sea.

"Don't you worry about the snow keeping us away," Fred said. "We have our snowmobiles."

George laid a gentle hand on her sleeve to slow her progress up the steps. He caught her elbow to steady her. "When's Barrett getting in?"

Her heart squeezed. Her father's command to smile whispered in her ears. She shrugged, putting on a mask of indifference. "Not sure. Guess we see him when we see him."

They turned around, following her up to the store porch and out of the elements. Victoria was relieved to get out of the wind, but she didn't relish the third degree on her and Barrett's lack of communication. She'd already read into it. The silence from Chicago did not bode well.

"Are you telling me you and Barrett haven't been burning up the airwaves?" Fred swore under his breath. "The man's an idiot, and I mean to tell him that next time I see him."

"Fred." Surprised from his outburst, she fumbled for words to calm him down. "I'm sure he has a good reason."

"Bull," he grunted out. "Oughta knock some sense into that fool. Been gone too long. Needs to be here for you."

Her cheeks heated despite the frigid air. She shot a pleading look to George. Ever the peacemaker, he was sure to call Fred to heel.

George's parka bounced as he lifted his shoulders. "The man speaks from experience."

"You got that right." Fred turned around, stomping down the steps to his machine.

Victoria swore she saw tears forming in Fred's eyes. A ridiculous thought. It must be the cold making them water.

"Cantankerous old fool." George watched his friend head across the parking lot. The snowmobile roared to life. He patted Victoria's arm. "Don't you worry. Snowstorm or not, we'll be there." His gaze spanned the parking lot and houses nestled across the street. "My money's on Barrett. He'll be there too."

Victoria smiled, leaning over she kissed his jaw. "Thanks."

Blushing, George nodded toward the skies. "You best get home quick. It's comin' in hard."

Harold stuck his head around the doorjamb. "Your order's ready. Got everything you wanted." Wrapped in his winter parka and snow boots, he was prepared for a trip to the Antarctic. "Closing up a little early tonight."

Victoria waved her hand. "See you tomorrow."

"You betcha. Helen has been baking all day." His eyes beamed, radiating warmth, and unspoken joy. "She hasn't spent this much time over the holiday, since...well, you know. Our boy, Tommy." The light on his face dimmed, then reignited. "It sure is a good thing to see." He paused, "Mind, you don't stay long."

"I promise. Just have a few things to finish up."

————

V ictoria tore her attention from the store's computer screen. She meant to spend a few minutes researching Chicago doctors and surgeons. Those minutes had turned into hours.

She didn't know if it was better to have headlines or not. For Barrett, there was nothing on the internet regarding physician misconduct. But there had been several news updates on Connor's activities. Chief Graham probably already knew the trouble her ex-boyfriend was in with the law. But just to be sure, she'd make a detour and swing by the sheriff's office on her way home.

On a last-minute whim, she clicked her email box. Recent reports on the investments she'd made for some of the seniors in town were bound to have dropped in. A smile lifted the corners of her mouth. Several seniors in Honeybrooke would be thrilled with her financial report. A very Merry Christmas surprise for many of them.

Scrolling through the numerous emails, her hand paused over the mouse. She didn't recognize the email address, but the subject line in caps read URGENT: DONALD BANNING.

Her heart beating like a scared rabbit, she prayed her father was all right. She clicked on the envelope. The chime rang and the email popped open. She sat back, pressing her fingers to her mouth, suppressing a cry.

The email contained a scanned photo of a wedding couple, the bride's head missing from the shot. Body parts were scanned and scattered across the page. Cut out words, spelled out 'In pieces when we're not together. V. Time to come home. To me.'

Scrambling for her phone, she dialed her dad's number. The air in her lungs burned, squeezing down a wave of panic. When the ringing stopped, she pressed her ear close to the receiver and listened to silence. "Hello? Dad?"

"Victoria." His shocked voice rumbled over the airwaves. "Are you in California?"

"Um, no. Still in Wisconsin." She ducked her head, focusing on the computer screen and rubbed her temples. The adrenaline that swamped her body had sucked back, emptying the reserve of energy she normally used when dealing with her dad.

"Thought maybe you were frozen out there and ready to come back to civilization."

Victoria closed her eyes, shutting out the image of Connor's email. "So, you're good? Healthy, I mean."

"Course. Couldn't be better."

"Okay. Good." Her heart racing, she plunged ahead. "Look, Connor is…"

"Sorry, Victoria, you caught me going out the door. On my way to Vegas."

"Dad—"

"Gotta go. We'll talk. Soon," he said and hung up.

She drew back and stared at the phone. "Happy Thanksgiving to you too." The air in her lungs burned, squeezing down a wave of panic. Connor had found another way to attack her.

Taking a deep breath, she hit forward and sent the email on to Chief Graham. A copy shot off the printer. It went into her purse. She would add it to the growing file of evidence at home. Scrambling for her coat and groceries, she fumbled her way out the market's door. She clutched the bags, the coveted turkey swinging into her leg.

The wind screamed against the door. She shoved, fighting it open. Snow pelted her in the face. She blinked away the flakes.

Cautiously, she stepped gingerly on the ice-covered steps. Her feet slid. Her purse snagged the railing, jerking her to the side, and the grocery bags swung out. Scrambling to regain her balance, she crab-walked across the empty parking lot. If it hadn't been near blizzard conditions, she would have kissed her little red car. "Please, God, get me home," she whispered.

———

B arrett hunched over the steering wheel as the truck crawled over the road. He planned to surprise Victoria and hadn't thought to call her. The five-hour drive had already stretched into eight hours. The snowstorm took a turn for the worse, creating hazardous conditions. Ice, sleet, snow, winds, and now whiteouts. It figured. No matter how bad he ached to get back to Honeybrooke Cove, the snowdrifts and ice remained relentless in slowing him down for miles.

Now, it was all he could do to keep the truck's snow tires on the road. The back end of the truck swung wide on a patch of ice. He let up on the gas and felt the tires straighten out. A sigh of relief passed his lips, letting him know he'd been holding his breath with every turn he took.

He grinned. The last turn would bring their cottage into sight. Anxious to have Victoria in his arms, he took the corner too fast. The tires bumped into a drift, shaking the truck's frame.

It didn't look like she'd tried to shovel the drive. Served him right for not calling ahead. The tires crept over the drifts, mashing them down, cutting a path to a dark house.

Headlights swept the area Victoria optimistically called her garden. This time of year, it looked like a snowman's playground. He flinched. He swore something moved behind the white vertical drifts. The snow pressed around Mag's memorial towers of stones, creating unbalanced snowmen. Snow-zombies. He half-expected them to move toward the light.

Barrett wiped his face, feeling every mile in his aching bones, and apparently his brain. He climbed out of the pickup. Lord, it felt like he'd come back home.

He tested the doors. The place was sealed tight. A tingle of concern shivered over his belly. Tilly stood on the other side, ferociously barking at his attempts to get in. The winds howled, forcing the blizzard into whiteout conditions. A gnawing dread tugged his breath. "Where is she?"

CHAPTER 31

Victoria chipped at the coating of ice on the windshield until she could no longer feel the ice scraper in her hand. Numb from head-to-toe, she scrambled inside her little car and stomped her boots onto the floorboard.

She blew on her frozen fingers, trying to get the feeling back into her hands. The wind howled and shook the convertible's roof. It had to let up soon. *Please, God.*

The longer she sat there, the harder the snow fell. Giving up the wait on the winter squall to pass over, she decided to skip seeing the sheriff and go straight home. Victoria took a deep breath. She gripped the steering wheel until her knuckles ached and inched out onto the snow-packed road. The tires spun and slid, catching just in time as she turned the first corner. Snowflakes came straight at her, creating a white tunnel until they struck the windshield. Visibility had reduced to where she could barely see the next turn. At least, she hoped it was the right road.

Victoria blinked, her eyes fighting the urge to stare into the storm. She glanced at the rearview mirror, made worthless by the layer of ice clinging to her car. She checked her side mirror. Something ghostly wavered outside, following her. At least she wasn't the only one out in this mess.

Headlights came closer and closer. She flicked the high beams on. Still too close. Her mouth dried as she questioned whether to step down on the accelerator. The convertible jerked from the impact from behind. Too late, her car spun and hit the ditch. The sound of metal scraping, hitting dirt and ice, the screaming engine registered in her ears.

The pressure behind Victoria's eyes tunneled through the darkness. She tried to force them open despite the evil elves working on the back of her head with little pickaxes.

Her arms were heavy, weighted with anvils, trapped by her sides. She couldn't remember when she'd had so much to drink. All she wanted was to sleep the pain away. No, wait. She hadn't been drinking. Never when she was behind the wheel. Nausea built when she moved her head to clear it.

She shivered. Her fingers were stiff. Numbness seeped into her boots. The furnace must have stopped working again.

"Barrett," she croaked. Hearing his name come out slow, like cold molasses, her brain began sorting through fact and fiction.

She was sitting up, not lying under a toasty comforter. Pushing against the lethargy, she fought to focus on her surroundings. She shoved the airbag out of the way. Blue dashboard lights illuminated the car's interior.

"Okay. In a car." She felt along the seatbelt. "Sitting in an angle. Car, not running." Rubbing her fingernail over the frosted window, she added. "Stranded in a blizzard. Not so good." Her teeth clattered together. "Freezing."

The details of how she came to be hanging by a seatbelt and draped over the passenger seat came back to her. She wasn't alone. "Help!" she called. "Is anyone out there?"

Dazed, she peered out the windshield, searching for the other vehicle. No headlights to light the way. No red taillights to lead her out of the ditch. Snow whisked across the deserted road. She couldn't think of one resident of Honeybrooke Cove that would leave behind a stranded driver. *Did I imagine it?*

The storm continued to blow and rage. The ragtop could only keep so much outside, and frost had already formed on the inside of the windows. The time to wait for anyone to come to her rescue had passed.

Victoria took stock of her body. Some sore muscles. A bump on the head. Her nose hurt. Her skin stung. But no blood.

Then she took stock of the car. It had taken the brunt of the impact. She tested the key. Nothing turned, and the interior lights flickered and dimmed. Time to call for reinforcements.

She snagged her purse strap and dragged it out from the pile of debris spilled onto the floorboard. Her hands shook as she frantically searched the pockets. No! Her sat phone was missing. She wracked her fuzzy memory, certain she'd picked up the phone on her way to the car.

Should probably stay here. Wait for someone to come by. The absence of the phone, always tethered to her side like a life preserver, made her vulnerable. Connor's last email filtered into her thoughts. She had to get home. Where it was safe. Although the snowdrifts and low visibility made everything look different, she was maybe a mile from home. Maybe less. Maybe more. "I have to try."

After gathering the groceries that had spilled over the floor, she dragged the twenty-pound bird across the seat. "You're coming with me." Angled in the ditch, the car made gravity her enemy. Bracing one arm into the center console, she unlatched the seatbelt and maneuvered one leg out the driver's side door.

The storm pushed her about like a bit of paper on the ground. The wind caught the door, slamming it into her leg, shoving her back into the leather seats.

———

B arrett stood in Mr. and Mrs. T's kitchen. The wind rattled the windows, spitting icy needles against the glass. On any given day, the sweet scent of butter and sugar would have made his mouth water. It mingled with the savory beef stew simmering on the stove. The smell of comfort food should have sent his empty stomach growling. Instead, he and the Tewilligers huddled together, worry marring their pale faces. Barrett glared at the phone in his hand. The constant ring on the other end of the call twisted his guts with each unsuccessful attempt to reach Victoria.

He looked up from willing the phone to make a connection. "When did you say you last saw her, Harold?"

"Right before I left for home. She was working on the store computer. Told her she should head out before the real stuff hit. Must be over an hour or two." He scratched his head, looking sheepish. "Might be a little more. I stopped at the Duck Blind."

Helen sucked in a short breath. "Why'd you do that?"

His already pink cheeks flushed to a cherry-red. He set his attention to an imaginary spot on the kitchen table. "Because I like Lyle's pumpkin pie and knew you wouldn't be making any."

"Harold Tewilliger. I would have baked you a pie if you said you wanted one."

Barrett nudged them back on track. An hour or two could be explained. But not answering her phone made the red flags wave. "Why isn't she answering?"

His phone rang. They all jumped and let out a collective breath. Barrett punched in the speaker.

"Barrett. It's me. Graham. You back in town?"

"I am. Glad you called." Static crackled over the airwaves.

"Good to hear it." Graham's voice garbled, cutting off his words. "Want you to keep a close watch on her. Hear me?"

"Graham." Barrett gripped the phone, his knuckles tightened. "We can't find Victoria."

"Are you sure? She sent me a copy of an email a little while ago. Brought my short hairs to attention."

"How long ago?" Barrett asked.

"About an hour and a half, maybe." Graham paused. "She's not answering her phone?"

"No." Barrett glanced at the window as he zipped up his coat. The wind was picking up speed.

Mr. T leaned into the phone. "Hey, Graham," he hollered. "It's me, Harold. I sure hope she hasn't tried to drive her bitty car in this stuff. I didn't see any snow tires on it. Not that they'd do much good in this storm."

Barrett shut his eyes. He should have winterized her car before he left for Chicago. "Are you where you can check on the store? See if her car is still in the parking lot?"

"Son, I'm on my way now. I'll make the circuit to her cottage. You stay put. I don't need to rescue anyone else out in this mess."

The Tewilligers offered each other a comforting smile. Barrett waved off the warning and narrowed in on something mentioned earlier. "Graham, what's this about an email? What do I need to look out for?"

Static crackled. "Her ex…"

Barrett stared at the dead phone in his hand. "What?" He rose, ready to bolt for his truck.

Helen gripped his wrist, tightening over his coat. "You heard the sheriff. You can't go out in this."

"My truck will handle it."

"A body can't see two feet in front of them."

"Son," Harold said. "At least wait to hear back from Graham. No point in putting yourself in danger if she is snuggled up on the office cot."

Barrett looked at the clock on the wall. It had been over two hours since anyone had seen or heard from Victoria. His stomach twisted in a knot. He shoved his hands under his arms to hide the tremor that radiated throughout his body. "I wish we knew what Connor had threatened this time."

Helen left the room and returned with an old shotgun. "Just in case," she said.

Barrett's thoughts galloped, speeding over worst-case scenarios. Each one was darker than the one before it.

Helen set the weapon next to the door and focused on making a fresh pot of coffee. Harold squeezed her shoulder, kissing her on the temple as he walked past. He went into the garage, shutting the door behind him.

The phone jangled in Barrett's hand. "Graham. Okay. No. Not yet. But. Look—"

Harold came back in, holding a set of snowmobile gear. "Tell him, you and I will be on snowmobiles and heading into town. We'll meet him halfway, whoever gets there first. And don't run us over."

Barrett held the phone from his ear before ending the call. "He's not too happy about it but said no promises."

Harold tossed him the suit. "Let's go." He wrapped his arm around Helen's waist. "Sweetheart, you keep that stew hot and your biscuits warm. We'll need it when we get back. Keep that gun handy too."

"Don't you worry about me." She cupped his gray-whiskered jaw. "You two go find her." Her lips connected with his for a lingering kiss before shoving him toward the door. "I'll have the lights on to help you find your way home."

Barrett followed, bemused. He had never seen them so kind and caring toward one another. He couldn't help but wonder if Victoria had something to do with it.

He ran to his truck and pulled out the emergency kit he always kept ready. Helen shoved a thermos and several blankets into his arms, adding to the load. Once they tucked their rescue gear safely away, he and Harold climbed onto the snowmobiles. They moved slowly over a drift and onto the road.

The terrain had changed in a matter of hours. Barrett followed close behind, impatient to rock the throttle. He took his cue from Harold. The man had lived in Wisconsin all his life and could track with the best of them. He prayed he was right.

————

Victoria rubbed her forehead. Her limbs didn't want to work. Someone had tied bricks to her feet while she slept.

Shivering, she scooted deeper into the car seat. "Sh…should have tried to make it." When the wind had caught the car door, slamming it into her aching body, she'd figured that was a sign that she needed to stay in the car and wait for help. She had crawled back into the car and prayed. "A sign from God," she said, her voice deep from the freezing air. She giggled, then frowned and patted the turkey sitting next to her. "Well, Tom, it looks like you might have a reprieve."

Her gaze caught on the darkness surrounding her. Black diamonds everywhere. Her heart ached for Barrett. Worse than her head. It no longer mattered why he'd been away for so long. The anger had died out, like the guttered flame at the end of a candle. She desperately wanted him to come home. He'd stolen a place in her heart. What was it that Mags had written about Barrett? That he had a piece of his puzzle missing. Somehow, Mags knew that missing piece was out there. And it was Victoria. She'd found the missing puzzle piece to her heart too.

A completed puzzle formed in front of her. A hologram. It was Barrett and her, spinning, holding hands, laughing, caressing, and loving. She stretched out a finger to touch it. It shattered. Icicles flew into tiny fragments. The completed puzzle was gone.

Frowning, her face scrunched in pain from the cold. Tears burned and cooled, leaving a slick trail of ice down her cheeks.

Her father's voice drifted into her muddled thoughts. *'Smile!'*

Victoria was too tired to fight. "I am Daddy. Maybe you should learn to smile...and love again, too."

———

Muffled voices urged her to wake up, prodding and poking her to respond. Light cut through the darkness. Aching warmth. Pleasure, then excruciating pain needled into her limbs. *God, I hurt.*

"Sweetheart." Warm liquid pressed to her lips. Forced down, it coated her throat. Revitalizing energy worked its way through her core. Her feet and hands burned as tiny fire ants marched across her skin.

She turned her head. Light glowed around a sparkly helmet. Blue eyes, the color of the Caribbean ocean, stared at her. "Barrett?"

His gaze flicked over her, moving nearly as fast as his hands. "Sweetheart, don't move. Just open your eyes."

Her heart began to beat a different rhythm, one that held hope instead of giving up. "You're here. You found me." She scrunched her face. "What took you so long?"

He lifted her hand to his mouth. "Baby, you scared us."

"I thought I lost my puzzle piece." She rolled her head, the weight of it extraordinarily heavy. "I'm so glad I didn't."

Lights swung into her eyes. White lines creased the sides of his mouth. "Baby, you have to stay awake now. Can you look at me?"

Roaming hands felt her up. She giggled and did her best to focus on the moving light. "Uh-huh."

"Are you hurt anywhere besides that bump on your head?"

"Just my heart." She captured his hand and moved it over her breast. "Why'd you stay away so long?"

Footsteps stomped behind them. Headlights cut through the

swirling snow. "Barrett, can we move her? They say in this weather the ETA for the ambulance is at least four hours away."

"Smacked her head pretty good. Looks like hypothermia is setting in." He glanced over his shoulder. "Graham, I've got my medical kit. I'd like to get her to the house and get her warm. If things deteriorate, we can make a different call."

"Put her in my truck. You can ride with her."

Victoria floated out of the car. The wind cut through her coat and brought another wave of shivers.

"It's too cold to mess with trying to tow your machine. We'll come back for it once we get her settled," Graham said over her shoulder.

"Wait!" She gripped the doorframe. "I can't leave the turkey."

"Victoria," Barrett growled under his breath.

"Thanksgiving."

Harold stuck his head over the procession. "I've got it. Don't you worry."

Satisfied, Victoria let them settle her into the backseat. Blankets wrapped around her shoulders and tucked under her legs. The warmth was bliss. Then the fire ants returned to bite her feet and legs.

Barrett sat next to her. He cupped his body around hers and blew into her palms. His protective arms held her as they followed Harold's snowmobile maneuvering through the drifts.

Victoria closed her eyes and let her body sink into the liquid heat.

"Baby," Barrett patted her cheek. "You have to stay awake for a little while longer."

She grimaced, wanting desperately to sleep.

"Talk to me. Tell me about the dinner you're planning."

"Mags's special menu. Some of the same guests she had one year." Victoria peeled her lids open. "Chief Graham is coming. Aren't you?"

Her announcement met with silence. She struggled to sit up

from the swaddled blankets. "It'll be just like Mags's Thanksgiving. Well, almost. The chefs have changed." She snorted, thinking she was funny. Graham took his eye from the road long enough to gauge her in his rearview mirror.

Barrett shifted so that he could flash the light in her eyes. "Who else is coming to this feast of yours?"

She started pulling names from a jumbled list in her aching head. "Me and you, Fred and George, The Ts, Teresa, and her son Jackson. And you, Graham. You have to come." She paused, her fingers still in the count. "I hope everyone can make it." She flicked another finger up. "Oh, and Hetty Eldridge."

The police car swerved. They swung wide, blowing out drifts, narrowly missing a fence line. Graham got the vehicle under control before they hit Victoria's mailbox.

He pulled into the drive, slid the gear into park before angling to stare at her over his shoulder. "Hetty Eldridge? S'pose her daughter has to come too."

"Susan? Yeah. Poor thing doesn't get out unless she takes her mother."

Disgruntled, he pushed out of the car, muttering under his breath, "Won't that be a hot mess."

CHAPTER 32

B undled in soft blankets, Victoria sat on the kitchen counter and did her best to focus on Barrett's finger. He stood between her legs. She didn't care if anyone else was in the living room. All she wanted to do was wrap her body around him and never let go. Instead, his serious side was out, and he was playing doctor.

Her gaze dropped to his mouth. How long had it been since their lips had touched?

"Your pupils are of equal size. That's good." He dropped his hand to her thigh. "You cannot really think there will be a Thanksgiving Dinner here tomorrow."

Ignoring the warmth radiating through a pair of gray sweats and two blankets, Victoria moved to shimmy down. "I'll do as I want, Barrett Collins. And I want the meal here."

His fingers braced against her knees, stopping her escape. "You need to rest. You've been through a lot tonight." Oblivious of her wrath, he stroked her jaw. "I'm worried about you."

"Really? Is that why you left weeks ago and forgot to call?" The heat in her cheeks, stained pink from the cold, heightened. She gripped the blankets wrapped around her like a royal cape and brushed his hand away.

"I couldn't break away. There were things I had to do. To set right. I told you that."

Jumping down, she took an intimidating step closer. "Oh, of course," she said, poking him in the chest. "You have this…" She forked the air with her fingers, "thing you had to fix on your own."

"I'm sorry. It became complicated when the attorneys were involved." He tugged on her hand. "Sit down. Let me finish checking you out and make sure you're safe. After that, if you still feel like it, you can rip my head off."

Turning her face, she offered resistance, fighting the tears. Her chin wobbled. She didn't want him to see how much he'd hurt her. "You didn't even call to check on Tilly."

When he brushed his lips over her knuckles, the irritation she'd been trying to hang onto deflated like day-old seltzer. "I knew I had left her in the capable hands of a strong, determined woman." He led her to the chair, gently pressing her down. "I need to examine you closer. You haven't had time to warm up all the way." He tilted her chin, turning it to the left and right.

She winced when he probed the bump on her forehead.

"Sorry. The swelling isn't too bad. Probably because your body temp had lowered. We'll put some ice on it in a bit. The bruising is probably more from the airbag." He spread an ointment over her skin. "Like a rug burn." He kissed the top of her head.

"Then there's no reason I can't go on with the plans."

"Why are we even discussing this? If the storm doesn't let up, we won't see anyone for a couple of days."

Victoria stiffened her back. "We will be eating turkey tomorrow. With or without you."

The Tewilligers stood in the doorway. Their eyes wide, their glances skimmed over Victoria's face. They cringed with empathy and shot their attention to Barrett.

Chief Graham parted them like the red sea. "Everything all right in here?"

"We're fine," Victoria snapped. "Just fine."

Graham nodded. "Think you can give me something to put in my report before I head out in this blizzard?"

She regretted her irritable response as soon as it registered. Unwilling to let them think she was ungrateful, she rubbed her temple. "Thanks for the rescue. All of you," she said. "How'd you know to come out in this mess?" The realization that they'd all been there for her deepened her guilt. "How did any of you know?"

"You can put it all on Barrett." Graham nodded toward the man standing in front of her. He had ducked his head and was busily putting his medical kit in order.

"Barrett?" she whispered. "How'd you know?"

A flush washed up to his ears, pinking the outer shell. His hands paused, stilling on the kit's latch. The depth of blue glittered back at her. "Baby, I just knew you had to be out there somewhere, and you needed me." Aware the Tewilligers and the sheriff were standing close behind him, doing their best not to eavesdrop, he cleared his throat. "Us. You needed us." He glanced up, locking eyes with a grinning Mrs. T.

"Seems to me, a reward is in order," Harold said, his voice gruff with emotion.

Helen elbowed him in the ribs.

"What?" The tips of his ears reddened. "All I'm saying is Barrett may get himself a little kiss, but I expect he'll require more."

"Makes sense to me." Victoria snagged the front of Barrett's shirt and jerked him down. Her strength returning, she captured the back of his neck and planted a long, deep kiss. Any icicles still flowing through her veins melted at the touch of their lips. A slow upsurge of liquid desire rushed into her limbs, into her stomach, warmed her heart. In an instant, she wanted everyone but Barrett out of the house.

"You get any ideas Harold Tewilliger," Mrs. T warned, "and I will smack that special pumpkin pie I baked for you over your head."

Harold laughed and scooped his wife into his arms. "Ah, woman, I am grateful you have a patient spirit."

Victoria released her hold on Barrett. Since he'd been leaning into the kiss, he stumbled toward her chair. Dazed, a corner of his swollen, kiss-stained mouth lifted in a hungry smile. Swirling tails of desire slid over her skin. She tore her attention away from the silent secrets he offered to share with her. "As for the rest of you, the offer stands. No matter the weather, I intend to have Thanksgiving dinner here."

Barrett stepped back, his arms folded across his chest. "We have to watch you, check on you every few hours for head trauma."

"Let us help, dear," Helen edged closer. "The bread and pies are done." Warming to her idea, she beamed with enthusiasm. "I can manage some of the sides." Seeing that Barrett was about to knock down her suggestion, she held her hand up. "If no one can get through the roads tomorrow, and it's just me helping out, Harold and I will still be able to make it over and nothing will go to waste."

"I say let's go for it," Victoria said. "Graham, you get all that down? You willing to push your way over here tomorrow?"

Graham held his pad of paper and pen positioned, ready to go. "I'll do my best. Now, if you would, Victoria. I'm waiting to take your statement. How'd you get in the ditch?"

She sat back in her chair and recounted the events of leaving the market. Sliding down the steps. "Bet that's where my phone is." She shot a glance at Harold. "Be careful when you're digging those steps out. You'll want to check the snowdrifts for my phone."

"And add some salt," Graham agreed. "Nearly broke my neck on those things."

Harold blanched. "I'll get on it." He was all too familiar with the threat of a lawsuit due to icy steps. "I meant to do it before I left for the day and forgot when I noticed my shovel and a new pair of winter gloves and boots were missing from the back steps." He swore under his breath.

Graham paused from jotting down his notes. "Theft?"

"Nah, probably just misplaced by one of the kids I hired for the holidays. I just need to have a look around the store." Harold turned to Victoria. "I'll look for your phone too. Should show up in the snow. It bein' bright yellow."

She smacked her palm on the table. "I can't believe I've lost it already."

"It's waterproof," Barrett added. "We'll see how good it really is."

"In the meantime—" Victoria said.

"I'm staying with you. I'll be so close to you; you can dial my phone through my navel."

"Folks," Graham said, "now that we have that settled, would you please let me have a few minutes with Victoria?"

Harold backed away, but Helen wouldn't leave until she had worked out the timing for tomorrow's meal with Victoria. A few minutes later, they were still making all the noises to leave and promises to contact each other if anything came up.

They watched the couple cross the yard. Bundled up the way they were, you would think they were one of the stone snowmen standing guard in Mags's rock garden.

"Okay, sheriff, I'm all yours," Victoria said.

"Anything else you can recall? Any little thing. It might seem like nothing, but put all together, it's what holds the puzzle together."

Victoria ducked her head, trying to piece the rest of the night. The fear of driving in the storm. The car moving out of control.

"Wait," Barrett said. His fingers tightened protectively over her shoulder. "Graham. You've seen her little car. It doesn't have the right tires. It has a canvas top, for God's sakes. Heck, she's never driven in this kind of weather, and we all can agree that she shouldn't have been out in it."

"Hey! That's not fair." Victoria threw off the blankets, rising from her throne like a vanquishing queen. "I would have made it home just fine if that idiot didn't have his high beams on." She stopped, her eyes widening. "Graham, there was another car. It came out of nowhere. I know that sounds cliché, but it's the truth. One minute, it's whiteout conditions. Then headlights. And..." She cupped her hands over her ears, rehearing the grind of metal.

"Someone ran you off the road, and you're just now telling us?" Barrett asked. He swept his hand over her head, rubbing the back of her neck. "Sweetheart."

Graham's frown deepened. "Now don't you fret, Victoria. Forgetting happens a lot. Especially when there's been a trauma." He caught Barrett's eye, motioning him to follow.

"Oh, no you don't," she said. "I want to know what you're thinking."

Caught in the act of concealing information from her, the sheriff paused and leaned against the doorframe. "I'm thinking that I want your car towed so that the snow can melt off and I can get a better look at it."

His phone jangled on his hip. Nodding, he took down some notes. "Yes, sir. Will do."

He hung up and headed for the door. "You get some rest, Victoria. I aim to have a fine dinner tomorrow night. And don't worry about your car. We'll take good care of it."

He turned, pressing his palm into Barrett's shoulder. "Walk me to the door, will ya?" He lowered his voice, but Victoria could still hear. "There's been a break-in at the Peabody cabin. Looks like someone might have done a little trespassing."

"Not a common thing around here."

Graham squinted over his notes. "Victoria tell you about the signs of a trespasser in the cellar?"

"Not yet." Barrett squared his shoulders. "Be one of the first things we talk about. Lord, what has been going on while I was out of town?"

"Appears that ex of hers has been mighty busy of late. Not say'n it's him. All I'm say'n is to stay on your toes."

"I'll keep close. You call me if you find anything out. I've got my phone on."

"Will do, Doc." Graham's smile reached clear to his toes. "Thanks for patching me up so I can still do my job. Good thing I'm not stuck in an easy chair watching the clock sweep away my life." He held out his hand. "I owe ya, Doc. I owe ya."

Barrett shook his head. "It's what I do, Graham. Can't seem to stop myself."

"Always said you make a pretty slick rocking chair, but I think it's high time you do what you were meant to do." He tipped his gloved fingers to his hat and headed for his truck. In a matter of steps, the whiteout swallowed up his shadowy figure. Barrett secured the door behind him.

"What does he mean, Barrett?" Victoria asked.

"Mags always said I was sent here for a purpose." The circles under his eyes were dark against his pale skin.

"What you were meant to do?"

They went to the kitchen, turning out lights as they went. The last bolt was clicked into place. Tilly padded behind them. The days and weeks away may have worn him out, but the last few hours had exhausted everyone.

"Practice medicine again."

He stopped. His fingers threaded carefully through Victoria's hair. Kneading the stiffening muscles in her neck. Before morning, she was apt to feel every jangled nerve ending.

"That's what you've been doing in Chicago?" She let him sink into her, absorbing him. He lifted his head to kiss her. The kiss of the weary. She returned the caress, placing tiny kisses along the creases of his eyes. The high cheekbones. Along his muscular neck. "Why didn't you just tell me? I would have listened." Her hands cupped each side of his head, pulling him up to look at her. "I'm proud of you."

"I let you down. You could have been seriously hurt because of me. Because I wasn't there." He tilted her face.

"But I wasn't."

His mouth contorted. "Not this time." He tenderly tucked a curl behind her ear. "You need to get some rest."

Victoria shook her head. "Come sit by me." She held out her hand and led the man she'd been missing, the man she'd been waiting for, to the living room. A fire in the fireplace made the room cozy and inviting. She vowed to never complain about Wisconsin's steamy summers ever again.

Barrett stretched out on the couch, his arms open wide for her to join him. Snuggled together, they watched the flames dance and waver.

Her head nestled on his chest, she whispered, "I missed you."

Barrett kissed her fingers. "There's no other place I'd rather be than by your side." His body grew lax as he settled into the cushions. His breaths evened out as he fell asleep.

Victoria listened to the storm outside. The winds rattled the roof tiles, finding every possible crack in the old cottage to push its way inside.

A dull ache bloomed at the base of her skull. She unwrapped Barrett's arm from her waist and slid off the couch.

On a mission to procure a few tablets to relieve the pain, she felt her way into the kitchen.

When she flipped on the lights, the glare cast a glaze over the windowpanes. Victoria never liked the inability to see out while knowing that someone standing outside could see in. It always made her feel like someone was out there, watching. The condo in L.A. was high enough off the ground to give you privacy. One of the reasons she'd liked it. She imagined that was what Connor liked about it too.

She tossed back the painkillers and drained the glass of water. The lists of recipes to prepare tomorrow whirled in her head. She was on the road to normal. Did she remember everything? A missing piece tickled her brain. Maybe it was in the notes. She turned to the cabinet that held Mags's cookbooks.

The cookbook with all of Mags's journal notes was no longer there.

CHAPTER 33

Victoria sat in the overstuffed chair, her knees drawn to her chest. Thankfully, she had woken up in time to properly baste and place the turkey in the oven. The tantalizing scent representing Thanksgiving and holidays filled the little cottage. Maybe she would channel her great aunt's ability to cook without mishap because without that cookbook, she hadn't a clue what to do next.

The wind had finally stopped blowing and allowed the snow to fall in an acrobatic dance. Nature's snow globe. The white flakes swirled and twirled until they stuck to whatever blocked their path. Mags's memorial stone towers now represented snowmen Picasso would have been proud to claim.

Although the storm clouds had cleared out, scrubbing the blue sky until it sparkled, she knew that Thanksgiving had all the signs of another crappy holiday. And it would be her fault.

She leaned her forehead on her knee, wincing when she bumped a bruise she didn't realize she had. How was she going to confront Mrs. T without hurting her feelings? There had to be a way to have it returned.

Barrett awoke, took one look at her and left for the kitchen.

Her heart warmed when he came back with an offering of coffee in two mugs. He held one out to her.

"Why the gloomy face? It looks like you have your wish. Company is coming for one of Mags's holiday feasts."

"Yeah." Victoria scowled, "Maybe the snow will hit again."

He stood up, clasping her hands, pulling her to his chest. "What's up?"

"The cookbook is missing. Mags's cookbook."

"So, you look up recipes in the other ones. Improvise."

She shook her head. "That's not just it. This cookbook had Mags's notes. Remember?" She paused, stretching out the phrase. "There. Were. Lots. And lots of her notes."

"Okay."

How could he still not get the urgency? She clutched his shirt and shook him. "Many are about people we know. As in 'guess-who's-coming-to-dinner'?"

Barrett's eyes widened when clarity hit. "Oh, no!" His knees melted under him and he dropped to the couch, taking her with him. He groaned at her nod. "Why? Why would you want to invite everyone she wrote about?"

Victoria ducked, resting her forehead against him. "I don't know. I wanted to get to know them. Understand why they had issues with each other. I never thought someone would steal the book from my home."

Barrett entangled from her arms and rose. "We have to get it back. Maybe Helen hasn't looked in it."

"We were getting along." Tears puddled. She blinked them away, smudging the traces onto her sweatshirt. "I don't want to lose that."

He caught her hand, pressing a reassuring kiss on her lips. "Don't cry. Let me think. I know. I'll go over, ask if she saw the book. Ask for it back."

"Don't make a big deal about it." She nodded, hope beginning to rekindle, then it flickered. "What if they ask why I didn't come for it?"

Barrett trailed his thumb over her cheek. "Because your head hurts, but you are still busy putting everything together. I'll tell them you are beside yourself with worry because you don't really know how to cook. We'll laugh about it and I'll slip out."

"Well, the headache part is true." She rubbed her temple and scowled. "I'm a much better cook," she lied.

"Of course, you are." He grinned back at her, like a cat with a secret. "It'll be great."

———

B arrett could not believe he was traipsing across the snow-packed garden, drifts thigh-high, with a cookbook shoved inside his winter coat. His boots skidded over the porch slats, only coming to a stop when his body slammed into the wood siding.

Victoria's brown head popped up over the kitchen windowsill. He choked back a chuckle. She looked like a wren. Her wide, almond-shaped eyes blinking back at him.

They turned at the sound of crunching snow. A pickup with the sheriff's badge emblazoned on the door pulled into the driveway and parked. Barrett was pretty sure retrieving your own property wasn't a reason to haul a person in for questioning. Of course, if you added breaking and entering, he might be in deep chocolate. He didn't think he would ever get Helen's pale reflection in the bathroom mirror out of his mind. And that was only the top of her head. Who knew the woman was bald as a cue ball?

"Barrett?" Graham called out as he walked up to the house. "What's wrong?" His eyes narrowed. "You look anxious about something."

"Nope. It's all good."

Graham whipped out a bag from behind his back. "I might run a little late tonight. Brought over some cornbread stuffing my mother always made. You don't think Victoria would mind, do you?"

Barrett held out his hand. It shook as if he had downed six cups of espresso. He forced his breathing to calm, steadying his heart rate and his hands. "She'll appreciate all the help she can get." He figured he better come straight with the man. "You do know she is not an accomplished cook."

Graham eyed him as if he wore a garland of gorgonzola and garlic around his neck. "Takes a good man to ignore the little things like burnt toast."

"And meat. And vegetables. Even pasta."

"She burns the meat," Graham sighed and shook his head. "Well, she can't be perfect. Bet she does a whole lot of things real good, though, doesn't she?" He leaned in, whispering, "So what you're telling me is, don't come with an empty stomach?"

Barrett tucked his chin, relief and guilt nipping at his conscience. He prayed the chef in question was not watching out the window. Or, listening.

"So why do you have Mags's old cookbook?" He pointed to the top of the book peeking out of Barrett's coat. "If Victoria needs it, why not give it back to her?"

The door swung open and Tilly ran out to greet their visitor.

"Chief Graham," Victoria called as she wiped her hands. "You're a little early, but you're welcome to come on in."

"No thanks, I have a few stops to make."

Barrett held out the bag. "He wanted to contribute to the dinner. Cornbread stuffing."

"Thank you." Victoria accepted the stuffing, cradling the casserole dish in her hands like a Fabergé egg. "Come on in. Get warm."

"That's all right. I have to get going." He folded his arms. "We pulled your car out of the ditch. It's at Mike's Gas & Garage. They'll let you know what the damage will cost to repair it." His frown deepened and he rolled his shoulders back. "Pretty good scrape on the side panel. Victoria, do you know anyone with a black vehicle?"

Three pairs of eyes turned to Barrett's pickup parked next to the sheriff's truck. His black pickup glistened in the snowbank.

"Just a minute," Barrett sputtered. "You'll see there isn't one scratch on my truck."

Graham bit the inside of his lip. His jaws worked as if chewing on new information. "I know, Doc. Someone else might know that too. Besides, I already checked it out while you were skulking around the neighbor's door. The truck is clean." His bushy brows arched. "I have to ask because…it's my job. What where you doing? Stealing Helen's secret to her perfect pie crust?"

"He was getting back a book that Helen lifted from my house last night," Victoria jumped in.

"How do you know it's yours?"

"It was Mags's." Victoria tapped her toe on the porch. "You sure you don't want to come in?"

"Nope. You say it's yours, I believe you. Sure you'll want to use it in case, you know, something goes amiss. Don't you fret." He patted her shoulder. "My momma never could serve up an edible turkey. Cremated that bird more times than we boys cared to remember." He patted her shoulder again. "Probably why we set so much store in her stuffing."

"Cremated?" Victoria whispered under her breath. The color drained from her flushed cheeks.

"Now, don't you worry. I'm looking forward to a meal just like my momma used to make."

"A great cook, was she?"

Barrett made a study of ignoring her glance and swallowed a groan. The sheriff needed to learn to keep quiet.

"I…uh…" Chief Graham cleared his throat as if reminded of that sacrificial meal and realized he might have stepped on his hostess's toes. He backed away, steering clear of the door. "I have a few things to check on." A blush began rising from his collar. He scratched at his ear, pulling on his earlobe. "I promised to pick up Hetty and her daughter on my way here tonight."

His gaze became serious. The police enforcement attitude had returned. "There have been a few incidents in the area recently. Theft, breaking and entering. Seems to be escalating. Can't have two women out on the slippery roads at night by themselves." He turned to leave. "You keep an eye out for each other."

Victoria lifted a hand to wave. "See you at six." Her mouth wobbled as she returned to her post by the stove.

To Barrett's relief, he heard her chuckle to herself as she poured over the pages in the cookbook. Maybe their Thanksgiving had a chance, after all. To be on the safe side, he planned to bring over a stack of frozen pizzas as his contribution to the meal.

———

The snow had stopped, the roads were clear, and everyone but Graham and his two passengers arrived on time.

Barrett came up, handing her a glass of wine, and whispered, "We've stretched it for an hour. Should we eat? I think your guests are getting restless."

Victoria couldn't have agreed more. Fred and George had begun a collection of empty beer cans on the counter. The drinking started the moment they heard Hetty would be joining them.

Helen stood in the corner, looking out the window at the lake. Her back was ramrod straight, and she looked like she could wring a chicken's neck with one hand. Harold grunted when she handed him a beer and he wandered off to kibitz with Fred and George.

That left Teresa and her son. Jackson had the teenager expression perfected. Bored. And hungry.

Barrett gave her a peck on the cheek. There had been a tension growing between them ever since Graham delivered the news that someone had clipped her car. They jumped with every little noise.

It was time to get this fiasco finished and put to bed for another year. Victoria cringed. Make that a millennium.

Unless someone came down with food poisoning, it couldn't get any worse.

She lifted her glass, "Everyone, let's eat."

That announcement seemed to have a magical effect. As soon as the words were out, a squad car pulled into the driveway.

Graham lifted Hetty out of the car and Susan rolled the wheelchair over the shoveled, snow-packed path to the house.

"Well, hell," Fred announced. "Look what the cat dragged in. Hetty." He knocked back what was left of his beer.

Hetty, ensconced in her chair, looked like a queen sitting on her throne. Judging by the shared glares, Victoria expected to hear Hetty announce, 'Off with their heads.'

CHAPTER 34

Victoria sat at the overly large round table. She loved to think about the equality it gave to everyone sitting down. No one at the end of the table to demand best behavior. No punishment held over your head if you spoke without invitation. No wonder King Arthur's Knights met around the round table. Equality. She prayed tonight that it would be the same.

Except for Jackson, everyone had coupled off. She and Barrett sat side-by-side. He caught her fingers and gave her an encouraging wink. Graham had Susan on one side, George on the other. Teresa sat down and Jackson soon followed.

Victoria held her breath when Helen sat next to her. She did a quick hand check, making sure the carving knife wasn't within Helen's reach. Harold joined his wife. They sat stiffly together, barely offering a glance to their mate. And God forbid, Hetty sat next to Fred.

Victoria let her gaze rest on each face, offering her best welcome to the table. Ensuring all the glasses were filled, she raised her glass in a toast. "I am grateful for new neighbors and friends. Thank you for joining me on this special day."

The conversation was stiff at first. The party manners were out in full form. "Please pass this. Please pass that. Thank you. Best food I've tasted."

But once the California pinot noir started flowing, everyone started to reminisce about Mags and her crazy ways. Victoria sat back, enjoying the conversations floating around her. The food was edible, and God willing, everyone would be happy and satisfied, their care packages of extra food tucked under their arms when they returned home.

"Mom," Jackson said, "I have some friends I need to see. Okay if I leave early?"

Teresa turned from her conversation with George. A frown cut a crease between her brows. "How will you get there? We have the one car."

George rested his hand over the back of her chair. "I'll give you a ride home."

He snatched his hand away at Jackson's frosty glare. "That's okay. I can take my mom."

"Jackson, George is kind enough to offer." She glanced, ducking her head, her cheeks slightly flushed. "If the offer still goes, George."

His fingers crept courageously over hers. "It'd be my pleasure."

"Whatever." Jackson scooted his chair from the table. He held out his hand. "Miss Victoria, I'm sorry I have to leave early. Thank you for dinner. It was really terrific."

"My pleasure, Jackson. I'll send home a piece of pie with your mom."

He took in the couple, a confused and dark mood shifted over his face. "Thanks." He grabbed his coat and keys in one motion.

An awkward silence filtered over the table as soon as the door ticked shut.

Hetty pulled herself up to sit straighter, ready to hold court. "You'd do well to control that boy, Teresa."

George spoke up for her, his arm rested, once again, over the back of Teresa's chair. "He's a nice young man, Hetty." He cut a look over to Teresa. "A son his parents should be proud of. Not everyone needs to be reined in so tight that they have no say for themselves."

"S'pose that's one of your dear Mags's sayings," Hetty huffed.

"I'll have you know she was one of the best."

"She was as fruity as a jar full of fruit flies." Her arthritic fingers gripped the wheelchair arms. "And she was a cheat. And a no-good man stealer."

"Mother." Susan's face blanched, and then heated, leaving two red splotches on her cheeks.

"I cannot believe you brought me here. I admit I wanted to see inside the woman's bordello. There had to be something that drew the men in like honey." Her mouth pinched. "Never saw anything special in that woman and I don't see anything special here."

"Hetty, that is downright hateful talk," George said.

Her gnarled finger poked the air. "You're one to talk. She pulled you away from your wife. Broke apart your marriage of over fifteen years."

"My marriage was broken way before Mags had anything to say about it." He threw down his napkin and rose. "She reminded me I deserved a good woman, and it was better to be alone until I found one than be strapped with a witch."

Victoria's stomach twisted. The meal she fought for, the food she prepared, the hours in the kitchen, was disintegrating. Barrett's hand stole under the table, squeezing, helping her to hang on. She blinked back the tears. "Hetty—"

Fred sat back and sighed. "What's gotten into you, Hetty Mae? You used to be the prettiest thing growing up. Pretty inside and out, that's our Hetty. Everyone knew who to go to for a shoulder to cry on or an ear to listen. People would say, 'yup, that sweet Hetty, she has a heart of gold.'" He lifted his beer and shook his head. "Now look at you. Just about eaten up with bitterness."

"What do you know about it, you, cantankerous old fool?" Hetty smacked her chair wheels. "Susan. Graham. Take me home."

Shocked by her mother's outburst, Susan's mouth opened and shut like a landed trout. "Mother—"

Impatient, Hetty started wheeling her chair away from the table. The wheels caught on the tablecloth and began to drag it with her.

"Stop right this minute, Mrs. Eldridge," Graham commanded. He leaned his elbows on the table. His fork and knife hung suspended from his brawny hands over his plate. "We were late because you raised a ruckus. Now you are doing the same thing to get what you want." He waved his fork. "Frankly, Mam, this meal is too good for a single man to pass up. Now settle down before I handcuff your wheelchair to the table leg."

Startled, everyone sat, wide-eyed, staring at each other. Who would dare speak and break the silence?

First a snort, then a titter. Followed by a chuckle. It wasn't long before everyone, but Hetty, was laughing at the ridiculousness of it all.

Fred stood and wheeled Hetty's chair back to the table. He bent down to whisper something in her ear that made a blush crawl up her neck, adding color to her cheeks.

"At least you didn't pull out your gun, Sheriff," George said. In the fracas, his arm had slid over the back of Teresa's shoulders. His thumb stroked her neck. She tipped her head to lean into him.

"My grandma held a tradition that we had to say what we were thankful for." Teresa cleared her throat, her eyes widened. "Course it might seem silly to you all." She cast a nervous glance at Victoria. "Sorry, I didn't mean to step on your toes. That's more of a hostess's topic, isn't it?"

Victoria offered a reassuring smile. "It's a great idea. I'll go first." She lifted her glass. "I'm thankful that we actually got to have Thanksgiving dinner. Otherwise, it would have been just a dinner party with friends."

Helen took up her glass. "I'm grateful Mags wrote what she observed, usually keeping what she saw to herself, and sometimes speaking out when it was needed."

Harold finally met his wife's gaze. He turned to her, holding her hand, gazing at her as if no one else sat at the table. "And I'm grateful that she gave us the gift of remembering that there are more good things that happen than bad." He leaned in and kissed Helen. The kiss lingered but no one minded. The couples shared that quiet moment until the Tewilligers separated. The applause caused their faces to flush. Or perhaps it was the promise of something sweeter, that everyone suspected would come as soon as they were home.

"Now that's what I'm talking about," Fred hooted.

Teresa cleared her throat as she played with her napkin. "I'm thankful that George shared the message that Mags taught him." She looked up. "There's room in my life now for a kindhearted man who is worthy of me." Her eyes shot to her hands again. "Somewhere."

George brushed his fingers over her cheek. "I'm grateful for second chances."

Graham laid his fork and knife down on his plate. The only sound was the silver tapping the china, the ticking of the clock. "If it weren't for the Doc, I wouldn't be here." He held up a hand against Barrett's protest. "Face it, Doc, we all know you used to have a practice. Something sent you here. Well, I'm grateful that you are."

Susan touched Graham's burly arm. "Me too."

His chest rose in surprise. "Really?"

She nodded, tears shimmered in her eyes. "Oh yes, really, really glad."

Hetty snorted beside her. "Well, I suppose I'm glad this is one Thanksgiving I don't have to spend in that depressing senior center."

Fred elbowed her arm. "I'm glad you're here too, Hetty Mae."

Her fingers plucked at the tablecloth. A smile ratcheted up the corners of her mouth.

Bemused, Victoria sat back in wonder. Had these people never talked? No wonder Mags felt the need to build stone towers to help her remember the good, even when bad things happen. It marked the victory after the struggle.

Barrett tapped his knife on the ridge of the wineglass. "It's my turn. I need to get my say in before you lovebirds fly off."

A nervous, self-conscious chuckle fluttered over the dining room.

Victoria had this odd, out-of-body, fear that he was going to announce their love for each other. Would he want her to proclaim her love? She cared for him. Deeply. But after Connor, she made herself a promise to keep things light and always stay in control of the relationship. Her fingers curled into her palms. Maybe he was getting into the mood of the dinner guests. All that self-proclamation of finding oneself. Finding each other. Cripes' sake, why couldn't they have saved it for their car rides home?

Barrett cleared his throat and waited, determined to have their attention. "I am grateful for Mags."

Victoria blinked. That was it? That was all he had to say? Wasn't that what she'd wanted a few seconds ago? Judging by the way Fred was ogling Hetty's cleavage, even they would get lucky. Darned if he wasn't already making that vinegary old sourpuss smile.

They lifted their glasses in unison. Even Hetty. "Cheers!"

———

Victoria and Barrett watched the cars file out of the driveway and into the snowstorm that started while they ate and reminisced. George and Teresa left first. That left Fred without a ride. Since he'd come with George, Graham opted to give him and the two Eldridge women a ride home. Before he left, he offered his reminder to lock the doors.

Victoria hugged herself. "I wonder if Fred will make it any farther than the Friendship House."

"I was wondering the same thing," Helen said beside her, eyes gleaming with wonder and mischief. "Who knew oil and vinegar would mix after all."

Victoria knew this was the time to bring up Mags's cookbook. She took a deep breath, bracing against a bad response. "Mags's cookbook—"

"Was intended to only help. I know." Helen patted Victoria's back. "The woman loved people. Some thought of her as a meddling busybody. I did too. Even had a thought or two about it this afternoon. And a few salty words. But as I sat around the table, I realized that all she really wanted to do was help. I think Harold realized that too."

Her husband came up at that moment and rested his arm around Helen's waist. "Lovely meal, Victoria." He nuzzled his wife's neck despite her feeble protests. "Entertaining too."

"I do my best," Victoria chuckled.

"Remember, what we talked about over washing the dishes," Helen said. "We are all going in for breast cancer screening."

Victoria rolled her neck. How did those women convince her to go too? She'd avoided dealing with breast cancer for the last couple of years. She dreaded it with every year that passed. Her mom had died from it. She'd seen the damage. And she didn't want to have to confront the beast. Ever.

"Hey, you're still here." Barrett slung the dishtowel over his shoulder. He shook hands with Harold as the Tewilligers prepared to leave. It was as if he was playing host in his own home. Victoria couldn't help wondering what it would be like, to have someone share everything with you, even the holidays, and still be speaking the next day.

"You look serious." He kissed her forehead. "What are you two cooking up now?"

Helen told them about the breast cancer screening they had decided to do as a group. The Women of Honeybrooke Cove's Booby Brigade. Victoria shut her eyes and shook her head slightly. She prayed Helen would get the female telepathy. When Helen paused, Victoria let out a tiny breath.

"You know us," Helen said. "We're always cookin' up something."

CHAPTER 35

The holidays passed with no events that made the front page of the Honeybrooke Cove Press. Otherwise known as tell-Lyle-at-the-Duck-Blind-Café-and-he'll-tell-the-rest.

Christmas and New Year's Eve came and went. The Christmas card from Victoria's father arrived in time for the New Year's Eve party. His message, 'Quit playing Nanook of the North. Time to leave the frozen tundra and find a position that represented her college tuition.' Evidently, he had forgotten that she and the scholarships paid for her degree. Not him.

On the days that Victoria didn't go into the Cove Market to work in the office, she stood at the window and watched the ice form over the lake. With each passing day, another ice-fishing shack went up. There were more strangers on her lake than when she'd moved to the cove. They unnerved her when they parked their vehicles on the icy surface. The three flourishing tourism seasons for Honeybrooke were summer boating, hunting, and ice fishing. The next season to come, she was told, would be tornado season.

She wanted to try her hand at fishing, but the visions of falling through the ice, well, made her feet feel like blocks of ice, and she couldn't move onto the lake for fear of sinking. That same block of ice kept her finding excuses for why the dates for the women's Booby Brigade would never work for her.

She hugged the nubby knit sweater that Hetty Eldridge had given her for Christmas. She should visit Susan and Hetty at the Friendship House. Maybe when it warmed up a bit.

Living in the backcountry of Wisconsin had a few drawbacks besides terrible phone reception and scarce Wi-Fi connections. They were finding it hard to get the needed parts and repairs for her red BMW.

Barrett had been hurt when she opted to stay in her little cottage and not move into his sprawling cabin. Maybe his delivery made her hesitate. It was about as romantic as 'honey-you-wanna?' Stubborn? Maybe. She wasn't about to move in with him because she'd have ready access to a vehicle or because that was the only way she'd feel safe from Connor. Nor did Barrett push his part ownership of the cottage. However, he didn't take her refusal lightly and he'd returned to his own home. But not until after he brought over a used pickup with four-wheel drive. Who was she kidding? She loved every moment they were together and missed him as soon as he walked out the door.

As if conjuring him up from her thoughts, the windshield of Barrett's black pickup caught the sunlight, reflecting it toward the house. The truck skidded to a stop, shooting packed snow and ice into the air.

The back porch door slammed as Barrett hurried through the kitchen. Tilly ran ahead of him, barking, her golden tail unfurling like a flag.

"Victoria," he yelled.

"In here," she said.

Barrett's tool belt hung at an angle. She still found it sexy and wanted to wrap her body around him. What did he look like in his doctor's coat or blue scrubs? Was he the doctor every estrogen-laden female wanted for herself? Her mouth, watering at the thought, she longed to hang on to him and never let go.

His cheeks were flushed with excitement. The blue of his ever-changeable eyes gleamed with raw excitement.

"We did it," he exclaimed, lifting her up by her elbows, and pirouetted around the room.

Dizzy, she laughed while they spun in a dance of joy. "Stop, or I'll throw up."

He slowed down but kept her suspended, swaying in a waltz, as he floated them to the couch and collapsed with her in his lap. "Kiss me," he demanded.

Her heart soared. Barrett had been so pensive the last couple of months. Refusing to talk about his concerns. She knew he'd been frustrated with the legalities of the medical field. He'd had a couple of trips to Chicago, but they weren't as long as the one before Thanksgiving. There were times when she could feel him pulling away. But this, this felt so good. Exactly where she'd wanted to be all along. A rush of love coursed through her limbs.

She kissed him, long and sweet. She caught the back of his head and sighed as he pulled her into his mouth.

————

Victoria draped her leg over Barrett's lap. He tucked her close and sighed into her hair.

She twisted, prodding him in the chest. "So, what did we do?"

He nipped her collarbone, causing her to shiver. She brushed the hair sticking to his forehead. Cupping his face, she brought his gaze to meet hers. "What's the news?"

Grinning, he bent down and tried to reach her neck. She pressed him back. He had that little boy look like someone took his best toy away from him. What if one day they had kids? Would they look like him? She hoped so.

He kissed one knuckle at a time. "I am no longer just a handy-man." He paused. "I can have my old position back. If I want it."

She caught his wrist. A deep ache gnawed at her stomach. Was he leaving again? "In Chicago?"

"Yes." He slid his arm around her shoulder, playing with the hair she'd pulled back in a ponytail. "But, I'm thinking..." He whispered into her ear, "I'm thinking, I should stay here, love on you, be your handyman for a little while longer."

Victoria's stomach bubbled with the thought of losing him. She ached to beg him to stay, turn his back on everyone and be her partner for life. But the man she loved lived to fix things. Especially people. And there were so many other people he could help. What if there was another little Jessica that he might be able to save?

She steeled her heart and prepared to tell the biggest lie she'd ever told. "I think you should move back to Chicago."

––––––

Victoria sat at the kitchen table and watched Barrett pace the floor. He reminded her of a caged lion. An angry caged lion.

"What do you mean you think I should take the position in Chicago?"

Handsome as ever, he'd paused, hands planted on his hips. His bare feet peeked out from his low-slung jeans. *Get your thoughts away from there, Victoria.* Once she went in that direction, she knew she'd never come back from it. She couldn't take back what she said earlier. She meant it. What if after all this time, the legal battle, the time away, the heartache, he woke up one morning and realized that she was his worst mistake?

"I never intended to stay this long. With spring coming, I think it's about time I start my own job hunt too. It's time." She circled her finger over the surface of the table. "Applications. Interviews. Trips out of town." She swallowed the lump lodging in her throat.

Maybe it was a piece of her heart. "Opportunities don't always come along, if I get an offer in another state, I'd have to take it." She swallowed the barbed words cutting into her heart. "And you'll want to do the same."

Barrett wiped his mouth. "All those things take time," he said, his voice an emotional growl.

"My, uh, dad submitted a few resumes for me. I, uh, already have a few bites."

"Your dad. He contacted you?"

"We, uh, decided that since Connor is no longer on the radar that he no longer poses a threat." She ducked her head to hide the lie.

Barrett smacked the counter. Head down, pressing his fists into the granite, his back to her, he said, "When were you going to tell me?"

She shrugged, praying she could pull off the biggest whopper yet. "If the position is in L.A., I can move in with my dad." Her voice shuddered. "We can put this place up for sale. Maybe rent it out as a vacation home."

He turned, leaning his hips against the counter. His blue eyes were red-rimmed. "How did this victory get so turned around that I feel like I'm losing everything instead?"

Victoria twisted the hem of her shirt and struggled to draw in a breath. "I know. I'm sorry."

He knelt in front of her. "Please, don't do this. We're good together."

Please, God, help me let him go, before it's too late and I tell him I love him. "I have t-t-to. It's the best financial decision."

"I see." His jaw worked, flexing and straining. He rose, grabbing his work boots and jacket, and turned. "If that's what you want."

Victoria swallowed the hateful knot. Bile burned the back of her throat. She waited, praying she could take the words back. And, praying that he would refuse to let her go.

Barrett kissed the top of her head, then walked out onto the porch and stood. His shoulders rose and fell as if he'd finished a marathon. After shoving his feet into his boots, he called Tilly to his side and climbed into his truck.

He didn't speed out in a rage. Instead, the truck rolled out, as if it knew it was taking the long way home.

————

Victoria sat at the desk, staring at the numbers on the computer screen. The figures danced in front of her. Her mind could not make any sense of them.

Seven days and she still could not focus. The to-do list never grew, and she never crossed anything off. Her attention tugged away from the tangle on the screen. She could overhear someone talking about Barrett.

"What do you mean we don't have a handyman to call," Harold yelled. "I need someone to fix the roof when the snow melts."

"…left town the other day."

"But I haven't seen Tilly at V—"

"Put things in storage."

The voices dropped to a whisper, but Victoria knew. She laid her head on her folded hands and wept.

CHAPTER 36

When Barrett left this time, he had checked the furnace and her pickup truck while she was doing the bookkeeping at the Cove Market. The first morning after he left for Chicago, she awoke to the delivery of a new sat phone. She waited for him to call, and he never did.

Once the word was out, the women of Honeybrooke Cove circled their wagons. They came in ones and twos, as couples and packs. Victoria recognized most of the women. She'd seen them at the market or the Duck Blind Café. The usual vague hello and good morning had been the norm of the day.

That was until they received the news that Barrett Collins had dumped her and returned to his life in Chicago. They all wanted to know the details. Victoria didn't have any to give.

In the first weeks, they shared their breakup stories and mammogram experiences. They spent the following weeks convincing her to accept their invitation to go to the breast clinic together. The women utilized guilt and trauma to gain her agreement, and she had gathered up the courage to go the day before. They'd celebrated with a glass of wine and a chocolate brownie at Lyle's cafe.

Checking the calendar had already become a compulsion. Soon, they would learn if someone had been splattered with the brush of cancer or whether they were all in the clear for another year. Once Victoria started down the road of self-checking, hiding her head in the sand was no longer an option. That's what her mother did, and it killed her.

She prayed they would beat the statistics and no one in the Honeybrooke Cove Booby Brigade would have to know that heartache and fear. For now, she waited like all the rest of the women in the cove.

Even Hetty Eldridge came out to offer her support. The latest, pounding on the service bell that Harold swore was vital to customer service.

Victoria scrunched down in her chair. She would have hidden under the desk if she thought it would dissuade Hetty from hollering over the counter that she needed to see Victoria immediately.

"It's an emergency."

What? Did she run out of foot powder? How the elderly woman sitting in a wheelchair, her head a foot lower than the countertop could project her voice to the back office, Victoria would never know. It must be an octogenarian trick. All the seniors in the cove appeared to have the skill mastered.

She scooted back her chair and prepared herself for the imaginary emergency. The smile plastered to her face she came around the corner, forcing exuberance into her step. "Hello lovely lady, what are you doing here?"

She leaned over the counter to shake the elderly woman's hand. Hetty should have been a stateswoman. Victoria wondered if Mags's old book might mention what the woman did before moving to the senior center.

Hetty's crab-like fingers gripped Victoria's hand. "Why'd you let that young man run off?"

Susan bustled over, blushing from the growing heat and her

mother's antics. "Mother, that is none of our business." She began rolling the wheelchair away from the counter, their progress through the store, slowed by Hetty dragging her feet.

They jerked to a stop when Chief Graham came through the door. Victoria noticed how the blush crept down Susan's neck, drawing everyone's eye to her cleavage. One, in particular, being Chief Graham. Soon as the snow showed signs of melting, Susan had taken to wearing dresses and lower cut tops. Maybe something good came out of Thanksgiving after all.

Victoria shuffled papers, sorting the receipts and orders while keeping an eye on the reluctant couple. The only thing standing in their way was the woman in the wheelchair.

Tucking the paperwork under her arm, Victoria pretended to straighten stock on the shelves and moved closer.

"Chief Graham," Victoria said. "Are you ready for the thaw? It looks like winter is finally over. Don't you think, Susan? Say, did she tell you about the creek that is rising near the Friendship House?"

"Pooh," Hetty announced. "Not doing anything it hasn't done before."

Victoria lifted a hand. "I haven't seen it myself, but I heard talk that it might flood." She caught Susan's eye. "Might be any time. Isn't that right, Susan?"

"We should probably check it out," Graham said. "Wouldn't hurt to get a reading on it."

Victoria nodded. "Why don't you go and do it right now. While there's still daylight."

"I don't know." Susan paused, judging Hetty's reaction. "We just got to town. Momma has some shopping to do. And…"

"We'll be just fine here. Won't we?" Victoria said, before Hetty could add her objection. "She can do her shopping while you and Graham take a run out to your place."

Victoria swore she saw sparks fly off Susan's pumps as Graham rushed her through the doorway.

"S'pose that makes you happy," Hetty groused.

Victoria grinned, and it felt like it came from her heart and not her dad's command to smile. Real. "Let's go shopping."

The cantankerous old woman flattened her feet to the floor, causing the wheels to move like they were pushed through molasses. "Guess I don't have much of a choice." An evil twinkle creased the corners of her eyes. "Course, you tell me what went wrong with you and Barrett and I might make it easier on you."

Victoria debated whether or not to leave her where she sat. Let her fend for herself. But she couldn't do it to the other customers. She leaned over Hetty's shoulder as Fred came through the door and whispered in her wrinkled ear, "I'll tell you, if you tell me about you and Fred."

Hetty surprised her with a swift nod and lifted her legs up with gnarled fingers. She settled her feet on the footrests. "Let's blow this pop stand."

———

"We go way back," Hetty said, fiddling with the silver band, worn thin from years of wear. It spun around her finger, revealing her weight loss. "Mags and I had issues way before my husband Hank passed." She waved her veiny hand. "Now, don't listen to the gossip. The only thing Hank was guilty of was complaining too much and wanting someone to listen. No, our issues started when we were kids."

She ripped open the packet of creamer and poured it into the mug Lyle placed in front of her. "You know it's a good place when they fill your cup before you enter the door."

Victoria wasn't sure about that. Being a creature of habit put you in danger when you had a nut-job threatening to make you see reason and demanding payback for what you took away. Thanks to Connor, she'd been learning about stalkers. Not great bedtime reading, but it was time she took control of the past that seemed to creep up on her from time to time.

"How about you, Ms. Victoria? Will you want a cup of coffee too?"

Victoria nodded. She needed something to keep her eyes open while she babysat Hetty.

"Fred was a looker back in the day. He always had an eye for the girls, and they for him. He knew it too. And your great-aunt Mags had that something the boys always liked. Drew them like bees to pollen." She blew on her coffee. "Me, I thought I was too good for Honeybrooke Cove. I had dreams and Fred was happy living in Wisconsin, never leaving the frozen winters, the summers buzzing with mosquitoes. This was the life Fred wanted. I see that now. Back then, I told him he was a fool. Me, I thought I should go to Washington, make a difference. Become famous. That's where I met Susan's daddy. Goodness, that was years ago." She huddled over her coffee, swirling her spoon, protecting her heart. "I returned during the summer of 1950."

She propped her chin on her hand and tilted her head. "Do you know what it's like to return to a community that knew you when you were a baby? But this time, it's not you that's wearing the cloth diapers. It's the little one in your arms." She sighed and shook her head. "Times have changed, and in some ways, they haven't. Hearts still break and people die."

"I came home, pretended my man had been killed in the war, and went to work for the Honeybrooke Cove Press. Mags surprised us all and went away to college. Met her sweetheart and came back the real war bride. She returned more sophisticated than I could have imagined for myself. She filled the reporter position I'd been working all summer for. It was hers." Hetty snapped her fingers. "Just like that." She picked up her purse, rummaging through the pockets, feeling the bottom layers. Her hand came back empty. "There are times when I forget I quit smoking. This is one of those times when I wish I still did."

She blinked, focusing on what wasn't in her hand, and sighed. "When I had returned, Fred looked different to me. He didn't seem to mind me having to care for a baby. We'd go on picnics just like we were a family. I thought him sweet on me but when Mags came back a widow, there was a mystery that stirred up the men in three counties. Fred included. The only one to give me the time of day was Hank. I up and married him as soon as he showed he was halfway interested in me. Probably the worst mistake of my life.

"Guess that's when the competition between Mags and me really took off." She lifted her head, rubbing her swollen joints over her lipstick-stained lips. "She sure had a way about wanting to help others sort out their differences. Everyone's but our own.

"Here's the thing, all that bickering didn't matter. Neither one of us got Fred. Been single all his life. Now Mags is gone. He's still here. I'm still here. We're both lonely. But we don't know how to get past the one barrier that is still there."

"Mags."

Hetty nodded. "I hoped writing to her people would set things right where she and I were concerned. Get some of that good Karma she was always yammering on about." She reached out, gripping Victoria's hands. "Listen to this old lady and don't let the hurt separate you and Barrett. Right now, it seems like there is all the time in the world, but you never know. Don't waste the years. Tell him how you feel. Before the walls are too high or you run out of time."

Victoria blinked the tears and looked away. Could it be that easy?

The moonless night closed in, shutting out the light and enveloping everything in darkness and shadows. Victoria paced the floor. She pulled out the sheet of paper that she printed off that afternoon when she took Hetty back to the store to wait on Susan.

Dear Ms. Banning,

We are impressed with your resume and would like to schedule an interview with you at your earliest convenience.

The return address was in Los Angeles.

She wracked her brain, sorted through files and the list of potential employers she'd written to for employment. None of them held this employer's name.

At first, it was exciting to know she had made it through the initial cut. By evening, when the rejections and offers started flooding her mailbox, she got that itch between her shoulders. She scrunched her back like a cat and then arched to move the tension out. It felt like someone was watching her, observing her mood. Was she ecstatic or in tears? Frozen in fear?

No. Right now, she was furious. She tossed the page on top of the stack of papers and carried them to the trashcan. This had all the stink of Connor's mind games. Staring out the window, searching for his face, she let the pages slide out of her fingers.

Checking the locks on the doors, she shut the windows and turned off the lights. The sat phone clutched to her chest, she curled into a ball, buried her face in one of Barrett's sweatshirts, and sobbed.

That night she dreamt of Barrett as they kissed under the warm Wisconsin sun. Barrett tickled with a blade of grass, making her laugh. "I miss you," he said.

"I miss you too," she whispered, waking to find her cheek damp with tears, the ache in her heart stealing her breath.

CHAPTER 37

"Did you hear the news?"

Victoria put down her pen and waited for George to spill it. She swore he looked younger than she'd seen him since they'd first met last summer.

She sat back and counted on her fingers. It'd been nearly nine months since she'd moved to Honeybrooke Cove. She'd survived Connor and heartbreak in less than a year.

Jackson came up behind George. Taller than his elder, he put his hand on George's shoulder. "Mom wants to know if you'll pick up more eggs for Easter."

George nudged him with his elbow. "Bet she'd like those white flowers, too."

Confusion coated Jackson's face. "But she grows them."

"Son, that's not the point."

"Victoria," Jackson said, "are you coming to the concert?"

Victoria bagged the odds and ends of their groceries. She enjoyed the warmth that had grown between Teresa's son and George. The teenager was becoming a solid young man. "I wouldn't miss it."

Leaning against the counter, her ankles crossed, she watched them leave. They moved fluidly, as if they were father and son.

Susan and Graham had become a hot item in the cove's gossip. Of course, nothing beat the news that Fred and Hetty, at long last, had gotten together. It only took them over thirty years to get it right.

Frowning, she straightened. George forgot to tell her his news. Puffing at an escaping bang from her ponytail, she chuckled under her breath. "Guess I'll find out, eventually."

The news came much too fast for Victoria.

It wasn't George's news. That she would have to wait on.

The letter from the diagnostic center lay on her desk. She nibbled the inside of her lip, fighting back the tsunami of emotions welling up inside. "I should have left everything as it was and not know." Her knees trembled as she melted into her chair. "This can't be happening." Flashes of her mother, too weak to move. Hair falling out. The surgery that didn't win the war.

She lifted the letter as if it was contagious. The paper quivered in her hands, making the print jump and blur on the page. Words like, suspicious … cancerous, caught her attention, pulling her under.

Her dad's voice echoed in her head, *"Smile! What do you have to be sad about?"*

Anger welled inside. She crumpled the letter and shoved it to the bottom of her purse. The breast care center had requested a retake, but it didn't say how soon. As far as she was concerned, she'd take her chances. *Never.*

She stormed out of the office. They had finally repaired her little car. The red convertible beamed like a rose amongst the standard, everyday four-door sedans. She ran to it and slammed the gear into first. The tires spun, squealing as she pulled out.

"No! No! No!"

She yanked hard on the wheel, dodging a black pickup, spinning the wheel to straighten the car. Horns blew as she sped past.

The wind tangled her hair, sticking it to her face. She clawed at it, surprise registering that she sobbed for the pain and loss. She didn't want to end up like her mother or Mags. She wanted a healthy life filled with love. And children. Barrett's children.

Downshifting, she pulled over to the curb. Hands clutching the steering wheel, she rested her head on her fingers. Rocks crunched under tires behind her. Lifting her head, she looked out the windshield. This was where she'd stopped the first night she drove into town.

Victoria shrieked when her car door opened.

"What the hell do you think you are doing?"

The man glaring down at her was the most handsome man she'd ever seen. "Barrett," she said, working to dig up some type of composure.

His nose flared. "You nearly killed yourself pulling out in front of me. Why didn't you stop?"

Victoria's eyes widened when he pulled her out of the car. This was not how she envisioned his return. She squinted up at him. Where the heck were her sunglasses? They would have hidden everything from his prying gaze. She jerked her arms out of his grasp and planted her hands on her hips. "I'll ask you one better. Why didn't you call and warn me you were coming to town?"

He shoved his fingers through his hair. "I didn't think..." He cleared his throat, glanced away. "You know...if you'd take my call."

Her anger deflated like a birthday balloon left in the sun. She'd missed this man so much. "You need a haircut, Doctor Collins," she said.

"Yeah?" he sighed. "I guess so. I've been busy."

She took a hesitant step forward, brushing the unruly bangs from his face. Her heart ached. "Yeah. Me, too."

"I, ah, thought you were leaving town. Had a job offer somewhere."

Her hand dropped to her side. Alarms rang in her head. *Please, God, don't tell me he wants me out of here so bad that he's the one who sent those resumes.* "What do you know about job offers?"

His head cocked to one side. "Remember? You're the one who told me you and your dad had everything worked out."

The lie she told came back to her in a painful flash. Relief washed the pain away. How could she tell him she had lied?

Hetty's advice came back to her. *Don't waste any more time.*

"I don't have any job offers." Victoria shook her head, cupping his jaw she lifted on tiptoes and kissed him. Stepping back, she gave him room. It was his turn to make the next step after she told him. "I lied." The stack of emails she'd tossed out made her smile and amend her confession. "No real job offers."

Hurt darkened his irises. "Baby, why?"

"You fought so hard for your position in Chicago. I didn't want you to regret what you gave up."

"The only thing I regret is not sorting things out before I left." He folded her into his arms. His voice deepened, resonating with emotion. "I missed you so much."

"I missed you too."

Barrett picked her up and carried her to his truck. "One sec." He ran back to her car. Snatching her things off the passenger side seat, he trotted back to the truck. Grinning, he shifted into gear and pulled out. "Baby, we have so much catching up to do."

Victoria clutched her purse. The letter from the cancer center burned a hole in the leather, branding her a coward. She dropped the purse on the floor, kicking it under her seat. Later. She'd deal with it much later.

———

B arrett entered the kitchen and began washing up from his latest repair on the furnace. A new ring tone, Boom-Boom-

Pow, chanted somewhere in the house. "Victoria, your phone!" It stilled after the fourth ring.

Victoria's soprano voice came from the bathroom. She sang a country song of midnight lovers. He cringed when she screwed up the lyrics. God, he loved her!

He shot straight up. The realization took his breath away. His heart thudded in his ears. It was as clear as a winter morning. He was in love. Grinning, he stretched his arms over his head. He couldn't wait to share it with Victoria. Would she laugh or push him away? His arms paused in midair. Or would she hold him and tell him she loved him back? He didn't think his heart could take her turning him away. Their separation had been torture. This time they would stay together. No matter what arguments she tried to put up.

The phone began its incessant Boom-Boom-Pow.

He scrambled around the empty kitchen table in search of the offending phone. It must be somewhere in the living room. The vibration came from her purse. He hesitated, remembering that his mother always warned him that a woman's purse was her private sanctuary. No man dares enter.

Shoving his hand in, he withdrew the phone and a crumpled sheet of paper. The phone quit ringing. The message light flashed. Fearing Connor was back at his games, he glanced at the screen.

Westbrooke Cancer Center.

A pit formed in his stomach. It pulled every bit of energy from his body. Swallowing, he sat the phone on the coffee table. Out of natural habit, he turned over the paper in his hand.

Wrapped in her thick housecoat, Victoria strolled down the hallway, singing the screwed-up song. Her slicked-back hair made her facial structure more pronounced. He looked closer. Had she lost weight?

She paused, radiant, relaxed, and smiling. "You're up." She scrunched her nose. "Did I hear my phone ring?" Her eyes fell on it and the letter in his hand. "Why do you have those?"

"Babe," Barrett croaked.

"You have no right." Her voice rose. "What happened to patient privacy?" She snatched the letter, shredding it into the trashcan. "There. It's gone."

He took a cautious step, closing in the space between them. "Sweetheart," he whispered. She turned to flee, and he caught her. "I love you."

A single tear streamed down her cheek. She stood rigid; her hands fisted at her sides. The shields were up. "No," she said, "I didn't want it like this."

Barrett winced, stinging from her denial. He wrapped his arms around her, holding her. "It's going to be all right." He bent, cupping her head to make her look into his eyes. "We will fight this. We will beat it together."

The shuddering breath shook her body. She nodded, "Together."

They stood in the center of the living room. Clinging to each other until Victoria's sobs faded into hiccups.

CHAPTER 38

Barrett gave up on sleeping a little before dawn. His heart ached for Victoria. Her fear was palpable. She was usually sensible and would have made a list of all the steps needed to combat the cancer. Where was the list of pros and cons of her medical choices, written out in her neat handwriting? It made no sense to him. Her list-making was part of the package that made her who she was.

He padded to the living room and dug the pieces of the letter out of the trash. Putting it together like a puzzle, he read the full report.

A plan of action began to form. Pulling out his phone, he began the necessary calls. Victoria didn't know it, but they were about to go on the offense.

———

Lack of sleep left bruises under Victoria's eyes. The crying jag didn't help either. It made them feel swollen and gritty. She was tired of having to fight for every little victory. First, there was the layoff, then Connor's betrayal and his threats. She thought she'd lost Barrett and had only found him, then to lose him again to a shadow on a mammogram. How had her mom survived the months, knowing that she would die despite all the surgeries, chemo, and radiation?

She wandered to the kitchen. Barrett had already started the coffeepot. "Bless him. It's like Christmas."

She could hear the shower running. The man's tenor voice sang the Alison Krauss's bluegrass ballad, "Baby now that I've found you, I won't let you go..."

Closing her eyes, she sipped her coffee and waited for the morning jolt to kick in. Life started to bubble back to her brain. Setting the mug down, she noticed the pad of paper. She spun it around on the table. The heading read, One Step at a Time. Underneath it...

Retest and biopsy, if necessary. Talk about the possibilities. Then take the next step. Together.

Her jaw clenched.

She marched down the hall to the bathroom and pounded on the door.

Barrett's voice trailed off. "...I need you now." After a moment of hesitation, he hollered, "Want to join in?"

"No," she snapped, folding her arms across her chest, protecting the body parts that might be mutilated by some surgeon because of some cancer that didn't cause any symptoms right now.

"Suit yourself." A loud bang let Victoria know that he'd just avoided the snapping towel cabinet.

She closed her eyes, breathing deep to find some moment of peace in her mind.

The bathroom door swung open. Barrett had already tugged on his gym shorts. He wiped the droplets from his face with the towel slung over his shoulder.

Victoria shook her head, trying to maintain her temper. "That's right. I will suit myself. I will do things my way."

"That's the problem. You aren't doing it your way," he said, tugging his fingers through his hair.

"What do you mean?"

"The lists. The organization. The 'let's take things by the horns and beat it' step."

She tried to keep her eyes averted from his sexy body, but the beauty of his strong back was too much of a distraction and she couldn't stay away. He rubbed dry his powerful, muscular thighs. The temperature in the steamy bathroom rose.

"What's your plan?" He waited, staring her down.

The man was not playing fair. Victoria narrowed her eyes. "You are infuriating. And bossy."

"Good." The towel dropped to the floor. "Be angry. It's better than hiding." He lifted her chin. "Sweetheart, you are not a coward and you're sure not a quitter."

Victoria focused on his lips. They had nibbled and made her tremble with desire. He'd led her to places she'd never thought possible. Her heart threatened to open, unfurling to offer her love. She never wanted that...to ever go away.

His thumb ran over her mouth, up her jaw, then to her cheek to wipe the tear. "Did you read the letter fully?"

Irritation bubbled again. "Of course, I did."

"Then why are you ready to give up? You just need to retake the mammogram, maybe a biopsy while you're there. Nothing is definitive."

"Yes, it is. I'm not going. Therefore, I'm fine."

"Victoria." He scooped her up. Bear hugging her, he lifted her off her feet until they were nose-to-nose. "This isn't just about you. I want to spend my life with you, and we don't have a chance until we talk about it and deal with it. That's what couples do."

She smacked his biceps. "Ha! You want to talk about it." Mounting the argument, she wiggled to get down. "What about what I want?"

Dragging in a ragged breath, her breasts pushed against his

bare chest. She braced her arms against him. "My mother died of breast cancer. I watched her die a little bit every day. I swore I would never put myself through that."

"Medicine has changed. You have a fighting chance. But you must go on the offense. Be proactive. Otherwise, it advances and we can't fight the whole body."

She shook her head. "I don't think I can..."

"It's not just about you. It's about us. About the people who care about you." Calming, he set her down gently. "I've seen the new treatments. And they work." His hand shook as he smoothed her hair, stroking her head. "They save lives, but only if they are utilized. Please. I made some calls. We can do this together. I promise to be there with you."

She ducked her head. An invisible hand squeezed her lungs. She struggled to draw in a breath. "Your practice. You're in Chicago. I'm here."

The blood drained from Barrett's face. He rubbed his mouth and grabbed the towel off the floor.

Avoidance? The man wanted full disclosure about breast cancer, and he was having trouble looking her in the eye?

"Spill it, Barrett."

"I, um, decided not to accept the position in Chicago."

Victoria blinked. "When did this happen? Don't you dare tell me you are doing this for me. What if a few months down the road you hate me for making you choose? I won't let you do this. I won't allow you to blame me."

Barrett straightened. Red warning flags stained his cheeks. "I made my decision weeks ago. I couldn't work with St. James. There was too much water under the bridge." His hands slid down, soothing her arms. "That's why I've been away. I've been setting up my practice the next town over. It's centrally located. But I'll be living in Honeybrooke Cove."

"See!" Victoria slugged his shoulder. "How can we be a couple? You didn't even talk to me about it."

"You said you were leaving. You told me to go. I told you I loved you and you turned me down." He turned, pushing past her to gather his clothes. "I thought you'd be happy about this. That we'd have a chance."

Victoria watched his sleek back turn the corner. "You told me you loved me?" She searched the hours they'd been together. "No," she whispered, racing down the hall after him. "Barrett, wait. When did you tell me you loved me? When you took off and left?"

"You tried kicking me out of your life the day you lied about leaving for another job. Remember? The trouble is, sweetheart, I've never stopped loving you. I've been trying to tell you and show you I love you, but you can't get past the past."

He shrugged on his shirt, leaving it unbuttoned. "How can you not believe me when I say I love you? I'm not Connor. I would never blame you for my mistakes, but I sure as heck will tell you how much I love and admire you. Every day."

Victoria's lungs squeezed, refusing to let her catch her breath. Tears slid down her cheek. "You don't understand...I—"

Snatching up his cell phone, shoes in his other hand, he headed out the door. "I won't force you to do anything you don't want to. That includes loving me back. Let me know when you've figured out what you really want."

He paused. "The phone numbers are on the pad of paper. You call me when you have the appointments set up. I'll be there."

Calling Tilly to his side, he walked to his truck.

Victoria's throat closed. How had she let fear mess everything up so badly? She ran to the porch. "Wait!" she cried. "Don't go. I love you."

But the tires sprayed gravel across the garden, drowning her out.

———

V ictoria swiped at the tears streaming down her face. Could she do what Barrett asked? Were there too many memories of her mother's lost battle with cancer to face? Barrett said he loved her. He promised to be there. She didn't have to face it alone.

Her chest tightened, making her fight for every breath.

What if she didn't have the strength to go through with the treatments? Would he think any less of her? She didn't think her heart could survive seeing him, living his life without her.

Her thoughts spinning in fear of the possibility of cancer and the unknown future, she pulled out her suitcase. The job-offer at her father's bank in L.A. might still be available if she moved fast. Connor's threats had gone quiet. She'd be safe enough now. Maybe she could work remotely for Harold and Helen and manage to cover them for a few months.

The air rumbled. Lightning streaked across the skies. Clouds barreled in from the west. The air shifted. It went from humid and warm to a chilly breeze. The bedroom curtains fluttered over the snapping blinds. She clicked the latch on her bag and turned when the rain struck the windowpane. Whitecaps formed on the lake.

Wiping her cheek on her t-shirt, mindless of the mascara that remained despite her hours of crying, she lugged the heavy bag to the door. She checked packing off her mental to-do list.

The realization hit her like a baseball hitting a windshield. She sank onto the kitchen chair. Barrett was right. She hadn't looked at the cancer scare like she normally would have—researching the facts, making a list, then formalizing a plan. Instead, she'd decided to run.

The pad of paper lay on the table where he'd left it. He'd pointed out the percentages of retesting done on an annual basis. He listed the stats for recovery with each treatment and possible scenario.

His last points on the list—Stay positive. Never give up hope. Never give up on us.

"Barrett," she whispered, stroking her finger over his scrawled penmanship. She had to find him.

Victoria grabbed her phone and purse. Her steps faltered. The skies had darkened to gunmetal gray. The rain had already filled the gutters and was pouring over the sides. She'd have to make a run for the truck.

A tree branch hit the house. The bent willow chairs Barrett made for her that first week tumbled across the garden. The roses, newly budded, were bent low, their canes twisting under the wind's force.

A siren blew. The piercing whistle raised the hair on her arms.

She ran to the garden shed, dodging downed tree limbs and broken branches. The wind picked up, pushing against her, combating every step. It tore at her hair and clothes.

Shaking, she fumbled with the latch and maneuvered the door open. The wall of the shed shook, breathing in and out like a giant accordion. She hunkered down and yanked on the metal ring to pull open the trapdoor leading to the root cellar. The wind caught it, jerking it out of her hands.

Her foot slid out as she stretched to pull the door back and she went down on one knee. Scrambling to regain her balance, she kicked out to untangle her foot. She looked into the cavern of the root cellar and screamed.

White teeth flashed from the darkness. Connor's pale blue eyes, wide and dilated, glittered under a matted head of hair. His hand encircled her foot like a vine.

"What the—" she cried. "What are you doing here?"

"V," he said, jerking her foot. "I've missed you." He dragged her toward the steps, twisting her ankle until it burned. "How could you tell that man you love him? How could you forget about us? All our plans?"

Cold metal brushed the side of her hand as he pulled her

down. The long wooden handle of Barrett's sledgehammer slipped through her fingers. She tightened her grip as her knees hit the first step. One arm stretched out, clutching the stair rail, the other held the ten-pound hammer.

The tornado siren continued to rip through the air, echoing her fear. Connor pulled her deeper into the earth. "You love me."

The wind caught the door. It swung out, then banged shut, sealing them from the danger outside. "Not anymore, Connor."

She held onto the sledgehammer as though it were a lifeline. Twisting to gain a better angle, she let go of the railing and swung. Connor's howl of pain filled the room, blending with the siren and the thunderous storm. His hold loosened and she fell to the floor.

Kneeling on the packed earth, she sucked in a breath. Overhead, the wind roared, taking on the personality of a beast. The hatch door shuddered, letting in brief glimpses of light and scattering debris. Her ears popped from the pressure.

"Why'd you do that?" Connor huddled in the corner, cradling his arm. "Don't you understand how much I want you? Need you?"

She turned her head, shoving her hair out of her face. "You'll stay there," she growled, eyeing his crotch. "Or I'll make sure I get your attention."

"But I love you," he said through clenched teeth.

"Shut up! You don't love me. You're incapable of love," she yelled over the deafening wind.

Crawling up the steps, she grabbed the trapdoor handle with both hands and shoved. The scream ripped out of her when the door lifted her off her feet. Sobbing, she prayed, "Please, God, I need more time with Barrett."

CHAPTER 39

The siren stopped. Silence came as suddenly as the roaring beast.

The trapdoor remained stuck against her efforts to get out of the cellar. The tornado left behind an energy that oppressed the spirit. Fear tainted the damp air. Only the sound of Victoria's ragged breaths cut through the eerily charged atmosphere.

Connor remained in the corner, his Adonis face covered in sweat and dirt. Blood smeared his cheek where he'd wiped it against his sleeve. His chest rose and fell in a jerky pattern. A wide, dark stain spread down his Dockers. What a fool she'd been. How did she ever believe she was once in love with that man?

Hesitantly, she slowly uncurled her cramped fingers. Her scraped knuckles were bloody from repeatedly hitting the door. She tried to stand, but her legs gave out from under her and she slid down to the packed earth.

Ducking her head, she buried her face on her knees. "I'm alive. I'm alive. I'm alive," she chanted.

The air ripped out of her lungs when Connor grabbed her ponytail.

"You have to listen to me." His fingers dug into her scalp as he forced her to look him in the face. "You're going to come back with me."

"No." She slapped at his hand and tried to stand.

"You should have answered my phone calls. My messages. You should have known I wouldn't just let you go." His knee plowed a path between her shoulder blades. Her neck burned as he bent her backward. His glassy eyes were wide and desperate. "We had a good thing. Remember? You'll help me get back everything I've lost because of you." He dug his knee deeper into her spine.

"Connor—"

"I've watched you. With him. With that handyman-loser." His mouth curled in a sneer. "V, you should have come home to me after you put your car in the ditch."

"My car...?" She searched his face, fearing what she'd see. A shiver of knowing ran up her arms. "It was you."

"You wouldn't listen to me. Wouldn't budge from your aunt's rundown house. No matter what I did. I went to a lot of trouble for you, V. I even set those traps." He lifted his head and took a deep breath. When he looked back down on her, his expression was calm, resolute. "Don't worry. I won't leave without you this time."

Keep him talking. "Yeah. We've changed, haven't we?" Victoria scratched the packed earth with her fingernails. There had to be something she could use to make him let go. "And you decided to find someone else."

"She came on to me, V." His fingers slid to her jaw. "And, you were never home. She's gone now. I made sure she got the message. For you. I did it all for you." He leaned over her, his mouth near her ear. "I want our life back. Just you and me."

Victoria swallowed the rising bile and searched for a way to put distance between them. If she turned far enough, his injured arm would be a perfect target. Or she'd aim for his balls. "You screwed up your life. Not me. We. Are. Over."

She cried out when he clamped down on her chin, digging into her flesh.

"I told you—" His nostrils flared. White flesh encircled his pinched mouth. "I'm not leaving without you. I want all the copies of the pictures you kept, too."

Her hand caught the table leg. If she rolled, she might throw him off balance. Maybe enough time to find the sledgehammer again.

Fortifying herself with a gulp of air, she threw her weight to the side, knocking him off his feet. She grabbed the orange five-gallon bucket filled with emergency food supplies and swung.

Connor grunted when it struck his injured arm. "You'll regret that," he warned through gritted teeth.

"I don't think so," Victoria said. She tightened her grip on the handle. The bucket arched, making an uppercut to his jaw. He froze. His eyes rolled back right before his legs gave out.

She winced when he bounced off the table and hit the ground. His chest rose and fell. He was alive, but not about to come after her anytime soon. She dragged the sledgehammer over to her bucket. If he had any more stupid ideas, she'd be ready.

Voices carried through the trapdoor and into the root cellar. "Victoria! Victoria!"

"I'm here." The words didn't come out as loud as she would have liked. Hauling in a deep breath, she tried again. "Down here. I'm down here. Please hurry."

"Victoria?" Wood scraped against wood. Dust rained down on her head. "We're coming, Baby."

"Barrett?" Victoria scrambled to her feet and shoved the door, but it wouldn't open. "Barrett, I can't get out."

"Hang on. There's a lot of debris in the way. We'll dig you out."

"Barrett." She pressed her hand to the panel as if it would bring them closer. "I love you."

"I know you do, Sweetheart, I know you do." He paused, his voice strangled. "I love you too. Are you hurt?"

She considered the scrapes, the bumps and bruises, and shook her head. "I'm fine. I just want out of here. So does Connor."

"What? Connor?" His voice deepened into a growl. "Are you okay?"

"I am now," she said. "I don't think he's going anywhere either."

"Someone get me a crowbar," Barrett hollered.

What felt like hours, in actuality was a few minutes. Victoria scrambled out of the cellar as soon as the trapdoor began to rise. She gripped Barrett's hand as he hauled her out of the ground. Behind her, Chief Graham led a very shaken Connor to the squad car.

Her arms wrapped around Barrett's waist. She clung to him, her face tucked into the sweet-smelling place where his collarbone met with his neck.

"Baby." His hands shook when he stroked her head. His legs trembled against hers. Someone led them away from the remains of the shed and out of danger. Their knees melted and they sank onto a pile of rocks.

"Are you all right?" they murmured. Their hands moved over each other. "Let me look at you."

Once satisfied they were both alive and safe, Victoria shifted her attention to her neighbors. The tornado had demolished part of the Tewilligers's garage.

"Helen and Harold?"

"A few bumps and bruises. Shaken up like the rest of us."

The storm had cut a path across the adjacent fields. It ripped out fifty-foot shade trees by the roots. One of them lay on its side, covering the remains of the rock garden. The memorial stone towers, commemorating significant events, losses and victories, were scattered across the yard. Many had landed on top of the building where she had taken shelter.

Barrett squeezed her hand and she turned to look at her home. The roof from another building had landed on top of the cottage, collapsing in the chimney. Her flattened BMW rested under the rubble.

She tucked her head on Barrett's muscled shoulder. Mags's root cellar had saved her life.

"We'll rebuild," Barrett offered. "If that's what you want."

"Maybe it's time to give it to the Cove." Victoria began stacking rocks, one on top of another. "Mags intended for the towers to help her friends. Maybe we can return the favor and create a memorial garden for her."

His arms tightened, his eyes shaded. "Does that mean you'll still be my partner?"

"Forever yours." Victoria raised her hand, drawing his face close to hers. "You can't get rid of me that easily." She kissed him, pouring out her love. "I intend to fight for you and for me."

Barrett held her tight, like he'd never let her go. Raindrops tickled her cheeks. Or were those tears of joy? He lifted her hand to his lips. "I love you, Victoria Banning, and don't you ever forget it."

They paused as one of Mags's crazy posted notes fluttered in the air, coming to settle at their feet. Victoria bent to pick it up and read aloud: *Embrace Life*. Barrett's brow arched at her giggle. Their gazes locked, sharing the undeniable fact that Aunt Mags must still be meddling from beyond.

Releasing the bit of paper, Victoria wrapped her arms around Barrett and intended to follow her aunt's instruction.

"I love you," Victoria whispered. "Forever and always."

ACKNOWLEDGMENTS

This book is the epitome of the phrase: It takes a village.

Honeybrooke Cove was indeed a full village project.

My BETA readers, editors, and proofreaders were amazing, and I can't thank them enough. Patty and Marilyn are my Wisconsin experts, and they give great insight to that beautiful state. Kim and Susie are proofreaders extraordinaire and keep me on my toes. Many thanks, go to my family, who cheer me on, wipe my tears, and tell me to get up and get going.

Some of my best memories and friends are from Wisconsin. I am forever grateful, and I am excited to explore more of the beautiful small-town living found in places like Honeybrooke Cove.

ABOUT THE AUTHOR

C.C. Wiley believes there are wonderful, caring, compassionate, courageous characters waiting for someone to tell their story. With each book she writes, she continues to find love and hope one story at a time.

ALSO BY C C WILEY

Historical Romance

Lilies of the Valley Series

Knight Dreams (Lilies of the Valley Book 1)

Would you give up your vengeance to save someone you love? The skilled archer, Terrwyn ap Hew, lost her young brother to the English years ago. Now, her night visions reveal that he is alive and she intends to bring him home.

Knights of the Swan Series

Knight Secrets (Knights of the Swan Book 1) Sworn to protect the crown, a Knight of the Swan must never surrender—not even to love . . .

Knight Quests (Knights of the Swan Book 2) For a Knight of the Swan in 15th century England, falling for the enemy is an act of treason . . .

Knight Treasures (Knights of the Swan Book 3) In 15th Century England, alliances can be deadly for a Knight of the Swan. Especially those made in the heat of passion...

Knight Furies (Knights of the Swan Book 4) For a Knight of the Swan, any mission might lead to fortune—but the chance for love comes once in a lifetime . . .

———

Contemporary Romance

Honeybrooke Cove: A Sweet Small-town Contemporary Romance Series

Hearts of Honeybrooke Cove Book 1

Coming Soon! Book 2

www.ingramcontent.com/pod-product-compliance
Lightning Source LLC
Chambersburg PA
CBHW020235180626
46810CB00006B/2198